GOD LEFT MANOR FARM

BY

CRAIG S. NELSON

Copyright © 2013 by Craig S. Nelson
ISBN 978-0-578-12663-0

Dedicated to Elizabeth

FORWARD

The small valley would have been an ideal place for a man to build a house. Instead, the animals, both wild and domestic, ruled here. The sun reflected off the water that dominated this part of the forest. A waterfall on the far side of the small lake created a white noise. Fish jumped every few minutes, desperately trying to grab a dragonfly out of the air. Birds sang and wild animals approached the water with caution, to hunt or drink.

The old Dog sat on the grass surrounded by young Pups. He waited for them to settle down, to stop rolling in the grass and nipping at each other. When there was silence and calm, he spoke in a soft, deep voice.

"Welcome to your first class on the History of the Pack," the old Dog said. "We will talk about how we came to be where we sit today. It is a long, sad story."

The Pups looked nervously at each other. They were not used to such seriousness, either in or out of school. Dogs still preferred play.

And the Dog began the story.

CHAPTER ONE – WHEN PIGS FLY

"Frank, you need to get out and talk to the Goats and Sheep," Cody said. "The Pigs have the Cows for sure. You need to go and work your magic."

"What? Wag my tail? Roll over? We are going to lose this election no matter what I say or do at this point. There is no use humiliating myself in the process. We need to give them what they want and they want change."

Cody cocked his head for a second and then decided to save his breath. He dropped down next to Frank on the porch. Chipped paint peeled off as his large paws scraped along the worn wood. Cody, a large German Sheppard, stood a head taller than Frank but weighed just slightly more. Brown and grey dominated his coat; a stripe of black fur ran along his spine. Sinewy muscle rippled on his tightly toned body. Cody was in the prime of his life. He stared at his mentor. He had never seen Frank resign himself to something before. It troubled Cody.

Frank's short black coat, graying on the muzzle, reflected the sun. He was the leader of Manor Farm for at least another couple of days. He had held this position for eight years, more than half his life. He had been the first Dog to hold this position in fifty years. The centuries of Manor Farm's history were dominated by administrations led by Pigs.

Cody sighed deeply, trying to relax. He had been born when Frank was already in office. Cody had risen through the ranks of the Pack and had led security for Frank for the last two years. Cody knew things would be different under Pig rule. He racked his brain for a way to win the election. Frank assured him that Manor Farm would survive.

Minutes after dropping to the porch, Cody bounced back to his feet and cocked his head at Frank. Frank opened one eye, the universal Dog expression for "What is it?"

"We can't give up."

"We aren't. The election is tomorrow. Everyone on the Farm has made up their mind already."

"No," Cody said more fiercely than he'd intended. "Some of the Goats are on the fence and the Sheep can be swayed."

Frank closed his eyes again. He had not lifted his head off the porch. Finally, he spoke.

"Cody," Frank said, "at some point, there will be bloodshed with the wilds, and the Farm will need your leadership in war. Be ready, as I don't have much energy left in me."

Cody growled. He knew that in any war, the Pack would be in the forefront. This was true whether a Pig or any other Animal led the Farm.

4

A week later, Preston, the second tallest and thinnest Pig to grace the acres of Manor Farm bathed before he assumed the power and prestige of leadership. He sauntered up the porch steps with a couple of much larger Pigs on either side of him. Carter the Goat, a few Rams, and various other members of the Farm community followed him up the steps. Carter, his hair shining with bath water, had a ribbon in the long hair hanging from his chin. The Ducks were only too happy to help him put it on for this auspicious occasion.

Preston turned and smiled from the high porch at the thousands of Animals of Manor Farm. He rose onto two feet and looked around, nodding at his supporters in the crowd.

"Look at that," Cody said. "I'd like to bite that smug snout right off."

Frank and Cody stood respectfully at the far end of the porch awaiting their role in the traditional Passing of the Gun. The ceremony symbolized the peaceful change of administrations. Frank held the shotgun, hundreds of years old but freshly oiled and in working condition, in his large Labrador mouth. Cody held a bag full of cartridge shells of the same age but of questionable utility. After waiting a suitable amount of time, Frank and Cody approached Preston and Carter. They placed the shotgun and the shells on the porch at their hooves.

"From the date of our independence, now centuries ago," Frank said, "this shotgun and shells have symbolized our freedom and power. The gun represents our independence from Man. The shells represent our subsequent freedom from the rule of Napoleon the tyrant. The gun passes peacefully now and forever upon each change of administration."

Frank pushed the shotgun forward with his large black paw. Cody did the same with the bag of shells. Frank and Cody solemnly nodded. Frank looked Preston in the eye, ignoring the condescension in the Pig's eyes. "Now the responsibility to protect and serve Manor Farm passes on," Frank said. "Guide us. Protect us. Keep us free."

The brief rite complete, Frank and Cody strode down the steps, heads held high, and joined the other members of the Pack at the very back of the crowd of Animals. They were gathered at the feet of, and in a large circle around, three Horses. With the Dogs were the fifty Cats of Manor Farm.

Preston took center stage, briefly stood on two legs again to look over the crowd and then began.

"Thank you, Frank. Thank you, Cody. Thank you to all the members of the Pack, the Cats and Horses who have demonstrated once

5

again the wisdom of the Pigs who founded this Farm. The Pigs had set down the means for all Animals to share in governing the Farm by holding elections every fours years and permitting the peaceful transfer of power.

To the members of the Farm who voted for me, a sincere thank you, thank you, thank you for your vote. During the campaign, I promised to do two things if I was elected. Carter and I promise to deliver on both. During the Campaign, Carter and I weren't just talking about change. We were already taking action to achieve our goals.

We promised to meet with our neighboring Farms such as Foxwood to seek a treaty. More importantly we committed to do the same with the other two major Farms, Snail Farm and Knight Farm. We promised to form alliances because we believe that there is strength in numbers. By joining together with the other major Farms, we will become stronger, safer. The weasels, rats and foxes will not dare to cross us. Even the wild dogs shall fear us."

Preston paused and gave the Pack a look that could be seen only as a challenge. "They will turn their cowardly tails and run from our united front."

Cody barely muffled a growl but Frank silenced him with a slight shake of his broad, grey muzzle.

"We believe," Preston continued, "that the wilds will see that finding a way to coexist is best for them. For while all animals are equal, some Animals are more equal than others. We must make sure the wild animals understand this."

"If the wilds dare to challenge Manor Farm, the wrath of Snail Farm and Knight Farm shall strike back in unison with us in righteous vengeance."

"The Animal lands are growing. The Humans have disappeared. The wild animals are becoming brazen. They do not fear dying. They do not value life. They do not think like us. We must unite to stop them. Isolating ourselves will no longer work. Fighting alone is an idea both old and tired. It is a new age, a new time. The violence must stop. Sending out our military might to seek out the wilds that attack us is like taking pain medication for a broken bone. It temporarily stops the pain but does not set the break.

Violence to stop violence is not the answer. Military might is a short-term solution. How many wars have Cody and his soldiers fought and won? How many times have the wilds attacked us in the last eight years? Ten times? Fifteen? Too many? We have lost a score of Animals in these attacks. This must stop. It will stop. I say we must have power through unity."

Preston paused for dramatic affect and scanned the audience. By this time, the Horses, Cats and the Dogs of the Pack sat in stunned silence. They had assumed Frank's air of patient courtesy, which none of them truly felt. The sun shone down brightly but the Animals were either too enthused by the passion of Preston's speech or shocked into a chilled anger to notice.

"'So,' you might say, 'Preston get off your high horse,' if you will pardon the expression, 'and tell us what steps you've taken or what this great plan entails.' Here is what we have done. During the campaign, Carter traveled to both Snail Farm and Knight Farm. Carter agreed to terms, subject to our election of course, of a compact.

The terms are as follows. If one of the three Farms is attacked by wild animals we will respond in unison. No Farm will fight alone. If Manor Farm is attacked, we will decide jointly, with the other Farms, on the appropriate response. We will include our allies in all decisions relating to the use of force. Only in this manner can we have the support of all civilized Animals. Only in this way can we demonstrate to our enemies that peace is the only answer. Wild animals must hunt only other wild animals. Animals with a capital A are off limits. The Farms will stand alone and only then will we be free from terror."

At this, the Animals raised their collective voices in support. Even a few of the Cats appeared to be persuaded and nodded their heads in support of Preston's logic.

"The ground rules of the pact are simple – acts of retribution are allowed only when at least two of the Farms agree that is the proper course of action. Of course, each Farm may defend itself from an immediate attack as they see fit.

This leads us to our domestic policy for lack of a better word. We promised to let all Animals share equally in what the Farm produces and for all Animals to be given the opportunity to hold positions previously denied to them. I know Frank and his team did what they felt was just, in keeping the defense of the Farm in the hands of the Dogs, Cats, Horses and a few select Pigs. However, I see things differently.

I believe Frank's practice is too tied to the old ways. It is true that prior administrations, led by Pigs, relied on the Pack for defense. But it is time for all Animals to serve in the defense of Manor Farm. A Chicken can act as a lookout just as well as a Crow. A Bull or a Cow can stomp through a pack of wild dogs just as well as a Horse. Our Roosters can keep rats and weasels out of the coop just as well as the Cats. Pigs can fight with our tusks just as well as a Dog can with its teeth.

Over the next couple of weeks all Animals interested in serving should seek an appointment with Carter. First, Carter will work with Cody to assess the needs of the Farm for its defense and then, based on interest, will form a team for defense of the Farm. The overall leadership of the defense of the Farm will be in my hands once we have a team in place. This role is much too important to delegate."

At this, Frank's thick black fur popped up briefly on his upper back before his mind told his body these were mere words. Cody was a better choice than Frank to lead the defense of the Farm, so Frank put him in charge. Frank understood that Preston knew this and was just taking a jab at him in front of the citizens of Manor Farm.

"We will also be looking at a more equal distribution of goods generated by the farm. Cows will now eat a like amount as horses. As the Cows will now participate in the defense of the Farm, they will need additional rations.

All Animals are equal. All Animals must share equally. We must no longer permit those that produce the least, eat the most eggs. No longer will Dogs receive the lion's share. We must no longer permit those that defend us to have a greater share of the milk than those who actually produce the milk."

Again the Cows, Sheep and Goats pounded their hooves on the ground.

"I promise you this – all of you will have an opportunity to contribute to our success and safety. No job will be unavailable to you if you can meet the minimum requirements. I believe all of us can be warriors. I believe all of us can be diplomats. I believe in all of you. You are my comrades."

Now the sound was deafening. When the Animal noises and hoof stomping ceased, Preston stood on his hind legs and held his head high. He dropped to the ground and mouthed "thank you" to the crowd as he descended the worn porch steps with Carter beside him. Standing about the same height, they wandered through the crowd. They thanked the Animals for their support, whether they had that support during the election or not.

"Congratulations Chief," Carter said as they made their way back onto the porch after an hour of small talk and hoof shaking with the other Animals.

"To you too, my friend," Preston said.

Carter showed even more of his criss-crossed teeth. They wandered into the old Farmhouse and found the whiskey that had not been touched for over eight years and raised their glasses alone to the new Manor Farm where all Animals would be given equal rank.

*   *   *   *

Manor Farm covered two thousand pristine acres. The majority was flat, vast fields of wheat and corn. The farmhouse stood a little over three football fields from the wide dirt road that ran along the Eastern edge of Manor Farm. The farmhouse was white and red but not by design. In many spots the white paint which had covered the house when the Animals revolted had chipped away to cover the house's original rust colored paint. Next to the rundown farmhouse stood a small corral and beyond that was the chicken coop, slightly larger than a small cottage. The coop had been well maintained over the hundreds of years since the departure of Man. Behind the farmhouse laid a vegetable garden covered in the greens of carrots, peas and tomatoes in late spring. Behind this was the Barn.

For centuries the Pack had spent their days and nights under the great oak, a stone's throw from the entrance to the Farm. Frank and Cody spent the night there with the Pack for the first time in many years. While leading the pack they had slept on the porch to watch the coop at night.

They woke the next morning and arranged with the other Dogs to take their shift guarding the coop and barn at night as this was the frequent target of the wilds. When in power they each had stayed awake half the night and watched the coop. They had no expectation that Preston and Carter or the other members of their administration would do the same. As added security, a member of the Pack spent the night at the door to the coop and another at the door of the barn. The shifts were two hours and they planned to contribute by taking a shift at the coop and the barn. This would also allow the other members of the Pack to spend more time guarding the areas surrounding the farmhouse and the Duck pond.

Frank was discussing the shifts with the Pack when he spotted Preston and Carter approaching from the house. The Pack turned in unison to follow Frank's gaze and fell silent as one. All that could be heard was the crunch of Preston and Carter's hooves on the gravel driveway.

"Good morning everyone," Preston said as he neared within twenty feet. "Beautiful day isn't it?"

"Yes," Frank replied looking up at the bright morning sun and dew shining off the yellowing grass under the oak tree. "I suppose it is."

"Am I interrupting something?" Preston asked seeming to forget that Carter was by his side.

"No it is something you should be aware of actually."

"What is it?" Carter asked when Preston did not respond.

"We are orchestrating the night watch. We should have better coverage now that Cody and I can participate."

9

"Well then the timing of our visit couldn't be better. That is the reason I came out to talk to you all," Preston said, surveying the pack of Dogs.

Besides a few Beagles, the Pack consisted mostly of large Dogs – two score of Labradors, Frank, Cody and Cody's wife. Cody's wife, Maggie, was a Rottweiler. She stood just a little shorter than her husband, but was nearly twice as wide. The Beagles, Maggie and Cody had escaped human farms hundreds of miles away as young Pups. They headed east until they arrived at Manor Farm. The Labradors were descendents of the second-generation of Dogs that inhabited Manor Farm.

"Okay let's hear it." This came out much harsher than Frank intended.

"I'd like to talk in private, one leader to another if that would be satisfactory," Preston said.

"Tradition requires that I honor such a request."

They moved down the gravel drive toward the entrance of Manor Farm where centuries ago a gate had excluded unwanted visitors. Preston's hooves were the only sound as even the wild birds had fallen silent to see what would happen next. They stopped out of hearing distance from the Pack but far away enough from the gate that the Horses who stood guard there could not hear either. The Sheep, Goats and Cows patrolled the perimeter during the day. The Cats assumed this role during the night. The Pack focused all its resources around the coop, barn and pond.

"As you know," Preston began, "I've promised that all Animals will have an opportunity to provide for our defense."

"Yes, I am well-aware of that," Frank said.

"Well, the Dogs have protected the coop and barn from the time of the Revolution; since Napoleon raised Pups himself. I think the best way for me to implement my plan is to exclude Dogs from this most important of jobs."

"But why?" Frank asked. "It makes no sense. We are the most qualified to serve in this role based on our God-given talents."

Preston tilted his head and regarded Frank for a moment. "You know my feelings about God, I would assume, Leader Frank." Preston smirked.

Frank waited in silence appearing to be lost in thought.

"But of course, I forgot that God is Dog spelled backwards," Preston said. Frank nodded slowly with a slight grin on his thick muzzle. The grin contrasted sharply with the fire in his usually sleepy eyes. He did not say a word in response.

10

"Look Frank, it's elitist," Preston said. "Why should the honor be bestowed only on Dogs?"

"The honor can be bestowed on other Animals without excluding Dogs entirely. Excluding Dogs will only put the Farm at risk. Why no Dogs at all?"

"If Dogs remain at the coop and barn the other Animals will feel as if they are being humored and the Dogs are continuing to provide the real protection."

"But if there is an attack on the coop and the barn there might be unnecessary causalities," Frank said.

"That is highly unlikely if the Pack does its job and responds quickly enough from the perimeter."

"The perimeter? What are you talking about?"

"Settle down Frank. I know it is hard but I am in charge now and I am going to make decisions that you don't necessarily agree with."

Frank smiled as only Labrador's can. He knew that Preston was attempting to be conciliatory in the bright, beautiful sun of Manor Farm. Preston wanted the Farm to start anew. But there was something in his attempt to do so that pushed Frank toward anger. Frank breathed deeply and watched the Cows taking their morning meal in the pasture.

"With all due respect," Frank said, "this issue is one of security and not equality. As the Leader, security must be your first priority."

"That was your first priority Frank. Mine, on the other hand, is equality and collaboration. The majority of the Farm agrees that is where our focus should be now."

"Yes," Frank said, "point taken. But please at least keep Cody and Maggie as part of the team that guards the coop at night. What if a fox attacks? Or a Coyote?"

Preston dropped his head and looked down his long, pink snout at Frank. "The Pigs, Cows, Goats and Horses can handle it," he said.

"Another thing to consider is you will separate the Pack. It will be much more difficult to respond in unison if we are separated on the perimeter and have no presence at the coop and the barn. It will be difficult for us to defend against a pack of wild dogs or coyotes."

"With the Cows and Horses to help the Pigs and Goats can handle it," Preston said now raising his voice. The Pack looked over and stared at Preston. Cody took a step toward Preston and Frank.

Frank silently and considered his options, while staring at Cody and the others. "Fine," he said softly, unable to look at Preston.

"Good," Preston said with a nod of his relatively thin and hairless head. He looked more like a Sow than a Boar. "Will you please inform the Pack that the perimeter is their sole responsibility? The Goats, Cows

11

and Horses will be moved closer to the coop and barn at nights, they are near the Boars."

"And the Cats?" Frank asked.

"They will continue to roam their assigned territories with the Pack. In our opinion the first line of defense must be the strongest. They will work with you to keep the wilds out at night."

"Why don't you see if the Ducks would like to take over that responsibility?" Frank asked.

"Because the Ducks need . . . " Before he even finished his sentence, Preston glared at Frank, turned his back and made his way to where Carter stood on the driveway a short distance from the Pack.

Preston and Carter quickly moved away from the old oak tree so they would be long gone when Frank broke the news to the Pack. Frank made his way slowly back to the Pack, to give Preston and Carter the time they needed to put some distance between themselves and the Pack.

"Well what did that pompous ass have to say?" Cody asked.

"He wants us to guard the perimeter so some of the other Animals can have the privilege of protecting the coop and barn," Frank said.

"That is absolutely ridiculous," Cody said unable to control the volume of his voice. "I swear to God Frank, I can't take this. They want us out on the perimeter? Away from the coop? Away from the barn? We can't stand for it Frank. It puts the Farm's smaller Animals at risk. It puts the Farm's supply of eggs at risk." The black strip of fur on Cody's spin stood up straight.

"I understand that Cody," Frank said trying to calm Cody by slowing the pace of the conversation. "But we have lived and will continue to live under the laws of the Farm. We must do our best to protect the Farm despite the policies of Preston and Carter."

"But . . ."

"Frank's right Cody," Maggie said. "We agreed to follow the laws of the Farm when we sought citizenship. Now that we disagree with the decisions being made by the leadership we cannot turn our backs on the other Animals. They are still our friends and fellow citizens."

Cody studied his wife. Her short black and brown fur gleamed in the morning sun. Her muscles rippled under her coat, even while standing perfectly still. Cody knew she looked beautiful to all the Animals of the Farm, not just to him. When she patrolled the grounds, the Animals stared in wonder at her raw power. It was commonly believed she could bring Cody down, and would have by now, if they had not fallen in love. Her ferociousness against the wilds was legendary. Cody led the Pack in combat but Maggie was the juggernaut. Cody stared at his wife and back

12

at his mentor in turn. The fur on his spin now flattened as quickly as it rose.

"I disagree. This is the beginning of the end. But I will defer to you two because I trust your judgment more than my own."

   *   *   *   *

An hour later, Preston and Carter walked past the Pack under the oak tree and to the front gate of the Farm toward the Horses. As they made their way down the gravel road they greeted all the Animals except the Pack. All but the Cats greeted them with unfettered enthusiasm. Bart, the coal black Stallion, stood head to head with the white Mare, Betsy, at the front gate. Their son, Buck, played with the Calves in a nearby field. When Preston approached close enough, Bart turned his head and said, "Good morning sir."

"Good morning Bart," Preston said. "I have some proposed changes for our defenses that I would like to share with you."

"Alright," Bart said.

Preston presented the same information he had shared with Frank. Pigs, Goats, Horses and Cows would now guard the coop and barn and the Dogs would join the Cats on the perimeter at night. Preston explained how this would give Bart and Betsy an opportunity to stand watch at the coop and barn.

"What about the Pack?" Bart asked looking down at Preston with one of his large, deep brown eyes. Bart had the kind of eyes that made it difficult to discern if he was wise and lost in thought or simply too dense to understand.

"I've informed them that they have had this honor for many years and along with it their deserved glory. Others should now share in the opportunity."

"But why exclude them?" Bart asked.

"So that others do not feel like they are window dressing," Preston said.

Bart and Betsy looked at each other for so long that Preston and Carter began looking to each other to say something. It appeared as if Bart and Betsy were carrying on a silent conversation.

"Well, what do you think?" Carter asked, unable to withstand the drawn-out silence.

"Not sure," Bart said. "Seems dangerous splitting up the Pack and having no Dogs at the coop."

"Are you saying the other Animals are not up to the task?" Preston challenged.

"Not sure," Bart said. "I reckon I might be."

"Well you don't have to volunteer for barn duty," Preston said in his sweetest tone. "You two can continue to guard the gate. We are simply trying to provide you with an opportunity you never had before."

Again Bart stood silently and stared at Preston with his huge brown eyes. "Let us talk about it," Bart said nodding toward his wife.

"Think about this," Preston said now speaking quickly, one word right after the other. "You have guarded the gate through Frank's eight years and through the eight years of a Pig administration before that. Not only should you have an opportunity to guard the barn but others should have the honor of guarding the gate. Don't you want to do something else?"

"Not sure."

Carter nudged Preston in the shoulder gently and then said to Bart, "Let us know in the next couple of days. We plan on redeploying everyone then"

"Alright," Bart said.

*   *   *   *

The next day, the bright sun contrasted sharply with the mood of the Pack and others on the Farm. The news of Preston's plan and Frank's response spread fast. Curiosity pulled everyone from their assigned duties, when it was announced that Bart would give a speech at the front gate at ten o'clock. Only once before had the giant Horse addressed the entire Farm. A little over eight years before, in one of the closest elections in the history of Manor Farm, Bart gave a one minute speech that turned all the Chickens from Oscar the Pig over to Frank's side. This turned Frank's looming defeat into a victory. Bart seldom expressed his opinion but, when he did, it was plain but thorough. He believed everything should be as simple as possible but no simpler.

At ten in the morning, the chill now lifted from the Farm, Bart stepped in front of the bright white gate, painted just the day before. Bart's hooves made a grinding sound as he stepped onto the gravel road. The Pack had gathered behind him on the dirt road outside the Farm in unintended symbolism. They knew no more than the others what Bart intended to say.

"What do you think this is about?" Cody asked.

"Not sure," Frank said. "I'm not sure if we should be concerned or excited."

"You know Bart better than anyone but it seems to me he always can see the heart of the matter," Cody said.

14

"True, but perhaps we are blinded and can't see what is best for the Farm," Frank said as he tilted his head toward Cody. They fell silent as they both realized the only thing they could do was listen.

Preston, looking somehow redder than the morning before, stood with Carter just behind the Cows. They were just in front of the rest of the Pigs and Goats. They were farthest from Bart but closest to the farmhouse. Carter's head swayed back and forth, impatient for Bart to start. Preston held his head high and looked down his snout at Carter. The Animals fell silent in unanimous respect when Bart stopped moving and looked out at the crowd.

"I seldom address the entire Farm but in this particular case I must," Bart began. "The Dogs have been directed to guard the perimeter. No member of the Pack can be or will be assigned to the coop. This is on the orders of the new administration. Instead, Preston and Carter have decided to spread the Pack about the thousands of acres of our Farm. Only the Dogs are precluded from coop duty. This concerns me and Betsy. This reminds me of the old quote, 'All animals are equal, but some are more equal than others.'

We have been asked to be part of the contingent assigned to protect the coop. This is a request we must refuse. We shall not be passive participants. We shall not be accessories. We do not want to return to the days where all Animals on the Farm believed that life would go on as it had always gone on – that is, badly. We will not lower ourselves to the petty place of inclusion through exclusion. Preston seeks to include all Animals by excluding the Pack.

We will maintain our positions as the guardians of the gate. This is the job we are best suited for and here we shall remain."

The Animals did not make a sound. Preston slowly made his way through the crowd to the front of the gate. He lowered his head, slightly closing his eyes in the direction of Bart. Bart stared down at Preston with the expressionless face of a horse. Preston scanned the crowd and then smiled.

"Thank you for your thoughts, Bart," Preston said. "I don't want to encourage any member of the Farm to exclude any other. We were elected on the platform that there would be opportunities for all. The Pack has been ninety-nine percent of the coop's defenses for centuries. I note that most of this time there was a Pig administration in the farmhouse. Others must be given a genuine opportunity to be part of the team that defends the coop and barn."

Now Preston's voice lost its conciliatory tone. "Bart's speech makes clear that the Pack, gathered around Bart in a show of unity, has trouble accepting any authority but its own. Clearly he is simply a mouth piece of the Pack. He is not the objective citizen we all assumed him to be."

At this many of the Animals made low guttural sounds in the direction of the Pack and Bart.

"Let's go back to the work of equality," Preston continued. "Let's not get sidetracked by self-interest. All Animals interested in serving in the defense of the coop, who have not done so in the past, please follow us back to the barn to apply."

Preston strutted quickly down the gravel path with most of the Farm at his heels. Frank, Bart and the rest of the Pack stood with the Cats and watched the others in disbelief.

"It was a good speech," Percy the Cat said to Bart. "For what its worth we know Frank didn't put you up to it. We aren't ones to follow the pack if you all will pardon the expression."

The Dogs all smiled. Percy's dry sense of humor appealed more to the Pack than it did to the other Animals on the Farm.

"Thank you, Percy," Bart said.

"What now?" Percy asked Frank.

"We do what Preston wants and protect the Farm as best we can."

"We will stay on the barn and coop portions of our zones and leave the perimeter to you all so at least the coop has some protection," Percy said.

"Good idea," Cody said. "That leaves the pond vulnerable but we have no choice. We can afford to put two members of the Pack at the pond but it will be tough to keep the rats away without some Cats there."

CHAPTER TWO – POP GOES THE WEASEL

"I've never seen so many rats in one place," Willie said. "It's giving me the frickin' creeps. There must be a thousand. No, at the very least, there's a thousand. I'm not sure I want to join forces with these guys. I tell ya, Al, I am getting creeped out."

"Look Willie," Alvarez said between licks of his burnt orange fur, "there is strength in numbers and we have a chance to finally get our due, to live high on the Hog."

Willie looked at Alvarez's large, brown eyes to see if he was joking. Alvarez wasn't joking. To Willie, the Hog reference would have been a joke. Alvarez rarely joked, which was unusual for a fox.

Willie and a score of weasels along with Alvarez and four other foxes were intermingled with rats along the banks of Beaver Creek. They were about a mile from Manor Farm. The sun had set just a couple of hours before.

An hour later, the last of the stragglers made their way into trees and onto the rocks and boulders on the banks of the creek. The harvest moon lit the night sky. These rats must have come from over ten miles away as they were smaller than the rats that inhabited the forest around Beaver Creek. Willie scanned the trees and banks in silence.

"Jesus, Alvarez," he finally said. "I was wrong. There are four or five thousand rats."

Rats covered the canopy of trees over the great rock in the middle of Beaver Creek. The great rock was the designated meeting place. Each branch had rats perched on it and to Willie's eyes they all stared hungrily in his direction. Thousands of red eyes reflected the moonlight. They were silent. Willie followed their lead and shut his mouth.

A few moments later, a rat as long as Willie and twice as wide barreled down the opposite bank from where Willie stood with Alvarez. The rat sprang ten feet in the air from the bank to the giant boulder in the middle of the creek. The moon seemed to shine directly onto the rat and the darkness surrounding the trees and banks of the creek seemed to intensify. The rat appeared to be in the Devil's spotlight.

"Good evening everyone," the rat said. He spoke softly but his voice carried enough so that the rat on the farthest tree could pick up his voice with its sensitive ears. "For those of you that don't know me, I am Sabean."

"Jesus Christ," Willie whispered, "you said he was big but my frickin' God."

"Shh," Alvarez said.

"First," Sabean continued, "I would like to welcome the foxes and weasels who have accepted my invitation. I would also like to welcome the bands of rats from all over the Animal lands that have joined us here tonight. Together we can bring down the wild wrath on those arrogant Animals of Manor Farm."

Sabean paused. "Everyone has their assigned roles. Manor Farm is vulnerable. They have a new administration. My rats have engaged in extensive surveillance over the last six months. They do not guard the coop or the barn with Dogs any longer. The Cats stay close to the barn and coop in the Dogs' absence. This leaves the pond vulnerable. As such, Manor Farm expects an attack on the nest of the Ducks and Geese in the pond. Our plan is a simple one.

"But before I lay it out in detail I'd like to provide all of you with context for this evening. This attack will serve not only the purpose of killing the Animals of Manor Farm but the much more important impact is the chaos and discord that will result. But this attack will garner the attention not only of Manor Farm but of Knight Farm and Snail Farm and all farms in between. This fear and their response to it will give us a chance to change the structure of our lives and the lives of generations of wilds to come. Why should the farm Animals control the land within their fences? Why have we never asked as a group, what about our rights? What about our equality? Things must change and tonight is the beginning of a new order in the Animal lands. No longer will we live in fear and in small numbers. We will form a collective force of such strength that the farms will be helpless."

Although not a squeak was uttered the rats were shaking violently in excitement.

"Now, the plan is simple. I will take my band of five hundreds Rats, with a capital R, and attack the pond from the East of Manor Farm. We will fight the Ducks and Geese and any Cats that come to their defense. The only Animals our forces must try to avoid are the Dogs. This is a war, not a raid. The rest of you, Rats, Foxes and Weasels will attack from the West once the battle at the Pond has begun in earnest. You will head to the coop and the barn and kill and maim as many of them as possible. Don't worry about food. This is an attack for fear not for food. A simple plan but we have surprise on our side. Manor Farm is much too pompous to expect such a planned assault from Rats, Foxes and Weasels.

"So let the games begin."

Sabean bounded back onto the bank of Beaver Creek and headed in the direction of Manor Farm. Thousands of wild animals followed in silence.

At Manor Farm, since the election, Carter led the first four hour watch of each night. He, a Cow and one of the younger, more aggressive Pigs were responsible for watching the entrances to the coop and barn. Initially, the Pig and Cow stood at the entrance of the coop and barn while Carter circled each building in turn. Now, six months later, the Pig and Cow laid down, often dozing off, at their posts and Carter watched from the porch. He figured the Pack only had a Dog at the entrance and that Cody and Frank slept on the porch so he and his team were doing much the same.

All the Sheep and Goats and a few Cows with calves slept in the barn. The remaining Cows spent their nights out in the pasture. The Chickens, led by a young, mean Rooster named Jack, were all asleep in the coop. Preston slept in the farmhouse in the master bedroom. He continued to sample the spirits brought in from Snail Farm on a nightly basis and snored loudly.

Despite Preston's directive not to get involved, Frank had the Dogs working double shifts every night. Forty Dogs awake at all times. The Pack slept most of the day so they could do their best to protect the thousands of acres of Manor Farm while guarding the miles of perimeter. Cody and eight or nine other members of the Pack slept during the first shift, as close to the barn and coop as Preston would allow. Unfortunately, this was hundreds of yards away at the old oak tree near the entrance to the Farm. Cody growled softly in his sleep.

Percy's Cats, all fifty of them, patrolled their territories diligently and approached the barn and coop as often as possible, without making it obvious to Carter.

Carter looked out at the beautiful night sky and couldn't believe his good fortune. He had met Preston at Snail Farm University and now was the second in command of Manor Farm. He never thought a Goat would have an opportunity for such an honor.

*   *   *   *

Just an hour after his speech, Sabean approached the Eastside of Manor Farm staying in the underbrush. Although nearly twice the size of any of the other rats in his band he was equally silent. He had superior strength and quickness to go along with his size. They regrouped a hundred yards from the fence in a small clearing under the bright moon. He divided his rats into five equal teams of one hundred. The leader of each group drew close to him.

"Alright, let's go over the plan one more time. My group, Group A, will head straight for the pond from the Eastside. Group B will follow behind and break off and approach the pond from the South and attack there. Group C will follow behind Group B and attack the pond from the North. Group D will circle all the way around and attack from the West. Groups A through D will attack the nests and Ducklings. Group E will follow behind Group A and attack the Ducks and Drakes." Sabean paused. "Any questions?"

He was met by four sets of burning red eyes. After a couple of seconds Sabean said, "Good. Happy hunting my friends. Welcome to the Rat Race." Sabean flashed a quick smile that even the group leaders found unsettling. He raced to the front of his group and waved his head dramatically in the direction of Manor Farm.

*   *   *   *

Jackson, a black lab, patrolled the area between the pond and the Northeastern fence line. His old body had quickly grown accustomed to the eight hour shifts. At fifteen years old he was still the fastest Dog in the pack for short distances. Jackson had trained Frank and Cody on the most effective tactics to protect the Farm from intruders from the time each was three months old. Jackson and the other members of the Pack had all fought wild dog packs, coyotes, foxes and knew the rules. First, alert the pack, then attack. Surprise attacks were for the Cats.

Sabean's rats were still outside the fence when Jackson picked up their scent. Jackson took a few steps forward, dropped down below a large wild rose bush and his eyes widened as the magnitude of the rat odor swept over him. He popped back up, spied four rats crossing the road that ran along the Eastside of the Farm and let out a growling yelp, "Rats incoming from the East – Northwest quadrant."

"That was fast," Sabean said calmly. "Let's pick it up. Remember, go for the nests. Engage with anything but a Dog; avoid the Dogs in battle."

Jackson waited for his message to move through the Pack to ensure he didn't need to repeat it. In accordance with Cody's standard protocol, the message "Rats-Northeast quadrant" passed around the Farm from Northeast to Southwest. The Dogs in the North and Southeast quadrant, bordering Jackson's quadrant, knew they must respond to the emergency. The Dogs in the Northwest, South and Southwest expanded their territories to patrol the North and Southeast quadrants and those patrolling in the interior held tight to their positions. The members of the Pack who were not on duty had their assigned responses. Two went to the coop and two went to the barn. The rest, about ten Pack members,

20

responded to the emergency.   Frank and Cody were the free roamers and reassigned Pack members as necessary.

*   *   *   *

Cody started from his sleep and watched Maggie and three large female Labs head toward the coop and barn.   Cody considered in a moment of pride the fear the rats would feel when they saw Maggie racing toward them with foam flying from the sides of he muzzle. Her jaws were like vices and she was nearly as quick as the Beagles. He saw Paulie, a Beagle, heading toward Jackson's position, her white tail bouncing in the moonlight. She let out a howl that would wake the family of humans lying in the family cemetery at the West-end of the Farm. Paulie fought rats with the ferocity of a Schnauzer. Paulie howled again, this time challenging Percy the Cat and the other Dogs to keep up with her.

*   *   *   *

Jackson hesitated briefly when he saw the number of rats crossing the road. He barked out loudly, "There are hundreds! Cats, be careful."

Percy heard this and thanked the Man-God that the Dogs were well-trained. He screeched loudly to the other Cats, "Pairs," an order he had never issued before. Cody had insisted that the Cats be trained to fight in pairs. Percy had relented despite such tactics being contrary to their nature. A minute later, Sammy bounded over a bush and joined Percy. Each Cat would now fight in pairs as ordered. Percy and the other Cats called this fighting "Dog-style."

With all appropriate signals relayed, Jackson hopped the fence of Manor Farm and wreaked havoc among the rats as they crossed the dirt road from the forest. Jackson had trouble mauling the rats with his mouth because the rats were too quick. So he crushed them one after another with his large black paws. He broke the limbs of at least ten and crushed two underneath his full weight before Sabean's forces were in the safety of the bushes of Manor Farm.

Percy and Sammy were not on duty so they also had responsibility to engage at the point of attack. The Cats on duty were to stay put. He and Percy were the only Cats who were not on duty tonight.

The two Labs for the North and Southeast quadrants raced into a stream of oncoming rats. The pond was in the North quadrant. The main body of Sabean's force, that was attacking the pond, was in the thick underbrush encircling the pond. They were searching for the nests of the Ducks and Geese. The two Labs had trouble stopping the rats because the underbrush slowed them down and the snapping branches alerted the rats to their presence. This gave the rats time to dart away into another bush.

The Ducks and Geese quacked and honked in panic and fear as the rats approached. The sound was like a siren warning of an air attack. Sabean and three other rats approached a Duck's nest. Sabean engaged with the Drake defending the nest, drawing him away. Sabaen darted in and out, avoiding the Drake's beak. The three other rats jumped on the Drake's back, surprising him as the Drake thought they were trying to get the eggs. The Drake fell to the ground under the weight of the three rats. As Sabean lowered himself to pound on the Drake's neck, Paulie darted through the underbrush, growling deeply. Paulie had a rat off the Drake's back before Sabean could get the words, "Dog, evasive action" out of his mouth. Paulie ripped the hind legs off the rat and tossed them into the pond. Sabean and the other rats darted away. Paulie turned to give chase and looked over her shoulder at the nest. The Drake stood in front of the nest bleeding, but unafraid. Instead of taking off in pursuit, Paulie howled at the top of her lungs, "Ducks and Geese push your nests into the water and keep them afloat. You can fight the rats in the water."

Jackson and the Labs heard this and went into action. They knew they could not help fight in the brush, that was for the Beagles and Cats, so they helped move the nests into the pond. There was a horrible scream more like that of a terrified human than a Duck as Sabean and four other rats murdered a Duck before she could push her nest toward the middle of the pond. Paulie howled letting the other Farm Animals know of the murder.

Cody heard this but instead of going to the pond he followed his instincts and headed toward the barn and coop. He barked out, "Pete and Patrick stay at the pond. All others compress the perimeter." The rats had made the mistake of all heading into the middle of the Farm and Cody intended to squeeze them toward the barn and coop where a group of Dogs and Cats would be waiting. Then they could avenge the murder of the Duck. First, ridiculously, he needed Preston's permission.

Pete and Patrick, Paulie's brothers, ripped across the Farm toward the pond from the orchard. Preston had made his way out of the farmhouse and up the gravel road toward the main gate. Preston met Cody about a hundred yards from the house.

"What's going on?" Preston asked sleepily.

"Rats are attacking the pond," Cody said.

"Attacking?" Preston asked. "You mean they are raiding the chicken coop."

"No, they murdered a Duck. Apparently the rules of engagement have changed. Please Preston, this doesn't feel right. Let some additional Dogs and Cats help at the coop and barn."

"Honestly Cody you worry too much," Preston said. "With your wife and the Lab we will be fine." We have all the help we need from the Pack right now. It seems the services of the Pack and the Cats are needed more at the Pond right now."

"Very well," Cody said quickly, "but I am following this order under protest. I tell you Preston something is terribly wrong."

The fighting at the Pond was ferocious. At first the Cats, Percy and Sammy, couldn't believe the Rats were engaging with them. Then once they had tasted rat blood and heard a Cat shriek in an agonized death a short distance off they descended on the rats like a whirlwind. While protecting each other's back, they maimed rats by the dozen as they circled the pond. By fighting in pairs they had surprised the rats. This tactic prevented further loss of life. The Cat they lost at the Battle of the Pond was a result of the rats cornering her before she could pair up.

About the time Percy and Sammy began slaughtering rats and Cody obeyed Preston's order and headed toward the pond, the second wave of rats with a number of foxes and weasels led by Alvarez and Willie moved in from the West. At this point the Dogs were spread out across the expanse of the Farm as ordered by Preston. Alvarez's forces were within a quarter of a mile of the barn before a pair of Cats spotted the force of thousands and sounded the alarm.

A suicide squad of ten rats engaged the Cats and faced certain death so the remaining thousands could pour into the barn and coop. Maggie spotted Alvarez as they approached. She initially darted after him but when she saw the magnitude of the invading army she realized it would not be her day to break the neck of the troublesome fox.

She retreated to the coop and her partner, Anne the Lab, headed to the barn. The five foxes and the ten weasels entered the barn with a thousand rats. The remaining rats, over two thousand in all, headed for the coop.

In the barn, the wilds wreaked havoc among the Goats, Sheep and Calves. They nipped at their hind legs and genitals. The Animals kicked and stomped and jumped as rats fell from the rafters onto their backs. For each they stomped on, five more seemed to appear. The screech of pain from the Animals and the death screams of the rats created frenzy among the rats and weasels as they fed off the fear. The foxes took calculated risks and ganged up on the smaller Goats and brought two to the ground and tore their throats out. Anne got a hold off a fox and broke his neck. She howled for reinforcements.

The rats poured into the coop from holes in the ground and in the coops, walls and roof. Maggie crushed a number of rats under her large paws but most were too quick for her. She growled in fury at the sound of eggs cracking and chicks and chickens dying. Blood, yellow with yoke, dripped from the nests onto the white hay spread over the wooden floor of the coop. In comparison to Maggie's relative ineffectiveness, Jack the Rooster inflicted significant casualties. Seeing this, Maggie stayed close to him so he was protected from a suicide squad. This allowed him to attack with no fear of a counter-attack. He picked the eyes out of nearly fifty shrieking rats. Among the chaos in the coop, Carter and the Pig were helpless to do anything but watch as the rats on the ground were too quick. Nor could Carter and the Pig get up along the row of nests to defend them.

Cody heard the attack on the coop and barn just as he reached the pond. Initially, he was perplexed at the relative quiet at the pond. He thought that the Beagles and Cats had turned away the attack. Then he realized that the rats had retreated once they heard the attack on the barn and coop. Cody ordered the Beagles and all Cats to the barn and coop with a vicious howl.

"Corner the foxes so Maggie can tear them apart," he growled.

The Beagles covered the mile to the barn and coop in less than five minutes. Cody wondered at their invincibility as the Beagles burst into the coop a hundred yards ahead of Cody and the Cats. As Paulie and her brothers tore into the rats, three Cats entered through the roof and dropped onto the shelf that held the nests.

Alvarez and the three remaining foxes had made their way to the coop from the barn and were jumping on Chickens and trying to break their necks. When Alvarez saw the Beagles and Cats, he shrieked the retreat signal in terror. The blood lust and this fear now removed any doubt about the wisdom of joining forces with Sabean and his rats. He hated the Animals and wanted war.

Word of the Beagles arrival reached Willie in the barn quickly. His face covered in the blood of Goats, Sheep and Cows, he yelped "Retreat." The Wilds disappeared from Manor Farm like a morning mist. In less than a minute there was silence. Thirty seconds later the silence was broken by the death screams of rats as the Cats killed the injured rats that could not make their way from Manor Farm.

CHAPTER THREE – PEACE AT ALL COST

The sun was a few feet over Pine Mountain, the tallest peak on the horizon, when Preston walked out of the front door of the farmhouse. He stepped slowly to the top of the stairs. He was to address the Animals of Manor Farm. Carter followed closely behind him.

Carter had spent the last two hours waiting for Preston to wake up. When Preston had stumbled out of bed, his face red and sweat lathering his body, Carter debriefed Preston on the casualties. Pursuant to Preston's orders, Carter had rejected the Dog's pleas for a pursuit team to go after Sabean, the weasels and the foxes. Instead, Carter asked the Pack to go and clean up immediately.

"The blood and dirt covering the members of the Pack will only cause additional unrest," Carter had told Cody.

Frank had tried to gain an audience with Preston immediately after the attack but had been denied access. Preston agreed to meet with Frank only after he had addressed the entire Farm. After somberly scanning the crowd, Preston began.

"My fellow Animals, what happened last night was a terrible, terrible tragedy. We lost fifty lives - two Ducks, a Cat and forty-seven Chickens and Chicks. We lost hundreds and hundreds of eggs and many others were injured at the hands of the rats and their comrades. We know that Sabean of Beaver Creek was behind the attacks as he was seen at the pond. The coordination and magnitude of this senseless attack is unheard of in the history of all the Animal Farms. This includes the ancient times, when this was one of the only Farms and held the name of Animal Farm. Rats satisfying only their blood lust, with no food as the target, with the help of equally vicious foxes and weasels would have taken any farm by surprise. So there should be no shame but only anger in our hearts. We fought bravely. At least five hundreds rats and a fox died at the hands of our security forces. For this we should all be proud."

Preston had stood in his excitement. Thick, white spittle had formed at the corners of his mouth as the passion behind his words intensified.

"But we shall not let this go unpunished. We shall seek retribution. Our wrath will be unprecedented. The combined power of Manor Farm, Knight Farm and Snail Farm shall fall like a hammer on Sabean and his horde. We are fortunate that our Administration had the foresight to enter into a pact for the support of all the major farms. We will stand united. A combined force shall invoke a vengeance that will finally lead to everlasting peace."

The citizens of Manor Farm pounded their hooves and sounded off with blood lust. The Dogs, Cats and three Horses stood silently. A few of the Cats hissed in disgust.

"Tomorrow, Carter will set out on a diplomatic mission to Knight Farm. There he will meet with King George and Louis the Wise, the ambassador for Snail Farm. I have chartered Carter to come back with a declaration of war."

Again the Animals voiced their support with unrestrained enthusiasm through noises, stomping and some Pigs even foaming at the mouth for battle.

Preston continued, still standing on his hind legs, in a loud voice, "Manor Farm, since the days of its founding and the first administration of Pigs has stood firm in the face of adversity. We drove out the humans and we will now drive out the wilds. Wild animals have tried to weaken us before and failed. I promise you my friends that they will fail again. United we will stand with our allies in the face of this despicable enemy. Let those of us who pray to the man-God to please do so and the rest of us will engage in a moment of silence for our fallen Comrades."

The Pack, the Horses and the Rooster Jack dropped their heads in prayer to the man-God while the rest of the Animals observed the moment of silence with their eyes closed but heads held high.

"Thank you," Preston said and walked back pensively into the farmhouse. He retired to the couch in the living room. Most of the Animals turned back to their work. Bart the Horse and his family returned to the front gate, moving slowly down the gravel path in silence. Percy and the Cats went to gather around the grave Cody had dug for their fallen warrior. They would sit and cry softly until sunset.

"Frank," Cody said as they took a few steps away from where the Pack still stood near the corral, "you have to address the Farm."

"Let me talk to Preston, see what he says and then we can decide on the best course of action," Frank said. "The last thing we want to do right now is undermine his authority."

"I understand," Cody said. "But this waiting makes no sense whatsoever."

"I know," Frank said and nodded in the direction of the giant oak the Pack called home. That was Cody's cue to take the Pack back to the tree.

Frank walked briskly to the House. At the porch, at the bottom of the stairs, he was met by a Boar with thick, course, black hair covering his massive body. He stood a head higher than Frank. Frank smiled a soft, Labrador smile.

"Hello Dutch," Frank said.

26

Dutch did not smile. "Preston is in a meeting with his advisors. He told me to tell you he could meet with you in twenty minutes to a half hour." The Boar stared at Frank.

Frank stared back and sighed deeply. Finally he said, "Okay Dutch, I'll wait." Frank barely muffled a growl.

"Fine," Dutch said. He walked up the steps and resumed his post on the porch. Frank dropped to the ground and made himself comfortable next to the bottom step.

"By the way," Frank said, "Cody sends his regards."

Dutch flinched at this reference to his closest friend. "Please send my regards back to him," Dutch said.

Forty minutes later, there was a muffled voice from the door of the farmhouse. Dutch stepped down a couple of steps. "Comrade Preston will see you now."

Frank started when Dutch's voice called out. He had managed to regain his composure after being told to wait and had fallen asleep.

"Thank you," Frank said, as he rose to his feet and stretched.

Frank entered the living room. None of the furniture had survived in this room. There was a large bed of hay, where the Pigs could rest and a tub of food – eggs, carrots, corn and other treats – so that Preston and the members of the administration could eat whenever and whatever they wished.

"We might want to have this conversation in private," Frank said, lifting his muzzle in Dutch's direction.

"Anything you would like to say to me can be said in front of Dutch," Preston said. Preston's eyes were bloodshot and he seemed tired for this hour of the morning.

"Is Dutch replacing Carter as your head of security?" Frank asked.

"No."

A few moments later, Frank understood. Dutch was now Preston's personal bodyguard. Frank barely suppressed a smile. His eyes flickered briefly with amusement but just as quickly regained their watery look of concern. The seriousness of the situation had also wiped any show of humor from Preston's now jowly face.

"I realize Preston that this is the second time in the six months you have been our leader that I have offered unsolicited advice. I want you to understand I don't do so lightly."

Frank paused to give Preston an opportunity to respond. Preston stared at Frank as if he was sitting through a long lecture on the history of man. "I offer this advice in the spirit of having carried the burden you carry."

"I value your counsel," Preston interrupted. "I truly do."

"Alright," Frank said, "this is my counsel. Don't wait to strike back. Strike back this morning while the scent is fresh. The Beagles can track their scent and the Pack can strike back quickly. By tomorrow, the rats will have disappeared into the forest and so will our opportunity for retribution. By the time we have a consensus with the other Farms, any hope of locating the real culprits will be lost. We will be in a position of trying to slaughter any and all wilds that might have been involved in the attack."

Preston sighed deeply and looked down his nose at Frank. Frank felt as if he was now in school and had ignored an obvious premise. "You know our agreement with the other Farms, Frank. We must build a consensus. It is the only way for long-term peace."

"But Preston, you told us we could defend ourselves from attack. As far as I am concerned staying on the trail of a retreating enemy is the same battle only on our terms instead of theirs."

"I don't see it that way," Preston said slowly. "That seems to be a selective reading of the terms of the pact. I did not promise to build a united front with the other Farms just to get elected as many in your Pack believe. I believe it is going to lead to a better life for all of us in the long run."

Frank felt the walls pressing in on him. He couldn't stand to be inside. "A large coalition of forces is not the way to fight a group of marauding rats who amazingly have teamed with foxes and weasels," Frank said. His voice now filled the room.

"I disagree and so does Dutch," Preston said. Frank looked quickly at Dutch who continued to stare at his former friend. "If we strike as a united force," Preston continued, "we can drive them from the forest into open ground and wipe them out."

"That's ridiculous. The forest is so big you would never know if you had Sabean in the group of wilds fleeing the forest. How can you believe you will root him out?"

The slight by Frank did not go unnoticed and Frank regretted his error immediately.

"Dutch has experience fighting with Cody and was trained by Jackson as were you. He is convinced this is the right way to fight the wilds and I am going to follow his advice."

"Dutch fights bravely but he fights large animals, wild dogs and raccoons. Neither Cody or Dutch fight rats well as it is not their specialty."

"If we form a tight enough line and there are enough Animals to march through the forest it will work," Preston said.

"I've never seen that work on rats," Frank said in a tone of resigned calm.

"It will," Preston said.

Frank thought for a moment and noticed that there was a blanket on the bed in the large room next door. He glared at Preston for a moment and then regained his composure. "At the very least, let one of the members of the Pack accompany Carter on his mission," Frank said.

"What are you saying Frank?" Dutch asked taking a step toward Frank and breaking his self-imposed silence.

"I am going to continue to be blunt," Frank said. "Dogs are better equipped to fight rats, foxes and weasels than Pigs. I am suggesting you let a couple of Beagles join you."

Dutch laughed. "Rats are no danger to a Pig, a Goat and a Bull," he said. "We'll be fine."

Frank looked at Preston and directed his words toward the leader again. Dutch had inched a little too close, and Frank couldn't stop the fur on his back from lifting just a little. "Preston," Frank said, "you are being obstinate and putting the Farm and your delegation at risk."

"That's enough, Frank," Preston said, losing his condescending tone. "This meeting is over. In the future, you can keep your own counsel."

Dutch took another step toward Frank and nudged him in the direction of the door. Frank jumped behind Dutch in a flash and bared his teeth at Dutch's vulnerable haunches before Dutch could turn his huge mass around. "Don't ever touch me again Dutch," Frank said with a snarl.

"Ah yes," Preston said laughing, "one must let sleeping dogs lie."

*　　　　　*　　　　　*　　　　　*

Frank padded slowly down the gravel road so he could regain his composure before addressing the Pack and their supporters. Bees hummed among the carnations lining the road but Frank could hear only his inner voice. As he neared the gate, he saw the Cats still paying their respects in the cemetery on the opposite side of the road from the Pack's oak tree. They intermittently howled and cleaned rat blood from their paws and turned their serious Cat faces to the focused morning sun.

Bart and his family stood at the gate. The Pack was gathered under the oak tree. Cody had a Dog looking West, East, South and North. The other members slept.

Those who were asleep woke as Frank's scent drifted into their sensitive noses. The Beagles, who had been growling in their sleep woke

29

and stood, ready to track Sabean's scent. The Pack knew if they could take out Sabean and a couple of the foxes the war would be over.

Frank sighed deeply, a slight growl releasing from his chest, as he tried once more to release, or at the very least hide, his anger. Cody looked at him, patiently at first, and waited for Frank to speak. Finally, Cody couldn't help himself and spoke first. "I knew it. They want us to sit tight while Carter seeks a consensus with the alliance."

Cody stood erect, his fur high on his back. Frank admired Cody's restraint. Just a year ago Cody would have flown down the gravel road, bolted into the farmhouse and ripped Preston's throat out. Frank looked at Cody with concerned, Labrador eyes.

"Cody's right," Frank said, turning his attention to the entire Pack. "Preston still believes the best way to confront the wilds is by uniting with the other Farms. He believes it is the only way to achieve everlasting peace."

"Is there such a thing?" Percy asked as he approached.

Frank did not respond.

"But why not let us defend ourselves by taking a war already begun right back at the enemy?" Patrick said from Cody's side. The Beagles had grown up with Cody and they all remained close friends but Cody and Patrick were closest. Although Patrick's sister was the master killer of rats, Patrick could track a wild over rivers and from tree to tree. Their brother, Pete, was fastest and tireless.

"Preston seems to believe that only by uniting and marching through the forest en mass and from three directions can the war be won."

"But a rat can hide here at Manor Farm and we may never know," Patrick said.

"I know Patrick, I know," Frank said. "I used that same logic and passion. I will concede this is Preston's true belief and not a political stance."

"I am not so sure about that," Percy said.

"With that said Frank, what should the Pack do?" Cody asked.

"I'm not sure. We will hold a debate and then decide. I am inclined to hold the course and let Preston lead. That is the will of the majority of the Animals on the Farm. I will take that position. Cody, would you like to take the position of tracking the wilds, counter-attacking, and then asking Preston and the administration for forgiveness?"

Cody looked at his friend for a moment, not breaking eye contact. "Typically I would agree to do so Frank," Cody said slowly. "But this is an issue where we should defer to your leadership and let no Animal or wild doubt that the Pack stands together with its leader and the Cats and

Horses." Cody dropped his head. Looking back up he said, "This is time to be more Dogs than citizens."

"Yes," the other members of the Pack said in unison.

"Very well," Frank said immediately seeing that his protégé saw the issue more clearly. "Cody, Bart, Percy – I would like your counsel." The other Animals moved a polite distance away so the four leaders could discuss the next steps to be taken without having to whisper.

"Percy, I'd like to start with you and to hear what you think is best for the Farm."

Percy stared in the direction of the barn. All of them knew Percy well enough to know he was formulating a response and not ignoring Frank. Percy licked his forearm a couple of times and used it to wipe his long, white whiskers against his jet black face. Percy was formulating an oral essay to set forth his opinion.

"As we all know, this was not your garden variety rat raid," Percy said. "No one will disagree with that. So I think letting them regroup and attack us or another farm is unwise. The force was at least four or five thousand strong and Sabean can probably raise a force twice that size once what happened here last night spreads through the Animal lands. I think we all agree that taking the fight to the rats is the best solution. The real issue before us is whether the situation is so grave that it warrants violating one of the ten laws of the Farm. Do we violate the tenet that we honor the orders of the administration? I think the answer must be yes for three reasons.

"First, we will not be able to find Sabean unless we move now. Second, the rats are united and will gain in strength if this victory goes unpunished. Many will join the cause if we let this fester. Finally, I am doubtful the three Farms will reach a consensus. I say we attack and beg Preston for forgiveness. It is the best course for the Farm."

Frank nodded and turned toward to Cody. "Cody?"

"I agree with Percy," Cody said. "This was not a raid but a declaration of war. It is a call to duty but one I believe the other two Farms will ignore. They will ignore it because Preston's battle strategy may work for a year but can only cause disaster in the long run."

"Okay, is that it?" Frank asked.

"Yes," Cody said. "Logic and my heart tell me that we must take this course of action if we want to avoid a disaster for our Farm."

"Alright," Frank said. "Bart, what is your opinion?"

"I must disagree with my friends. I have seen many things during my decades on the Farm. This attack was something unusual, I must confess. However, in all crises we have followed the laws of the Farm and allowed the administration in place at the time to govern. Manor Farm

31

must be first and foremost a democracy. It is not right for us to fight a good fight without official sanction. It is our duty to let Preston lead and help him be successful."

Bart flipped his tail casually, knocking the flies off his hindquarters but his eyes burnt with a sad resolve. Frank looked at his friends and advisors for a moment, and regretted for the first time that he did not try to sway more members of the Farm to vote for him.

"Okay, anything else?" he asked.

They all shook their heads.

"Let me think on it for a bit," Frank said.

He walked down the gravel path and out the gate and spread himself on the dirt road running along the fence. He looked at what had been the corral hundreds of years ago but now was the lushest field of green grass on the Farm. Cows walked slowly around nibbling the springtime treats. Frank allowed the pros and cons of each course of action to roll over in images of result through his brain. He started to doze.

When Frank woke he was no closer to a clear answer. He had only had a counsel once before where he had encouraged a debate with his advisors. Frank believed one's initial reaction to an issue should form the basis for a decision. He was gifted with vision. However, his instinct to chase down Sabean, despite Preston's order to the contrary, couldn't overcome the bias he had developed as leader of the Farm. A leader should be allowed to lead, Frank thought.

Frank, his black fur now covered with a thin layer of dust, padded slowly back to the Pack, Percy and the Horses, who still congregated under the giant oak tree. Percy was the only Cat that had left the gravesite of the fallen warrior. Frank glanced at the open gate as he re-entered the Farm. It had stood that way for hundreds years and was rusted and covered with brush. To Frank, the open gate represented Manor Farm's power. Never to be closed again, it symbolized the Farm's strength and lack of any lingering fear of man or wild beast. Now Frank had the urge to order Bart to pull it close.

He spoke softly when he reached the Animals gathered in the rays of light filtering through the branches of the oak. "My Animals in Arms, this is what I believe. Our ancestors put a system in place hundreds of years ago to govern Manor Farm. It has worked over these centuries because all Animals could rely on each of the other Animals to defend Manor Farm and comply with the directives of the administration. It is not for us to change the rules and laws now because the current administration is making a decision we believe foolhardy. We must stay the course, defend the Farm and follow Preston as our duly elected leader."

The Animals stood silently. Not one protested. Not one shouted out in agreement. Frank stood for a moment and then made his way to the far side of the oak tree, closer to the fence that still surrounded Manor Farm. Cody followed and looked down at Frank. Cody stood over him with a look Frank had never seen before.

"Are you okay?" Cody asked.

Frank smiled. The look on Cody's face was one of concern and indecision. "Yes, my friend, I am fine. Please don't worry. I am just not sure I've made the right decision."

Cody nodded his large, triangular head. Frank was amused that, even when sad and uncertain, Cody looked fearsome. Ah, to be a German Sheppard, Frank thought.

"I may not agree with this decision or others you have made, Frank, but I want you to know one thing," Cody said. "I, and the other members of the Pack, will follow you. You are our leader until you say otherwise."

"Or I die," Frank said with a twinkle in his eye.

"Or until you die," Cody said with a bemused smile. Cody plopped down next to Frank and they remained silent until sleep overwhelmed them in the warm early afternoon heat.

CHAPTER FOUR – A KNIGHT'S ERRAND

When Carter woke early the next morning, the Farm felt eerily mundane. Carter was met at the barn by Dutch and Alexander, a giant, black Bull. Carter had laughed when Dutch told him of Frank's request that a Dog act as a guard. Carter knew that the three of them could manage against a pack of wild dogs and perhaps even against a pack of wolves. They sauntered down the gravel road through the front gate with pride.

"Best of luck," Bart said as they passed by.

"Thank you Bart," Carter said.

Dutch nodded in the Horse's direction. Alexander smiled at Bart but did not speak.

The journey to Knight Farm was a day and a half at a walking pace. They would need to stop along the road for the night. This made both of them a bit nervous despite their prodigious mass.

Alexander asked what the approach would be at Knight Farm with King George and Louis. Preston had been clear in his instructions, Carter explained – come back with an agreement for war. The best option was an all out attack on Beaver Creek Forest from the West, East and North. The other option was an agreement to await the fleeing wilds as Manor Farm's forces pushed through the forest from the West.

"What if they don't agree to an all out war against the wilds?" Alexander asked.

"The current plan is then we sit tight, wait for a different farm to be attacked and then we forge our alliance for war," Carter said.

"That does not seem like a sound fallback position," Alexander said.

"Don't worry Alex, they will agree to war," Carter said.

They walked along the road in silence. Beaver Creek rushed along to the South of the road.

*   *   *

Preston stepped out to the top of the porch stairs to address the Farm two hours after Carter had set out on his mission. During his six months as the leader of Manor Farm, he had implemented many of his domestic policies. From the date of his election, the Goats received as much oats and hay per Animal as Bart and his family. However, some of the Cows and Alexander shared with the Horses to keep them well-fed. The Cats received as many eggs per Animal as the Dogs. Of course, Percy gave the overabundance to the Pack. The new system's fragility was masked by the citizens' generosity.

"This is a time for reflection," Preston began. "Have the policies of the past come back to haunt us? Have our overreaction to the attacks of the past resulted in our current, everlasting state of conflict with the wilds? I am not saying the violence imparted by the wilds was in any way justified. I am simply asking if the killing of twenty rats for stealing a few eggs for a meal was justified. As you all know that has been our response on numerous occasions.

I say perhaps we have played a part in this mess by unilaterally deciding on the punishment for the rats. We need our alliance to check our actions. It is time to develop a new strategy. We will present a united front. We will defend ourselves but shall no longer act alone to impose our own brand of justice in the name of vengeance."

Preston's speech went on like this for some time, but he merely repeated the same theme in a variety of different and flowery ways. Most of the Animals did not understand what Preston was trying to convey. Despite their confusion, they shouted out agreement at the end because Preston always appeared on the side of equality and justice.

When Preston finished, Cody stood and made his way down the gravel road. He was intercepted by Roger, the Drake who typically spoke for the Ducks. Roger stared at Cody.

"He's right you know," Roger said.

"What's that Roger?" Cody asked.

"Your Pack and the Cats have always overreacted. It was those actions that pushed the wild animals to unite."

"You can't believe that," Cody said. "We struck back forcefully to make sure all wilds knew the safety of our Farm should not be breached."

"It is always revenge with you Dogs," Roger said. "Have you ever considered what it feels like to be a rat out in the wild? Show some sympathy."

"Come on Roger," Cody said his fur rising up on his back. On his large Sheppard frame, the long hair looked like wheat blowing in the wind. "We defended you and yours and the rest of the Farm."

Cody wished he could will the hair on his back to flatten along the curve of his muscular back. But it was too late.

"I see that Cody," Roger said with his head cocked to one side and his eyes locked on Cody's back. "Violence is always the answer with you and the Pack."

*   *   *   *

"Let's stop here for the night," Carter said with a sigh.

"Alright," Dutch said. "Let me find a good spot off the road for us to sleep."

Dutch moved slowly through the brush. The forest grew silent as he worked his way deeper into the trees and away from the road. Sensing danger, Dutch turned his head east, toward Manor Farm. He spied three pairs of eyes gleaming in the moonlight. Jackson had trained him well during better times and Dutch knew the eyes belonged to raccoons. Jackson had also taught him that even a manageable threat should be met with the necessary precautions. Dutch knew he could take six or seven raccoons but decided not to take any chances. He trotted through the forest, making no effort at silence, and found Carter and Alexander still in the middle of the dirt road.

"What's the problem?" Carter asked.

"I saw three pairs of raccoon eyes," Dutch said.

"So?" Carter said.

"I think we should continue on for a mile or so and sleep in the road with a watch," Dutch said.

"But they're raccoons," Carter said. "What could they possibly do to the three of us?"

"Probably nothing but I am not taking any chances," Dutch said. "Your safety is too important to the Farm."

Carter grinned as only a Goat can. "Fine, you are the head of security. I'll defer to you."

Carter turned toward Alexander expecting to see the Bull's teeth in the moonlight, contrasting against his jet black coat. Instead, Alexander was already stepping forward down the road in clear agreement with Dutch.

A half an hour later, Dutch stopped and lay down in the middle of the road. "Alex, you take the first watch, then me and then Carter," Dutch said.

"Alright," Alexander said.

"Is a watch really necessary?" Carter asked. "I need my rest for the diplomatic discussions."

"I think it is," Dutch said. "Plus the delegate from Snail Farm will arrive later than us and we should have some time to rest before the talks. This is the case even if Louis left as soon as our Crow arrived at Snail Farm. That message wasn't sent until King George agreed to meet."

"That's true," Carter said too tired to argue the point.

Each Animal took a turn staring into the forest on either side of the road. They did not hear a strange sound or eye a dangerous wild the entire night.

*   *   *   *

The next morning, Frank and Cody sat under the giant oak. The rest of the Pack slept quietly in the bright, morning sun, a short distance away. Dew covered the grass but Frank and Cody wanted to be alone so they ignored the chill caused by the moisture and the shade of the oak.

"It's infuriating Frank," Cody said.

"I know, but the Animals will always believe what makes them feel safest. Preston created a sense of fear during the election to get votes and now he is doing the same."

"How so?" Cody asked. "It seems he merely tried to make us look incompetent and out of touch with current thinking."

"Well, he ran on the platform that our policies drove the wilds to raid us time and again," Frank said. "He used the Animals' fear of the wilds then and he is doing the same now."

"But why? He has won the election."

Before Frank could answer, Patrick and Paulie ran through the gate with their tongues dangling on the sides of their mouths despite the brisk morning air.

"Well?" Frank asked.

"It was strange," Patrick said. "We trailed them like you asked us too. Just as the sun set we picked up the scent of some raccoons. A bit later, Dutch went into the woods, I think to find a place for them to sleep."

Patrick paused for a few seconds to catch his breath. Sensing Frank and Cody's impatience, Paulie picked up the story. "We went into the woods about two hundred yards behind Dutch. We approached slowly and just when we could make out Dutch's huge black frame we saw the strangest thing. The raccoons, three of them, were in a tree watching Dutch."

"So?" Cody said.

"The fact that they were in a tree watching Dutch was not strange but what they did after was very unsettling. When Dutch spotted them he high-tailed it back to the road. The raccoons jumped from the tree and trailed Dutch like they were stalking prey. Luckily Dutch understood there might be danger and took precautions."

"Interesting," Frank said. "I guess Dutch really paid attention to Jackson's training."

"Seems so," Cody said.

"It is a shame he fell into Preston's camp," Frank said, despite his run-in with Dutch. "He is an excellent fighter."

"Yes but all species end up sticking together," Cody said. "Always have and always will."

"Alright," Frank said to the Beagles, irritated he let himself get sidetracked, "then what happened?"

"Dutch went back to Carter and Alex and they walked for another mile and made camp in the middle of the road with a watch," Patrick said.

"Smart," Cody said.

"Then what happened?" Frank said, impatient with any commentary, even from Cody.

"Nothing," Patrick said. "The raccoons did not follow once Dutch regrouped with Carter and Alex and we didn't catch the scent of a wild the rest of the night."

"Thank you," Frank said. "No watch for you tonight."

"Thank you," they said in unison.

"Excellent work," Frank said.

After a few moments of silence, Cody moved off to be alone in the sun, out from the shade of the giant oak. Frank padded after him a couple of minutes later.

"What's on your mind?" Frank asked.

"It's strange."

"The raccoons?"

"Yeah. Strange they tracked Dutch."

"Well, raccoons eat a lot of things," Frank said.

"Yes they do. But a full-grown Boar is not the best thing for three raccoons to try to eat."

"What are you saying Cody?"

"I'm not sure. It's just strange. I feel like it's related to the attack on the Farm."

"I think you are being paranoid, my friend," Frank said as gently as he could.

After a long pause, Cody said, "Yeah, maybe I am."

CHAPTER FIVE – A KING'S CASTLE

King George moved slowly through the darkness of his private quarters, his dark face hidden but the black curls that covered his body seeming to give off light. Although he had lived less than two-thirds of a Longhorn Sheep's average lifespan, tonight he felt much older. The Owls that acted as his spies had brought news of the attack on Manor Farm. His Owls had shared the news early that morning, long before the Crow sent by Preston had arrived asking for a meeting of what only Preston and Carter call "The Alliance." The Crows let him know that the second in command at Manor Farm, the Goat named Carter, would arrive within a few days. Louis, the Ambassador from Snail Farm, would arrive sometime shortly thereafter. It seemed tranquility at Knight Farm would never last long enough for King George to enjoy the Farm's prosperity.

The muscles on his large frame managed to express their power through his thick coat as King George made his way through the outer rooms where his twenty-two Lambs slept. A number of them were too old to be referred to as Lambs, but he still thought of them that way. His quarters were grand, made entirely of stone many centuries ago by human hands and later by Animal might.

The castle had a great stone hall, an eating area and three wings with many rooms in each. His extended family lived in the other wings of the castle. The Great Hall, as it was called, was often filled with advisors and other Animals close to the King. It had grand banners hanging from the rafters glorifying Knight Farm as the first farm to free itself from the oppressive reign of man. He often wondered why a history had never been written about this greatest of Animal feats, when the revolution of Manor Farm centuries later continued to be the subject of much folklore and had been immortalized by man.

But today, a different string of thoughts ran through his mind. He found it both amusing and troubling that the problems he faced ruling his kingdom were the same as those faced by farmers during the reign of man – disease and wild animals. Today, the topic of discussion with his advisors would be the same as that of his great-great-great grandfather who had freed the Farm nearly four hundred years before. How do we deal with the wilds?

These thoughts drifted away as his cape brushed the ground and he clacked down the stone steps into the Great Hall. His personal guards, two Giant Schnauzers, fell in behind him as he stepped off the last stair. The light of a new day peered over the mountains from the East and into the Great Hall. Two Cow-sized Mastiffs, standing as tall as King George, cast giant shadows on the hall floor from their position at the great wooden doors leading out to the courtyard. His closest advisors: his brother, Prince James, and Sir Andrew, a Llama, stood at a giant stone table at the far end of the hall.

"What is the news James?" King George asked his brother, as he took the final couple of steps up to the table.

"They will arrive mid-morning tomorrow," James said in a baritone even deeper than George's. "Sir Andrew will meet them on the outskirts and escort them in with a team from the Royal Guard. We will allow Louis to arrive on his own so as not to insult his sensitive disposition."

"And then what?" King George asked.

"We will all dine together and let them rest for a night before we begin the talks," Prince James said matter-of-factly. Politics bored King George's brother.

"Thank you, James," King George said. "Sir Andrew, what is the state of our security?"

"We have doubled the guard around the perimeter. Each emissary from the other Farms will have their own guard."

"What about lookouts?" King George asked.

"Yes, your Highness, we will have four Owls by night and four Hawks by day circling the Farm," Sir Andrew said.

"Excellent," King George said. "Now, I would like your advice on what our original stance should be on this issue. It seems there is little doubt as to why Manor Farm called this summit. Sir Andrew, what should be the starting point for our discussions with Manor Farm?"

Andrew stood over the two Sheep, slowly chewing his cud, his long fur white as clouds. The color made the King's coat appear to be a dull black. Fortunately, vanity was not one of King George's character flaws. Sir Andrew's pale blue eyes moved back and forth from King George to Prince James as he thought.

The stone table had two maps spread over its surface. One map was of Knight Farm and other of the parts of the world where Animals ruled and of which man had stopped thinking about long ago. Sir Andrew stared at the second of these maps while he gathered his thoughts.

"My military opinion is this," Sir Andrew said. "A full-scale war, based on the alliance of the Farms, to destroy or bring a group of loosely associated wilds to the table to talk peace makes little sense from a long-term point of view."

"Yes," King George said. "You made this opinion known forcefully when Manor Farm proposed the alliance. Now the question is how do we respond, given we never finalized a treaty but we agreed in principal that we would work hard to form such an alliance."

King George did not want to revisit an old issue but wanted to focus on the issue at hand.

"Well, with all due respect, Your Highness," Sir Andrew said slowly, "at this point they are one and the same."

King George realized Sir Andrew was not rehashing old arguments as it related to the proposed alliance. Sir Andrew believed that Preston sought such an alliance so that a war as the one to be proposed could transpire. "I think I see where you are going with this but please elaborate," King George said.

"I raise this, your Highness, in order for you to see the source of my concern as it relates to pursuing the course of action I believe Manor Farm will advocate," Sir Andrew said. "I believe they will seek a united effort to seek out and destroy Sabean and his followers. More than this, the proposal will be a wide sweep through the wild forests to drive them out. I believe this is not a prudent course of action and thus we should not adhere to the spirit of a treaty we have not yet agreed to."

"And delineate for me why it would be unsound to join Manor and Snail Farms just to destroy Sabean's forces," King George said.

"Because the trail is lost Your Highness," Sir Andrew said. "Even if we could find them we could not force a battle."

"Why not?" King George asked.

"For a number of reasons," Sir Andrew said. "First, they will retreat into the man lands. We will not follow. Their alliance is very loose and based only on attack and not defense. Rats don't think the way we do. They won't defend land, they won't defend each other and they certainly won't protect the foxes and the weasels and same holds true in reverse. We could do a lot of damage and maybe get lucky and find Sabean but that is doubtful. We will probably be able to track down some foxes and weasels but will they be the right ones?"

"But won't pushing them into the man lands give us peace as Preston and Carter suggest?" King George asked.

"In my opinion, no," Sir Andrew said. "If we don't get Sabean we will always be on alert for a mass attack. Even if we do get him, the rats will cross back into the Animal lands over time and things will be as they always have been."

"Why?" King George asked with a raised Sheep eyebrow.

"Men are better at killing rats than we are."

"Then what course do you suggest?" King George asked.

"I would join a limited mission to find and kill just Sabean."

"An assassination you mean?"

"Yes," Sir Andrew said. "That is the word for it, your Highness. I suggest we send some Owls and a few Schnauzers to hunt with the Manor Farm Beagles and Cats for just Sabean and not his army.

"Thank you, Sir Andrew," King George said with a smile. King George was unable to contain his amusement at Sir Andrew's cold, calculating Llama brain.

"James, what are your thoughts?"

"I respectfully disagree with Sir Andrew," Prince James said. "Not so much with his military analysis but on the proposed course of action. I think agreeing to a full-scale attack on Sabean and his force is the correct solution for two reasons. First, we made a pact with Manor Farm and if Sabean's attack does not warrant a unified attack then what does? Second, an attack, even if only successful in driving the rats out of the Animal lands for a short period, sends a very strong message that we are united and will strike back fiercely."

"Thank you, James," King George said. King George knew his brother would have said more if there was more to say. "Anything else either of you would like to add?"

"Yes your Highness," Sir Andrew said. "I think a mass attack would result in as many casualties as we inflict."

"How so?"

"Rats are difficult to catch and I get the feeling they have trained themselves to isolate individual soldiers and subject them to an overwhelming attack. Therefore, a mass attack where we spread ourselves thin might not be advisable. More importantly, I think this will start a war with no end if we push through the forest and drive all wilds, affiliated with Sabean or not, out of the forest."

King George stood silently for a moment, his big, black eyes shining in the morning light of the Great Hall. "I see," he finally said. "Well, I am not sure I know the right course of action. Let's see what the summit reveals and we shall then decide accordingly."

*   *   *   *

The contingent from Manor Farm made their way down the dirt road at a brisk pace in the late morning sunshine. They had started out before sunrise. The sky was a deep blue, seeming to reflect the multitude of lakes surrounding and inside Knight Farm. A quiet "Caw" broke the silence, and the Goat, Boar and Bull turned in unison to watch a large Red-tailed Hawk glide over them and land on a thick branch of a dying redwood tree. The branch was ten feet high and nearly crossed the dirt road. The Hawk landed facing the opposite direction and popped around to face them.

"Greetings, honorable visitors from Manor Farm," the Hawk said in a thick Knight Farm accent. "I am David of the Royal Guard."

Carter was happy he could understand the words through the thick accent. "Greetings David," Carter said. "I am Carter, First Advisor to Preston, the leader of Manor Farm. This is Dutch, who is in charge of security at Manor Farm and reports to me, and this is Alexander, part of our watch and my personal body guard."

"Greetings Sirs," David said with military politeness. His black eyes seemed to look through to their innards despite his deferential words. "I have been instructed to tell you that Sir Andrew and other members of the Royal Guard shall meet you about a half a mile from the gates of Knight Farm. Expect them a bit after the road turns to stone."

"That is very kind," Carter said. "Thank you."

"Standard operating procedures for a dignitary but you are most welcome Sir," David said with no hint of sarcasm.

David jumped off the branch of the tree and swooped down to within a few inches of the ground before a tilt of his long, brown wings took him soaring into the sky with a shriek. As he bent against the air to head toward Knight Farm, he was joined by two Hawks on either side of him. The visitors from Manor Farm had not been aware of their presence until they flew in behind David.

"A very polite Hawk," Carter said to neither of them in particular.

"I got the distinct impression he would rather poke our eyes out than talk to us," Dutch said.

Carter ignored this and said, "Well, let's go then."

Neither Dutch nor Alexander said a word. They continued walking down the dirt road. They had rehearsed their roles and the party line so many times even Carter managed to bite his tongue.

Carter let Dutch continue to lead them and watched the giant Boar intently. It amazed Carter that the giant Boar with the grotesque, black hair could move so nimbly. The muscles of his haunches shimmied with each step Dutch took. Carter could tell that even Alexander looked upon Dutch with passive admiration.

As they had made their way from Manor Farm to Knight Farm, they had climbed about two thousand feet. The woods of oak and maple had slowly turned to a forest of sequoias and redwoods. This close to Knight Farm, the trees towered over the well-used road that now turned to gravel. The road was well-groomed by the Animals of Knight Farm. Carter, who had been here twice before, knew that within a half mile of the farm the gravel would turn to stone. In addition, a rock wall, six feet high would protect travelers from the dangers of the forest. On Carter's two prior visits, he had been a student and then an envoy for a candidate who had not yet been elected. On the first occasion there had been no escort. On the second occasion, Dutch and Alexander had accompanied him to the gate and stayed there while Carter met with King George.

A short time later, Carter spied the escort at the top of a hill a few hundred yards ahead. The escort, led by Sir Andrew, started down the hill toward them. Carter glanced at Dutch, about to point them out, but he could tell by his narrowing eyes that he had spied them long before Carter had.

Sir Andrew, his white coat making him hard to define in the bright sun, was flanked by two Llamas who each stood a foot shorter than the lead of the Royal Guard. Behind the Llamas strutted four full-sized Schnauzers. The Schnauzers, despite their generally pleasant appearance of grey coat and bright eyes, set Carter's stomach empty. Dutch pushed forward, clearly unimpressed.

When they were within ten feet of Sir Andrew and the other members of the escort, Dutch stepped aside to allow Carter to greet them. Carter stood tall, his stomach now firm, and lowered his head as custom dictated when greeting royalty. Carter waited for Sir Andrew to speak. Sir Andrew waited a bit longer than Carter would have liked.

"Greetings, First Advisor," Sir Andrew said. "It is a pleasure to see you again, Carter. Welcome to Knight Farm. May I introduce Captain Neal and Sergeant Emerson?"

"A pleasure," Carter said. "May I introduce Dutch, who is in charge of security for Manor Farm, and Alexander, one of our guards and my personal body guard."

Sir Andrew nodded to Dutch and Alexander but did not address them. Nor did he mention the presence of the Schnauzers. Two of the Dogs had moved behind the Manor Farm contingent and assumed positions at the rear of the group.

Carter and Sir Andrew started toward Knight Farm. The other two Schnauzers jumped onto the ten foot wall with ease and walked along it a few yards ahead of the group, with their noses and eyes focused on the forest.

"Your soldiers are incredibly well-trained," Carter said nodding toward the Schnauzers. "I wish I could control our Dogs that way."

Sir Andrew looked down at Carter, his blue eyes twinkling with a look of amused astonishment. "All members of the Royal Guard act out of a sense of duty, Dogs included," Sir Andrew said. "I do not control them in the slightest. I never forget they'd rip the tendons from my legs if they ever decided my leadership was lacking or that I ever held them in anything but the highest regard."

"Well, what I meant to say . . ."

"How is Leader Frank enjoying retirement?" Sir Andrew interrupted.

"It is difficult to say," Carter said. "He doesn't act as if he trusts our administration to lead the Farm."

"Interesting," Sir Andrew said looking straight down the now stone road. "What makes you say so?"

"Well, he realigned the Pack's security responsibilities despite our request to keep it the same. We had moved the Dogs from the protection of the barn and the coop so he increased the watch on the perimeter of the farm."

"Why would you and Preston see fit to remove the Dogs from their assignments at the barn and the coop?" Sir Andrew asked. "Isn't this the most vulnerable and susceptible location for attack?"

"We believe many Animals are capable of performing those duties and our administration passionately believes in equal opportunity."

"I see," Sir Andrew said.

They walked in silence for a time as they made their way to Knight Farm.

*   *   *   *

The stones laid to make the road to Knight Farm were white from use and were anywhere from six to ten feet in length and three to five feet in width. They had been put in place by the Animals of Knight Farm, shortly after their independence over four hundred years earlier. In addition, a stone wall surrounded the entire two thousand acres of Knight Farm. The wall stood ten feet tall and was four feet wide. The wall had stood the test of time through war and sometimes vicious storms.

For Animals too big to crawl between the stones and unable to scale the wall, there were only two ways into the grand farm, the front and the rear entrances. The front entrance faced west toward Manor Farm. The East entrance faced east toward Snail Farm. All visitors must enter through the front or West entrance. Any visitors approaching from the East were sent around the Farm by security so they could enter through the main entrance.

The purpose of this restriction was twofold. First, security within the Western edge of the Farm was much tighter because that was the location of King George's castle. Second, and more important to Sir Andrew and Lord Winston who led the Royal Army, was the majesty of the front entrance. It signified the strength of Knight Farm and showed all who entered that in the Animal Lands, Knight Farm stood alone as the leader.

The wall made defense from wolves, coyotes and wild dogs much easier for Sir Andrew than for Cody and now Dutch at Manor Farm. Because of this, Knight Farm's largest security issue was rats. Rats found their way into the Farm over, under and through the stone wall. The rats figured out that the Schnauzers could not get them inside the wall and there were enough holes for the rats to navigate through to escape. Cats did not reside at Knight Farm.

Occasionally a pack of wolves or dogs would attack Knight Farm but these were quickly and bloodily quashed. The Mastiffs and Schnauzers of Knight Farm relished the opportunity to fight these wilds. Llamas released their hidden energy by stomping the wilds to death.

Over the centuries the Guard and Army of Knight Farm had perfected their tactics in fighting the wilds. Individual Mastiffs and pairs of Schnauzers would engage a wolf or wild dog. Once each attacker was engaged or otherwise distracted in battle, the Llamas, led by Sir Andrew or one of his predecessors, would join the fighting and kick and stomp on the attackers. The first time this tactic was implemented, the forces of Knight Farm killed thirty of the seventy-five members of the attacking pack of dogs before the leader signaled the retreat. As time went on, the tactics of the wolves and wild dogs changed as they attacked with the goal of a kill and some food. They would try to isolate a security force out in the forest to avoid an all-out battle.

Sir Andrew led the contingent up a small hill and stopped at the top. He allowed Carter, Dutch and Alexander to take in the majesty of Knight Farm. A giant stone castle stood a few hundred yards inside the giant wooden gate that currently stood open. Leading to the gate was a stone bridge over a creek than ran just outside the Western wall of Knight Farm. The castle had two large wings pointing forward toward the West. Many large and small residences could be seen as one's eyes moved east. The houses appeared on the horizon as far as the eye could see. Nearly all of the homes were made of stone. These sat among the rolling hills of apple and peach orchards and wheat and corn fields. Even Dutch raised an eyebrow at the spectacular sight. The extent of Knight Farm's accomplishments was unfathomable to the Animals of the other Farms.

The wooden gate, fifteen feet high, was attached to pillars of stone standing a few feet higher by huge rings of iron. Dutch now realized his eyes had played a trick on him. He thought there had been two statutes of lions carved into the bottom of each pillar. Instead these were two of the largest Mastiffs Dutch had ever seen. Last time, he had arrived at with an

46

escort of Schnauzers to take him, Carter and Alexander through the gate, where he and the Bull waited for Carter to return. He hadn't noticed the Mastiffs six months before.

Dutch gave a slight grunt when he realized they were Dogs. Their loose, tan fur drooped from their faces but was pulled taut over their chest and haunches. As they entered Knight Farm, passing by the giant Dogs, the Mastiffs continued to stare straight ahead into the forest, their sad eyes watching for any sign of danger. The Dogs did not acknowledge Sir Andrew and would not do so unless he gave them a military command. The Mastiffs were on duty.

They entered through the gates into a sprawling courtyard. They stood a few hundred yards from the King's castle but only a hundred yards from its shadow. At the entrance to the castle sat two Mastiffs somehow larger than the two at the gate. Halfway between the gate and castle was a large fountain with green mermaids shooting water from their outstretched hands. Carter made a mental note to ask someone how they had managed to maintain the fountain in working order over the many centuries.

To the right of the castle, stood a building nearly as large but built of stone bricks ten feet by ten feet and as plain as the palace was majestic. The Royal Guard's Llamas lived on the bottom floor while the Mastiffs and Schnauzers of the Royal Guard lived on the second floor. The top floor was the administration building for the Guard and the Army.

On the left side of the courtyard, the Administration building for Knight Farm stood two stories high but its soaring ceilings of the entry stood as tall as the three-story quarters of the Royal Guard. The Administration building was also used to house visitors. The group turned in this direction. It was nearly as magnificent as the Palace but lacked the giant doors of the Great Hall and the magnificent approach that defined the castle. Many of the top administration officials, who were not members of the Royal family, the Guard or the army, lived in this building.

When they were within fifty yards of the Administration building, Sir Andrew stopped and turned toward Carter, Dutch and Alexander. "Sergeant Emerson shall escort you to your quarters," Sir Andrew said. "We will dine in two hours. We will have a bath made up for each of you." This was said more as an order than an offer.

"When can we meet with King George?" Carter asked.

"We will meet first thing in the morning. The Snail Farm ambassador will arrive this evening. The rules of engagement we agreed upon during your last visit require that we wait for a quorum." Sir Andrew looked down at Carter with an amused smile.

"Yes, but we need to act quickly."

Sir Andrew chewed his cud and then responded. "It is much too late to speak of acting quickly. Sergeant Emerson, please show our guests to their quarters."

Sir Andrew turned sharply and moved lightly toward the castle.

"If you will follow me, gentle-Animals," Sergeant Emerson said as he turned toward the Administration building.

Sergeant Emerson led them into the expansive marble foyer. The first floor was made up of meeting rooms, eating rooms for the residents and the staff, offices and bathrooms. Emerson led them up a marble staircase lined with deep, burgundy carpet that was less than ten-years old. Carter could not believe the portraits along the walls leading up the half circle of stairs. The first third were of the humans who were master of the farm many centuries before. The remaining paintings were of members of King George's family who had ruled from the time of the first Animal revolution that took place here at Knight Farm. Carter found it difficult to comprehend that the Animals here, even the Owls and Hawks, had lived like humans for so long.

The tapestries were clearly centuries old because the designs were of humans hunting wolves. However, they had been cleaned and cared for so well they seemed only decades old – loved but at the beginning of their usefulness. Carter's legs relaxed as he stepped on the cushioned carpet. It was a welcome relief from the dirt, gravel and stone he had walked upon over the last two days. Throughout the building, red, purple and a deep green were the only colors to be found expect for a rich, dark mahogany that ran along the floor, ceiling and the parts of the wall that were not plaster. The doors and banisters were made of the same dark, shining wood. Emerson took them down a long hallway and then turned and stopped.

"Here you are, Mr. Carter," Sergeant Emerson said.

He managed to turn the knob deftly with his large Llama toes and push the door open to allow Carter and the others to enter before him. Carter was not surprised to see that, like the room he'd stayed in last time, it had a human bed, a dark writing desk and a large, forest green sofa.

"Thank you," Carter said looking over his shoulder, hoping that he and his escort would be left alone quickly.

"You are most welcome," Sergeant Emerson said. "We shall come and escort you to dinner at seven. One of the Guard shall be outside your door should you be in need of anything."

"Thank you," Carter said with a nod of the head.

"I will see you at the feast," Emerson said.

Emerson shut the door with his hind leg as he exited. Carter couldn't fathom how he had managed it.

Ambassador Louis of Snail Farm made his way slowly down the gravel road heading West. It was a day and a half journey, for the average Animal, from Snail Farm to Knight Farm. The distance was just slightly longer than the journey from Manor Farm. It had taken Louis and his entourage two days. They approached the rear gate with Sir Andrew as an escort. Sir Andrew had decided an escort was prudent and decided to provide one despite Louis's sensitivity.

Louis's personal guard, two frighteningly large Poodles, pranced nervously by his side. Although the Poodles had made many trips to Knight Farm, they had also fought a bloody war against the forces of Knight Farm, just a few years before. They had met Sir Andrew and his Schnauzer escort on the battlefield. Many of the Poodle's comrades had fallen that day.

Louis's belly nearly touched the ground as he waddled over the tiny, jagged rocks. He held his snout high as he came from a long line of government officials. Both his father and his grandfather had led Snail Farm during their lifetimes. Louis's great-grandfather had led a rebellion a hundred years before which led to the overthrow of the Snail Farm Royal Family. The rebels had started a government similar to the one Preston sought to implement at Manor Farm. The government's success had been mixed over the last couple of hundred years.

Louis considered himself lucky to come from a family that had ties deep within the group that controlled Snail Farm. He had studied hard in school and been a successful student and warrior. He garnered the most joy from tutoring university students. Most of these came from Snail Farm, but some came from the other farms that were willing to send their young scholars to Snail Farm for an advanced education. Manor Farm's Pig families and some of the other herd Animals often sent their brightest sons and daughters to study at Snail Farm University.

Louis adjusted his red scarf. It has significance that the casual observer might not understand. It denoted that he was a scholar at the University just as his huge frame with multiple layers of fat signified his high rank and prestige within the ruling party of Snail Farm. His pink flesh was no longer entirely covered with coarse black hair. His sides and back were rubbed bald from a life of leisure.

Sir Andrew led Louis and the two Poodles into the Administration building and up the marble staircase. Louis's stomach caught the carpet as he did his best to keep up with the Llama. The Poodles remained a respectful distance behind Louis despite his occasional mishaps.

"Where is my nephew's advisor staying?" Louis asked Sir Andrew between hurried breaths when they finally reached the top stair.

"He is in the first room on the left down this hall," Sir Andrew said. "We will pass it on the way to your quarters. If you would like to visit him before the evening meal, I will see if it can be arranged."

"Can we stop and pay our regards now?" Louis asked with an amused tone.

"I believe he is in the bath, preparing for dinner as we speak," Sir Andrew said, calmly chewing his cud.

"I see," Louis said.

"We have baths prepared for you and your escort as well," Sir Andrew said with a quick Llama smile. The white fur around his mouth seemed to move without Sir Andrew's own body being aware that a smile was forthcoming.

"Actually they are my personal guard just as King George has his personal guard of Schnauzers," Louis said.

"I see Ambassador. I beg your pardon. I find it so very difficult to recall the appropriate titles chosen over the last hundred years or so since the revolution."

Louis stared at the giant Llama. Sir Andrew met his gaze and continued to slowly chew his cud. Louis could no longer keep his bloodshot eyes on Sir Andrew's sparkling blue ones. Sir Andrew swallowed his cud quietly as Louis looked away.

"Right this way, Ambassador," Sir Andrew said.

They had stopped walking during this exchange and Sir Andrew started off again. The Poodles appeared not to notice that the two statesmen had even been talking. They walked the rest of the way in silence. When they arrived at their quarters, two Mastiffs stood on either side of the mahogany door. Louis marveled at the fine wood work despite his strong desire not to do so. This door was a scene of a Lamb kicking an attacking lion in the face. Sir Andrew opened the door and allowed Louis and his guard to enter.

"We will be by in a little less than an hour to escort you to the Great Hall," Sir Andrew said. "In the meantime, Zack and William will be right outside your door in case you need anything."

"Thank you," Louis managed.

"As I mentioned, there are baths drawn for you and your guard," Sir Andrew said. "It is our custom to bathe before the evening meal."

"Yes, Sir Andrew," Louis said quickly. "I have visited your Farm on over twenty occasions and I am well aware of your customs and taboos."

Sir Andrew looked down at Louis and locked his blue eyes again on the Ambassador. Louis felt as if he was looking at a picture. Sir Andrew should be beautiful with his snow white coat and eyes the color of Robin's eggs. Instead, the magnificent beauty made the Llama's size and strength more daunting. Louis looked away for a brief moment, then made eye contact again.

"Right," Sir Andrew said. "I shall return shortly"

Louis was shocked by the Llama's dexterity as Sir Andrew pulled the door closed behind him.

*   *   *   *

The Poodles helped Louis remove his red scarf. Louis managed to pull himself up onto the large four-poster bed without their help. Louis sprawled out on the bed, rolls of lard draped off his stomach, neck and back. His wiry hair was no longer flat against his skin now that he had stopped sweating. From a distance, he looked like five or six giant layers of mashed potatoes with long, black chives mixed in heavily in certain areas.

Louis moaned from the almost intolerable pain in his legs and back. He had not walked more than a mile in a day for over a year. He had covered over fifteen in each of the last two days.

"Urgent," the Crow had said when he arrived at Snail Farm. As a result, Louis had to forego his normal mode of travel, a cart pulled by two Donkeys. This took the two strongest Donkeys at Snail Farm hours just to cover a few miles at which point they would be exhausted. It would have taken at least three days and would have meant delaying the first day of the summit.

If Preston had been less demanding or deserving, Louis would have taken his time because he knew there was little that could be accomplished without his presence. But Preston was his nephew and the best student of political philosophy that Louis had ever taught. So he had walked to show his support and to demand, along with Carter, that Knight Farm form a unified front in the face of Sabean's audacious attack.

Louis stopped reliving the last two days long enough to open his eyes. He saw Jean and Marcel staring at him from the door to the bathroom, upright and alert as if they had just slept for ten hours after a large meal. If his safety did not depend on them and they had not demonstrated their loyalty time and again he would hate them for their incredible resiliency.

"Alright gentlemen," Louis said with a toss of his head. "Subject yourselves to pneumonia."

51

Jean and Marcel nodded their heads in unison. "Thank you, sir," they both said.

"Please try to get some rest so you are at your best during the evening meal," Jean said.

"I shall," Louis said.

Jean and Marcel pranced into the bathroom and slid into the baths that had been prepared for them. Dirt drifted off their black fur and turned the water a dark brown. When they stepped out of the water they were darker and more regal than when the dust had lightened their curls.

Louis had dozed off, the only sound was the panting of the Mastiffs outside the door and the only odors were those that emanated from his own body. Much too soon, Marcel woke Louis up and he and Jean, smelling repugnantly like soap, helped him with his scarf and licked down what remained of his coarse black hair. Five minutes later, there was a knock on the door. Louis knew this must have been the second knock or his Poodles would not have woken him.

"Good Evening," Louis said when Sir Andrew opened the door.

"Good evening, Ambassador," Sir Andrew said sniffing the air. "Did you have a pleasant bath?"

"I did," Louis said. "Jean and Marcel do excellent work."

"If you will follow me please," Sir Andrew said, motioning toward the door. "We are following just behind the delegation from Manor Farm."

"Excellent," Louis said. "It will be nice to see young Carter again. Who else is in their delegation?"

"Dutch, a Boar who is in charge of security for Carter, and a Bull named Alexander," Sir Andrew said.

"A Bull?" Louis asked, not expecting a response. "Interesting."

Jean and Marcel flanked Louis who walked behind Sir Andrew. The two Mastiffs who had been at the door took up the rear. They would not leave Louis and his contingent for the duration of the summit. Unlike the Schnauzers who had escorted Louis and the Poodles into the Farm, the Mastiffs were able to mask their disdain for the Snail Farm citizens with calm indifference.

The wealth of Knight Farm nearly suffocated Louis. The mahogany, the marble, the jeweled dress capes on Sir Andrew and other royalty, the majestic stone buildings, the abundance of food and the flowing fountains were a reminder of Snail Farm's failures. He started to breath loudly and rapidly as he struggled to keep up with Sir Andrew. The quicker Louis gasped, the faster Sir Andrew seemed to move. They made their way into the courtyard; the fountain in front of them was alight with electricity. The water reflecting the man-made light mesmerized Louis.

He turned his eyes to King George's castle and beheld the splendor of the façade bathed in fire light. It stood five stories and had hundreds of rooms. The smooth stone blocks weighed over a ton. They had been brought in by man centuries before. The Animals had taken these and built the castle that King George and the rest of the royal family called home.

Exactly one hundred yards from the fountain, the cobblestone of the courtyard gave way to smooth, black stone. It was the blackest marble Louis had ever seen.

The castle was one hundred yards from the end of the courtyard. Rose bushes in full bloom lined the marble drive, alternating red and white. Every ten yards, on each side of the drive, burned a torch. Under each torch sat a Schnauzer who did not acknowledge, and were not acknowledged by, Sir Andrew. Each of the Dogs' collars gleamed with blue sapphires the size of rat eyes, indicating they were members of Lord Winston's elite attack squad. This squad, like Sir Andrew's Royal Guard, was feared by all Animals for hundreds of miles in every direction. Jean and Marcel stared straight ahead but Louis was certain they were noticing the animosity emanating from the Schnauzers.

Two Mastiffs sat upright on either side of the massive, carved doors leading into the great hall. The entryway was large enough for three elephants to enter side by side. A Ram's head in profile graced each of the doors. When the doors were shut, it appeared as if the Rams were engaged in combat, head-to-head. The handles the Mastiffs used to pull the doors closed were made of solid gold and polished each day. Each handle had two grooves in it as far apart as the muzzle of an extremely large Dog. The grooves were slightly larger than the teeth of a Mastiff. The centuries had seen this happen.

Louis followed Sir Andrew into the Great Hall. Song Birds sang from the corners of the roof two stories overhead. Red and blue tapestries, the length and width of the barn at Manor Farm, hung from the wall. Sewn into these were scenes of Rams, Llamas, Mastiffs and Schnauzers engaged in battle with man, various Animals such as Pigs, Poodles and Goats as well as wild dogs and wolves. In most of the scenes, Hawks soared overhead engaged in battle with Crows. Owls perched nearby waiting to take the place of the Hawks when night fell.

The hall, which was empty earlier that morning, now housed a score of tables, each twenty feet long. These were scattered about the cold stone floor. Each had a table cloth, silver candle sticks and bowls of gold that glimmered in the bright light of the torches and the fire roaring in the hearth. The hearth was as tall as an elephant and as wide as a hippopotamus. The logs in the hearth were as large as Jean and Marcel.

Louis could see King George at the table farthest from the entry, and closest to the fire. Next to the King sat Carter, Preston's closest friend from Snail University and also one of Louis's students, a few years behind Preston. On the other side of King George was an open seat for Louis. Next to this empty seat sat Lord Winston, an aged, scarred Schnauzer. On the other side of Lord Winston sat a Boar as large as Louis; however, instead of layers of fat this Boar was entwined with massive ropes of muscle. That must be Dutch, Louis thought. He could barely suppress his feeling of irritation when he saw how charmed Dutch was by Lord Winston. The old Schnauzer looked upon Dutch with his one good eye and seemed equally impressed.

Also at the table of honor were a large Bull, Prince James, King George's wife, Queen Anne and Lady Maria, Sir Andrew's wife. Next to her was a chair reserved for the pompous Llama. Sir Andrew showed Louis to his seat. The Poodles worked their way around behind Louis and sat at attention. The Mastiffs each assumed a position behind the Poodles.

"Quiet please," King George said in a baritone that was rarely disobeyed. Each voice in the hall fell silent, as if by magic instead of command. King George stood on his hind legs and rested a hoof on the table. The other hoof somehow held a tankard of ale.

"May I propose a toast," King George said a little louder, "to the Ambassador from Snail Farm, Louis Proust. He joins us to determine the best course of action against Sabean and his followers for their despicable attack on Manor Farm. Join me now in drinking to Ambassador Louis's health."

King George raised his cup high and looked at Louis. "To his health," he said firmly.

Louis nodded his head as was customary and said nothing in return except "Thank you" and took his seat between King George and Lord Winston.

"Have you met Lord Winston?" King George asked Louis when they had all sat in the hard, carved chairs and voices again filled the hall.

"Yes," Louis said. "We met briefly on a visit ten years ago and I also know him from his reputation as a fearsome warrior on the battlefield. Suffice it to say that Winston has a place in the history of Snail Farm."

Louis looked down his snout at Lord Winston and waited for King George to respond. When he was met by silence, and despite numerous promises to himself not to do so, he went on. "Yes, in fact, there are many Poodles at Snail Farm who wonder why their father or mother, or sometimes both, will never be coming home. All their new guardians can reply is 'That is a question for Lord Winston.'"

54

Lord Winston's right eye, the one closest to Louis, was a slit and it was impossible to tell if he had heard Louis's little speech or was simply able to hold his tongue better than the Ambassador from Snail Farm. Lord Winston did not move a muscle but stared straight ahead with his good eye.

Queen Anne, apparently sensing her husband on the brink of cracking a hole in Louis's skull while Lord Winston ripped out his intestines, spoke up to break the silence. "Now Ambassador, I think it is in the interest of all the Farms to put the past behind us – both the distant past and the near," Queen Anne said. "Reliving old wars and battles opens old wounds and creates a desire to inflict new ones."

"Yes your Highness," Louis said regaining his sound judgment. "You are quite right. Please accept my apologies to you and the King."

A feast of vegetables, eggs, bread, platters of wild deer and goblets of ale was served. Louis ate with reckless abandon. Twice he spied Dutch watching him eat with a looked of amusement on his fearsome face. Each time, Louis responded with a wink. Dutch just continued to stare in return.

Queen Anne had wool of the lightest brown and, instead of coal black eyes like her husband, hers were a beautiful emerald that contrasted with the coffee color of her face. All the Animals in the land spoke of her beauty and grace and looking at her eyes was like looking into the eyes of one's mother – one felt instantly loved but also as if one should remain on their best behavior.

A dessert of berries and yogurt, eaten even by the Cows whose milk it came from, was served. When all the guests had finished their dessert the tankards were refilled and King George climbed up on the table, now on all fours as was customary, for the final toast of the night. He bent toward his wife and she pulled his cape loose with her mouth and King George allowed it to fall onto the now soiled cloth covering the stone table.

"I stand before you as an Animal," King George said. "We are Animals. We are free."

"Praise Mother God," all the Animals responded with the exception of Louis and the Poodles. Carter caught himself in mid-response when he saw Louis's lips pulled tight on his face. Dutch no longer looked at Louis with amusement. Louis attempted to glare back but quickly turned away.

Carter watched Louis as if his dead father had floated in. Carter mirrored Louis, sitting stoically, and looked to see if Alexander and Dutch followed suit. Alexander watched King George with what could only be described as admiration. Dutch looked at Louis with disdain. They each echoed King George's words as custom dictated.

King George looked down on Louis, his obsidian eyes sparkled with neither amusement nor anger. He moved his eyes to Carter and then slowly, with hundreds of Animals watching, his eyes settled back on Louis. Louis tried to understand the look in King George's eyes. Despite the heavy meal and the numerous bowls of ale, Louis finally realized he had seen the look before. It was a look of resolution. His mind drifted back to the prior time he had observed this same expression on the King's face.

*   *   *   *

King George and Prince James had both fought bravely in the Battle of Beaver Creek just a few years before. The story is an unfortunate one for Snail Farm. Snail Farm had claimed the mile of land between its walls and Beaver Creek. This was a blatant violation of a treaty signed a hundred years before in which Snail Farm and Knight Farm agreed to leave all lands outside the walls of their farms wild. The leadership of Snail Farm believed that relations were so good between the two Farms that the desire for peace, and the need to maintain the exchange of commerce and ideas, would trump any desire of the Royal Family of Knight Farm to enforce the ancient treaty.

Snail Farm had underestimated King George. Instead of ignoring the wall the Pigs, Goats and Poodles of Snail Farm were erecting along Beaver Creek, King George sent the Premier of Snail Farm a message that was simple and direct. It read:

"Pursuant to the Treaty on Expansion, Knight Farm demands that Snail Farm cease construction of the wall along Beaver Creek and tear down what has already been built. The failure to do so within three days will be considered a declaration of war."

The Premier, shocked and angered, called Louis to his residence and solicited his advice.

"The King is bluffing," Louis had said. "He will not call his army to war over land he does not want or need. We need the river so that we can use its water to generate power. We should stand firm for we have much to gain. On the other hand, King George has little to gain from preventing us from doing so."

The Premier consulted with his General who agreed with Louis's assessment that ultimately Knight Farm would not fight.

"Alright, General," the Premier said. "Move your troops to the river and we will hold them there if they decide to attack."

"Yes sir," the General had said. "From a military perspective it is an ideal spot to make a stand."

"Good," the Premier said. "Then I will expect a victory if war comes."

While the Premier was meeting with Louis, King George had Lord Winston and Sir Andrew draw up a plan for war. Its simplicity caused Snail Farm to be caught off guard. King George and Prince James led the main force of Rams, Llamas, a few Mastiffs and a scattering of a few hundred Schnauzers. The force gathered along the opposite bank of Beaver Creek from the Snail Farm army.

A squadron of Hawks worked diligently to clear the air of Crows for a ten mile radius around Snail Farm. It was clear that Knight Farm had a smaller army on the West side of the river than that assembled by Snail Farm. The advantage was about three to one, with Snail Farm having a thousand more soldiers assembled. As King George gathered his troops on the bank, Lord Winston had led his elite squad of Schnauzers and Mastiffs across Beaver Creek four miles up stream. The squad was made up of Winston's best fighters. The squad was often used for surprise attacks on wild dogs, wolves and rats that ventured too close to Knight Farm or made the mistake of killing, or attempting to kill, one of King George's subjects. They worked in teams of four made up of three Schnauzers and a Mastiff. Lord Winston and his second in command made up the remainder of the team.

King George led the charge down the bank and into the river that was inaccurately called a creek. Hundreds of snarling Poodles moved to the edge of the creek waiting for King George's army to make it across. As King George reached the opposite bank and lowered his head into the breast of an eighty pound Poodle, his personal guard of Schnauzers tore into its flesh.

At the same time, Lord Winston led a charge from upstream and his battle hardened Mastiffs and Schnauzers ripped into Snail Farm's rear guard of Pigs and Goats. The tactics of Lord Winston's squad were for the Mastiffs to break the necks of the Goats while a team of three Schnauzers ripped a Pig apart. Then the team would regroup and attack again.

Reacting to the shrieks of the Pigs and the horrifying sound of snapping Goat necks, the Poodles disengaged from battle with King George's troops to rescue their comrades. As expected, King George's troops were exhausted from establishing a beachhead on the Snail Farm side of the river. Therefore, pursuit was slow.

In anticipation of this, Sir Andrew had hidden in the forest with his Royal Guard behind the main army. Now they sprinted from the cover of the trees into the river and toward the fighting. There were Llamas, Mastiffs and Schnauzers in the Royal Guard and all were seasoned warriors. Unopposed, they crossed the river easily at it shallowest point

57

and reached the East bank still filled with animal blood lust. The Royal Guard tore up the bank in pursuit of the Poodles.

Lord Winston's squad and Sir Andrew's Royal Guard now attacked the Poodles from opposite sides, while King George's army fought the Pigs and Goats. Mastiffs crushed Poodles one by one while the Schnauzers isolated Poodles and attacked them in groups of three. Llamas stomped and kicked Poodles into the river. Many of them did not make it back out of the water.

The carnage continued for twenty minutes until the Premier finally raised a white flag from a hill in the distance. Louis sat at his side.

*   *   *   *

Just prior to the fighting and massacre, while looking through binoculars at King George, Louis had seen the same look on King George's face. King George began his speech.

"Citizens of Knight Farm, I honor you and your fathers and your fathers' fathers."

"And we honor you," the crowd responded. Despite his recollection of the terror of the Battle of Beaver Creek just a few moments before, Louis rolled his eyes.

"Please raise your glasses," King George said. He paused. "I must confess, I initially intended to simply honor our distinguished guests and sit down. However my heart tells me that tonight is a night to speak plainly, and not stand on ceremony. To state clearly what I believe while respecting opinions that are contrary."

King George looked down on Louis and this was not lost on anyone in attendance.

"Over five hundred years ago, our forefathers rebelled and pushed man from Knight Farm. A century later our fellow Animals of Snail Farm broke the chains of man and a century after that Manor Farm did the same. Over the last three centuries other Farms followed the three major farms so that now there are thousand of miles of land controlled by Animals. Man leaves us alone. Why? Because what we have done does not coincide with man's preconceived notions of reality. So what do they do? They pretend it never happened. They simply do not enter our lands because in their minds it does not exist.

"So what has happened? What have we accomplished in our five hundred years of freedom? We have adopted the ways of man." Some of the Animals grumbled in reluctant agreement.

"Do not misunderstand me," King George said a little bit louder, his baritone now reverberating off the stone ceiling. "Some of this was planned, correct?" The Animals nodded in agreement.

Watching King George, Louis's sense of superiority began to wane. Sensing this, Carter began to twitch nervously. Neither knew where King George was headed with his speech but the hostility from their hosts was now palpable. Dutch's eyes bored into Carter, the Animal he was duty-bound to protect.

"But in ways no one could have imagined we have become like man," King George continued. "When the first member of my family became King, he had no idea that we Animals would adopt the lofty ideas of man; that we would presume that the rules of our species, the Sheep, living together could somehow be applied to a multitude of species living together. But so far, somehow, it has worked.

"Equality in man makes sense. Equality of Animals in their rights within the Farm is an inalienable right. So is equality of opportunity. Yet somehow there are certain Animals who are confusing equality just as man did. What success man is having with this new definition of equality is unknown.

"We must not presume there will be equality in all manner of things: not of station, not of food and goods because we are not equal in ability. This is at odds with nature. Man has a name for this social/political philosophy but I do know what it is. But we can assume it will never work. Station must be earned in some way, shape or form."

The Animals stared at King George. Although he often addressed the Farm on matters of state, this was the first time he had discussed political philosophy. It was both awkward and exhilarating.

"'Okay your Highness,' you might say, 'how is it that you have earned the right to be our King?' My response is this; that is a very good question." Many Animals laughed at this.

"But it is one that I have an answer to," King George said. "The answer is that I have not or at least when I ascended to the throne I had not. My Family has ruled this Farm for centuries. My Father earned it by leading a rebellion and being put on the throne by a vote of the Animals, a democratic monarchy if you will. Our rule has been good and fair. Kings have led the defense of our newfound freedom from man, fought the wilds and have led the troops to victory in three major wars with Snail Farm in order to stop the expansion of farms into the wild lands."

King George smiled down at Louis.

"During these times our Farm has successfully advanced technology far beyond that employed by other farms," King George said. "Am I boasting? Yes, for the achievements of my ancestors. But I point out that during our history it has often been a younger sibling or a cousin who was selected by a King to be elevated to the thrown. This was done because it was thought best for the Farm. All I can offer as justification for my leadership is that I hope to have earned it both before and after I took the throne."

Now the Animals looked at each because they would never even think to question King George's right to rule the Farm. The speech was starting to make some of his subjects nervous.

"Why my Family?" King George asked. "Because Sheep are natural leaders and know how to pick a leader among their own species while looking out for the herd as a whole? Perhaps, but this is also true of Dogs and Llamas and others. The fact is our forefathers, Dogs, Sheep, Llamas, Chickens and all the other Animals decided on a monarchy ruled by a Ram. Amazingly, this continues to work.

"My Family understands that the Dogs and Llamas can remove us from power anytime they wish. My Family could not stop them. Sir Andrew would concede that Dogs could lord over even the Llamas should they elect to do so. But they do not. My Family has earned the respect and loyalty of the citizens by continuing to make fair and honest decisions. Our system works and until it does not work we will continue on as before. I will always look out for the best interest of my subjects."

The Animals now saw the picture King George was painting and roared their support. "Why, you might ask," King George said. "Why does it work? That answer is that we allow all Animals to do what they are good at, what nature has put into their nature and their natural ability. Not all Dogs are soldiers but most of them are. Not all Hawks are scouts but most of them are. Not all Sheep are in Administration but most of them are. Llamas are split between soldiers and technological advancement as are the Owls. Yet some of the best administrators have been Dogs and some of our best soldiers have been Sheep. Why? The answer is that we encourage all our citizens to do what they excel at doing.

"Others have a society wherein you get to do whatever you choose regardless of competence. Unless, of course, one wants to work in the administration of these societies and then one must be a Pig or a Goat. This results in weakness and holes in society because tough decisions are difficult to make and even more difficult to implement because they end up having the wrong people doing the wrong job with no one left to do the hard work. Most choose to eat, drink and talk instead of act. This leaves a farm vulnerable to its enemies.

"So I raise my glass to the wisdom of our forefathers and the wisdom of Frank, the former leader of Manor Farm."

The Animals of Knight Farm raised their tankards of ale in the air with a cheer and then drank deeply. Even Louis and Carter raised their bowls and drank. A failure to extend this courtesy would have been impossible for King George to ignore.

The remainder of the evening passed without incident. The King and Queen retired early so that the rest of the Animals could enjoy themselves without worrying about protocol. King George bid both Louis and Carter goodnight as if nothing had passed between them. Sir Andrew also retired early.

Dutch, Alexander, Jean and Marcel watched Carter and Louis drink ale deep into the night engaged in a quiet conversation. The murmur of their words was only occasionally broken by one of Carter's Goat snickers. They paid no attention to their hosts and purposely avoided Lord Winston's attempts at polite conversation. By the time they retired for the evening, each of their escorts would have been happy if their masters had died at the table.

CHAPTER SIX – A SWEET REVENGE

Sabean emerged from a deep complex of tunnels followed by a contingent of twenty rats. His black fur melted with the night. He and his followers made their way to the creek and Sabean took his place on the large stone in the middle of the flowing, brown water. He waited. An hour later, three raccoons bounded onto the large rock; they hardly acknowledged the twenty rats who served as Sabean's personal guard. The raccoons were bigger than the full-grown Beagles who resided at Manor Farm.

"Well my friends," Sabean said slowly, "what is the latest news relating to Mr. Carter's journey?"

"Well my Lord, as you know, we tracked Carter and his escort most of the way to Knight Farm," the largest raccoon said in a voice barely above a whisper. "Their security is minimal with no Animals to provide a viable defense against smaller animals such as us."

"Yes, we received word of this through the outposts," Sabean said. "This is important information that we may be able to use when they journey back to Manor Farm. Were you able to get any information relating to whether we might come under attack?"

"It is too early to say either way, my Lord," said the largest raccoon. He was clearly the leader. "We couldn't get close enough to hear anything that is happening inside Knight Farm. And unlike other farms the citizens do not have loose lips. However, we did manage to overhear a conversation between some of Knight Farm's Mastiffs. They would never discuss matters of state in the open air but they did gossip. Apparently, Louis managed to insult King George and Carter watched in amusement."

"Really?" Sabean said with a smile that displayed his pocket-knife-sized incisors. "That is very interesting. How so?"

"The usual, my Lord," the raccoon said. "Louis insulted Lord Winston. Of course, Lord Winston appeared not to even notice the slight. That loony old Dog lets his actions speak for him." The raccoon said all this with clear admiration in his whispering voice.

"Yes he does," Sabean said. "So it seems unlikely that a consensus will be found when the Animals finish with their series of meetings if Louis started the talks off with an insult. Excellent."

"Yes my Lord," the raccoon said. "Shall we return and see if we can find out more?"

"I don't think so," Sabean said. "I am formulating a different plan. Return here tomorrow night with as many raccoons as you can round up who are willing to fight for the rights of wilds to live as equals."

"Are you offering any incentive for them to come and fight my Lord?" the raccoon said so quietly that Sabean could barely hear him.

"Chaos, carnage," Sabean said. "You know, the usual."

"I believe that will be the perfect reward for my kind, my Lord," the raccoon said with just a hint of a smile. His voice seemed to flow out of his vocal chords in harmony with the rushing water of the river.

"Until tomorrow then Brutus," Sabean said.

"Until tomorrow my Lord," Brutus the raccoon said. He turned and jumped from the rock to the shore in unison with his lieutenants.

Sabean motioned to two rats on the shore. They scaled the distance to the stone throne.

"Yes, my Lord," one of the rats said.

"Send out a message to the Foxes and the Weasels and the Generals," Sabean said. "Tell them there will be a meeting here tomorrow night. Also send a message to One-eye and tell him that I request an audience this evening on the top of Pine Mountain. Let him know I will be there in a few hours."

"Yes, my Lord," the rat said.

He and his companion jumped toward the shore but landed in the water, intentionally getting wet to face the heat of the race through the forest to gather the wilds and then make the journey to Pine Mountain.

*   *   *   *

A few hours later, Sabean worked his way over pine needles and boulders in silence. Fresh out of winter, the needles on the trees were a dark green and appeared black in the night. Many of the trees rose over one hundred feet into the clear, bright night sky. The higher Sabean climbed, the thicker the mist he created with each breath. He had left his guards at the river, a mile below the designated meeting spot at the top of Pine Mountain.

Sabean stopped a hundred feet from the summit to catch his breath. He looked over the Animal Lands. To the West, he could see Manor Farm, only its farm house lit by lanterns. To the Southeast was Knight Farm. Its magnificent man-made light and firelight created a glow in the night sky. The castle was lit up like a full moon and the torches in front of the other residences appeared as stars in the sky. To the East, far in the distance, he could see the torches on the main residence of Snail Farm that formed the shape of the hoof of a Pig clasped with the paw of a Poodle. Sabean smiled and took a long drink from the stream of running water making its way down Pine Mountain to Beaver Creek. He sucked in the cool, night air to catch his breath and to find a calm rhythm.

Sabean made his way out of the shelter of the pine trees and into the maze of boulders that covered the top of Pine Mountain. Along the way he jumped onto an oversized boulder to get a look at the top of the mountain. On a boulder larger than a chicken coop sat an animal Sabean could think to describe only as beautiful. The wolf had a coat of snow white with a stretch of grey and black fur running along the back of his neck and back. The wolf stood taller and weighed more than the giant German Sheppard that defended Manor Farm. Sabean knew this wolf had seen decades of battles.

"So One-eye," Sabean whispered to himself, "you decided to come. Good. Very good."

Sabean raced up the last fifty yards, looking more like a jackrabbit than a rat as he bounded from boulder to boulder. A dot of red gleamed from One-eye's good eye clearly tracking Sabean's progress. Sabean stopped on a boulder about ten feet from One-eye and took a quick look around. He saw many places to hide from One-eye should this conversation head in the wrong direction. He looked at One-eye who simply stared back, the breath from his nostrils released in steady, even streams into the air between them.

"Thank you for the audience, Caesar," Sabean said.

"The pleasure is mine, Lord Sabean," One-eye said without sarcasm. "I am pleasantly surprised you have taken timeout from your war to pay a visit. To what do I owe this honor?" One-eye showed his canines as he asked the question.

Sabean hesitated as he was not sure if the canines were a smile or a snarl. "Well Caesar," Sabean began, "my visit has to do with my war, as you call it. I come here with information you may choose to use or you may not."

Sabean waited for One-eye to respond. The wolf simply stared at Sabean and continued to release deep, powerful streams of mist from his nostrils. When it was clear that One-eye would keep his own counsel, Sabean continued on. "As you apparently know Caesar, we attacked Manor Farm just a few nights ago."

"And quite successfully, I heard," One-eye said. "Very impressive, Lord Sabean, you accomplished what no pack of wolves or dogs have been able to do."

"Thank you, Caesar," Sabean said.

He was not sure if he had been subjected to One-eye's sarcastic wit for a second time but it didn't matter. His response would have been one of appreciation for the kind words in either case. Again, One-eye sat in silence and Sabean was forced to continue on. "After the attack on Manor Farm, Preston, the leader of Manor Farm sent . . ."

"I am up to date on farm politics," One-eye interrupted. "Of that, I can assure you."

"Of course Caesar, my apologies," Sabean said quickly. "The major Farms are having a summit to determine how to respond to my attack."

One-eye looked away from Sabean and into the night sky. "If this is the news you bring me, it is fascinating but of little interest," One-eye said with his canines glimmering in the moonlight.

"Caesar, please humor me for but a moment more."

One-eye nodded his head quickly, communicating to Sabean to proceed but to make it quick.

"My spies tracked Carter to Knight Farm and they are but three – a Boar, a Bull and Carter the Goat. But this is my concern and not yours. I know you find it best to keep your distance from Manor Farm."

Sabean could not resist taking a jab at One-eye's two disastrous attempts to attack Manor Farm over the last three years. Each time they had been turned back by Cody, the Pack and the horses, without bringing home any food. In order to deter further attacks, Frank had the Beagles lead the Pack in pursuit and Cody and Maggie had torn the slowest member of One-eye's pack to pieces.

If One-eye registered the meaning of the remark he gave no indication. He continued to stare over Sabean's head into the night sky.

"However, of great interest to you Caesar," Sabean continued, "is that Louis, needing to get to Knight Farm quickly, traveled only with his personal guard of two Poodles."

"Now you have my attention Lord Sabean," One-eye said looking at Sabean with his good eye.

"I thought this might be of interest to you."

"Why did he fail to travel with his usual escort of twenty-five elite fighters?" One-eye asked. "This would not have slowed him down."

"I believe there are two reasons," Sabean said now speaking with confidence. "First, after our attack, security at all the farms is very tight. The Premier of Snail Farm probably wanted the elite squad for defense in case of attack. Second, I think Louis has diminished in value in the eyes of the party at Snail Farm after the Battle of Beaver Creek."

"I see," One-eye said. "So what you are telling me is that my old friend has become expendable?"

"It seems so Caesar."

"Well Lord Sabean," One-eye said, "this is fascinating and interesting news. What I do with it remains to be seen. As you know we are but twelve these days."

65

"Yes, but twelve versus three if you count Louis," Sabean said, stating the obvious.

"I have heard Louis is no longer a warrior but has turned into a fat Pig like the other leaders of Snail Farm," One-eye said. "Do my spies speak the truth?"

"Yes Caesar."

"Too bad."

Sabean did not understand what One-eye meant so he did not respond. After a long silence, Sabean said, "That is the news I bring. Do with it what you will."

"Yes," One-eye said, now back to staring into the night sky over Sabean's head. Sabean gave a slight bow and bounded from rock to rock into the forest and back to his guards waiting for him at Beaver Creek.

*   *   *   *

The following evening the setting sun turned the sky purple and tried to hold off the chill of the night air. Sabean bounded onto his stone throne and waited. His personal guard spread out on the banks of the river on trees and on rocks. The remaining members of his tribe were spread out in the forest to watch as the allies streamed into the area for the meeting.

Thousands of rats lined the creek as midnight approached. The moon lit up the creek and also Sabean who still sat alone on his throne. The rats on the shore were covered in the darkness of the trees and bushes. Oaks, maples and many other native varieties grew close to each other in the well fertilized, damp soil. A stone's throw downstream a hundred of raccoons sat on the branches of an ancient oak tree that spanned the river. Always in battle mode, the raccoons were ready to drop into the water and swim to the safety of either bank at the first sign of danger. Their eyes reflected blue in the moonlight.

Sabean counted the raccoons and smiled or did a rat's best imitation of a smile. The hundred raccoons were twice as many as he had anticipated. Willie the Weasel and Alvarez the Fox were upstream and behind the throne with the ten weasels and five foxes they had managed to get to join their ranks. After six months in partnership with Sabean and the aligned rat tribes, Willie and Alvarez were more trusting of the rats but Sabean could tell that Willie could barely stand being in his presence.

As if on cue, Willie whispered to Alvarez, "I just can't stomach a rat that weighs twice as much as I do, Al."

66

Alvarez merely smiled in response as he did to all of Willie's amusing quips.

Just as Sabean stepped forward on his throne, General Nicholas, the rat who led his army, jumped from the riverbank. General Nicholas had grey fur and scars along his haunches.

A few years before, the General had led an unsuccessful raid on Manor Farm and barely escaped with his life. Sabean had saved General Nicholas's life by biting the leg of the Cat who had desperately wanted to break General Nicholas's neck. This act of valor led Nicholas to lead a revolution of consolidation to allow Sabean to rule the Beaver Creek packs of rats as one tribe.

General Nicholas whispered into Sabean's ear. Sabean froze for a moment or two, apparently lost in thought. Then he stepped forward to the edge of the stone so that the water rushing against his throne threw drops onto his ink colored fur.

"Friends, I have splendid news," he said in a powerful whisper. "In addition to our allied forces, we have been joined by over one hundred raccoons led by Brutus. This alone will strike fear into the hearts of the Animals who occupy the farms. However, General Nicholas has just informed me of an unexpected coup. It seems lady luck is smiling down on us and approves of our endeavor."

The other wilds looked upon Sabean in anticipation. "Swimming down the river from just outside Snail Farm are a thousand rats led by Poseidon himself. Revenge will be sweet my friends and it appears that at least a few of the enemies of Snail Farm plan on taking full advantage of it."

The rats squealed with delight. The raccoons, weasels and foxes did not respond. They looked on with rapt attention. They did not understand this high level of excitement. Sabean, who assumed that the raccoons, foxes and weasels would not understand the significance of this, went on. Sabean hoped to finish his explanation before Poseidon and his tribe arrived so that all they heard were the squeals of delight upon their arrival.

"My friends, the raccoons, foxes and the weasels are entitled to an explanation so that they understand the importance of Poseidon's pack of rats joining our cause," Sabean said to the rats to explain why he was speaking of things all rats knew.

"Ten years ago, Poseidon united a number of packs of rats, leading thousands in a common cause. Like us, he saw the need for strength and understood that this could only be achieved through unity. Unlike our mission, his was one of defense and not offense.

It was during one of the terrible times of Snail Farm's aggression and expansion. The Pigs of Snail Farm believed their politics could work for all Animals and all wild animals as they prefer to describe us."

The wilds gathered at Sabean's throne released a terrifying sound in unison. From them came squeals, hisses and growls which in unison sounded like a band of Hollywood monsters.

"We call ourselves free animals. We do not live trapped behind walls coddling to Dogs or suffering the consequences of failing to adhere to the ridiculous political philosophy of Pigs."

The wilds squealed with delight as Sabean hit his stride.

"So during this time of aggression, an army of Pigs, Poodles and Goats pushed out from Snail Farm. Those free animals that remained in the occupied territories were forced to subject themselves to the authority of the ruling party of Snail Farm. Others fled the occupied lands and were forced to fight other free animals for hunting territory. Two groups stayed and fought bravely, the rats and the wolves. Both would concede that the Snail Farm forces were on the brink of victory when King George and Lord Winton earned two consecutive victories to win the War of the Territories. Eight years later they again defeated Snail Farm at the Battle of Beaver Creek. Again, only the rats and wolves stayed to fight.

"Poseidon is the first rat to join packs of rats together in a large enough force to battle a farm in a true war. His rats inflicted scores of casualties upon the arrogant forces of Snail Farm but his numbers were depleted from nearly ten thousand to just a few hundred before King George's army entered the fray. He is the elder statesmen of rat politics if there is such a thing. If we could have silence to honor his approach it would be much appreciated. After his arrival I have intelligence I would like to share with all of you."

Only the running of the river over the rocks could be heard as the wilds waited. As the crickets adjusted to the silence and began to sing their night song once again, Poseidon and his pack floated into view like a thousand pieces of driftwood. The rats allowed the river to do the work of swimming until Poseidon floated to the large stone that served as Sabean's throne.

"Permission to join you, Lord Sabean," Poseidon said in a voice raspy from old age. He said it loudly and clearly so that the other wilds could see the deference he was paying to Sabean.

"It would be the greatest honor I could imagine, King Poseidon," Sabean said louder still.

Willie the Weasel leaned in close to Alvarez the Fox and said as quietly as he could, "This pomp and circumstance is a bit much." Alvarez shushed him with genuine fear.

Poseidon climbed up nimbly and stood next to Sabean. His grey fur, soaked through with water, reflected the moonlight in sparkles of light in contrast to the jet black sheen of Sabean's coat. Sabean bent down and put his muzzle briefly to that of Poseidon. Poseidon looked like a newborn next to Sabean. However, as Sabean would acknowledge, Poseidon's exploits made Sabean's seem almost childlike. In Sabean's mind that would change very soon.

"My friends," Sabean said, "may I present the greatest rat in all of history, Poseidon."

Again squeals of ecstasy from the rats as if a boat full of eggs had miraculously floated down the river for a midnight snack.

"Thank you, my fellow free animals," Poseidon said.

Poseidon stood on his hind legs to his full height so that he now was eye level with Sabean.

"I am a rat that is disinclined to make speeches. I say this: Let's bring the fight to the arrogant Animals that populate the farms. Let's destroy their arrogant peace. It is a peace based on the tenet of man, the very animal they sought to free themselves from. I see the irony, why don't they? I will follow Sabean in this war for our freedom and I ask all of you to do the same."

The response was deafening. Willie couldn't believe that rats could be so loud. A chill ran down his back and his fur stood on end. It was fear and not animal lust that caused it but the hundreds of rats close enough to see him thought he had gone into battle-mode. He thanked the man-God, whom he did not believe in, that none of the rats had heard the snide comment he had made earlier. When the last squeal of delight and growl of anger subsided, Sabean hopped forward to the edge of his stone throne.

"This is what I know," he said. "All of you should know this so that you see that we have allies who are not our friends. Ambassador Louis, Poseidon's enemy from the past, shall be making his way back to Snail Farm from Knight Farm with only his personal bodyguard of two Poodles. If all goes as we hope, Sir Andrew's scout parties will not be providing protection either as additional defense or as scouts. It seems Louis is doing all he can to aggravate King George and his advisors. It seems the likelihood of joint action by the Farms is very low. Louis seems to want the alliance to fail."

Sabean scanned the faces around him and saw that very few of his followers understood the significance of this.

"You see," Sabean said, trying to keep his voice from sounding condescending, "Sir Andrew had little interest in the Ambassador's safety when there was the specter of an alliance. Now, if no agreed upon course of action springs forth from this Farm summit he will have no concern for Louis at all. The hawks will not even track Louis's return."

Sabean now saw the rats nodding in understanding.

"I made a trip to inform One-eye of the likelihood that Louis would be traveling the roads alone, with only his personal guard. I do not know what he will do with this information but I have a hope and strong belief that One-eye will not let this opportunity pass him by. One-eye can exact revenge and at the same time wreak some havoc on Snail Farm.

"You see, the Premier of Snail Farm may have decided that Louis is expendable but I don't think the Poodles have. It seems the Poodles of Snail Farm remain fiercely loyal to Louis despite his excesses over the last six or seven years. They will insist on retaliation and will not be dedicated to the Premier until he does something to right the wrong of leaving Louis unprotected. So if Poseidon's pack of rats were to attack Snail Farm for a raid only the Poodles are unlikely to engage in a pursuit once the attack is thwarted. A raid is one more way to cause confusion within a farm and further our hoped for dissension among the Poodles and Pigs of Snail Farm."

Poseidon nodded at this line of thinking. Sabean could not hold back a smile.

"For the rest of us, we wait for Carter's return journey from Knight Farm. We expect Frank will be sent out with some Beagles as an additional guard, but if not, we will be poised for attack. In either case we shall try to find a way to take Carter out. Without Beagles we may be able to take on the Boar and the Bull he calls his escort."

The rats, raccoons and weasels nodded in understanding. Good, Sabean thought, they are not as slow as I feared.

"I ask each of you Generals who have joined the cause to keep your armies ready to move at a moment's notice. We will need to act swiftly should the opportunity present itself."

This is our best chance to turn the tide and return things to the way nature intended. We can return the land to free animals where the strong survive and don't need walls to do so. No longer will Animals use man's ways of walls and unity to exclude us from their farms. We too, the free animals, shall move across their fertile land unencumbered by the fear of reprisal from ruthless Dogs and Cats."

Again, the deafening sound of rats screaming in unison rushed through the forest. This time the raccoons and weasels joined in. For miles around, rabbits, frogs and other animals of the forest froze in fright.

70

CHAPTER SEVEN – ON FEAR

Frank padded up to the farmhouse and asked the two Boars guarding the front door for an audience with Preston. The requirement had initially amused Frank. Now, he could no longer prevent himself from treating the guards with disdain. A few minutes after asking to see Preston, the Boars escorted him into Preston's private chambers. On the floor next to Preston sat two empty bottles of alcohol. Apparently, they had managed to make alcohol using some of the information contained in the books in the farmhouse. It was not the ale that was typically bought from Snail Farm.

"Welcome Frank," Preston said. "Did you come for a sip of this?"

Preston did not stand to greet Frank but remained on the floor entangled in a pile of blankets. It appeared to Frank that getting up onto the human bed in the other room had become too much trouble for Preston.

"No thank you," Frank said. "I must tell you something that I did without your approval and also ask you to let me help you."

"Well?" Preston asked gruffly.

"First, I sent the Beagles out to follow Carter to ensure his safe arrival at Knight Farm."

To Frank's surprise, Preston did not react to this but just stared impatiently at Frank.

"Carter and his party arrived safely at Knight Farm," Frank said.

"Yes Frank, my Crows told me as much."

"But there is more. Raccoons trailed them during the night. Luckily, Dutch spotted the raccoons and insisted they sleep in the open space of the road."

"Really, Frank," Preston said slurring his words just slightly, "what could raccoons possibly do to a Goat, a Boar and a Bull? I know losing the election was painful, but I'm in charge now. You need to enjoy the freedom from responsibility that you have now."

Frank nodded. "Thank you for the advice."

"Indeed," Preston said. "Now you said you had a request. What is it?" Preston asked looking out from heavy eyelids that were starting to drape over his bloodshot eyes.

"I do," Frank said ignoring Preston's disrespectful tone. "Humor an old Dog and send some Dogs to help escort Carter and his guard home."

Preston stood up, struggling to gain his balance among the old, brown wool blankets. "No," he said firmly. "You really are an arrogant bastard. I have the situation well in hand. There are no wild dog packs near Manor Farm or Knight Farm from what the Crows say. And the nearest wolf pack is One-eye's and they are on the Eastern side of Pine Mountain. Carter and the others are in no danger. I have the situation well in hand."

"What about raccoons and foxes?" Frank asked, still remaining calm despite Preston's outburst.

Preston snorted, sending mucus flying out of his snout. "You've become paranoid, Frank."

Frank bared his teeth and said, "You are scared and fear banishes wisdom from one's heart. You have turned to man's bottle for strength," Frank's voice mirrored his words. "You will ruin our Farm if you don't quit that and open your door to the other members of the Farm, and your mind to sound advice."

By now the two Boars had entered the room and were on either side of Frank. Frank looked at first one and then another. They moved slightly back so that Frank could turn to go.

"No additional escort," Preston shouted at Frank as he left Preston's private quarters.

Frank turned at the doorway and said with sorrow, "As you wish. You were elected to lead the Farm and there is nothing I can do about that now."

*   *   *   *

Louis woke with a start. Marcel, awake at the door, looked over with what appeared to be genuine concern. "Are you alright Ambassador?"

"Yes Marcel," Louis said between labored breaths, "I am fine." After a couple of minutes passed, he started to enjoy the comfort of the bed again.

"Where is Jean?" Louis asked sharply.

"In the bath," Marcel said.

"Again?" Louis said with undisguised disgust. "Very strange, the affinity you both have to the ways of Knight Farm."

"Perhaps it is simply our instincts taking over Ambassador," Marcel said. "Poodles have historically been water Dogs as you well know."

"Yes, perhaps that is the case," Louis said sleepily.

He rolled out of the bed and made his way over the lush, multi-colored rug to a basin in the corner. He swiped his face back and forth briskly and then drank deeply with long, deep slurps. Marcel looked away in disgust.

"How much more time before our escort to the talks arrives?" Louis asked.

"We have sent them away four times already, Ambassador," Marcel said matter-of-factly. "They will return in half an hour."

"What on earth possessed you to send them away?" Louis demanded as he quickly turned from the basin to face Marcel.

Despite being surprised by Louis's nimble movements, Marcel responded calmly. "I felt you should be fresh for the talks, Ambassador. You have made it perfectly clear how important these talks are."

"Well, you clearly know little about politics," Louis said regaining his composure. "I have now lost face as it appears I am unable to hold my liquor."

"I used my judgment Ambassador," Marcel said. "I beg your pardon if I have erred."

"You did err," Louis said bitterly with a hint of sarcasm. "I suggest you leave the politics to me and focus on what you do best."

"And what might that be Ambassador?" Marcel asked.

"Why," Louis said, "protecting me of course."

Marcel hesitated. He knew the Premier had sent him and Jean on a mission which might end in death, so he decided to speak. "If I may be so bold Ambassador, it seems you need to learn to hold your tongue as well as to hold your liquor."

Louis stepped forward within a couple of steps of Marcel who held his ground. As he did so, Jean, dripping water from his dark curls emerged from the bathroom. "Good morning Ambassador, have you decided to join us?" Jean asked.

Louis did not like his mocking tone but he could not battle both his bodyguards when the odds of victory against one of them were little better than a fifty-fifty chance. He could not understand his guards' hostility but thought it better to focus on the summit. It appeared he had done something to offend or embarrass the Poodles the night before but making amends would have to wait.

"Yes Jean," Louis said softly. "Would you gentlemen help me with my cape?"

Louis's cape of green and red that hung on the clothes-horse in the corner of the room reflected the sunlight in waves.

Marcel nodded at Jean. "Of course Ambassador," Jean replied.

A moment later, Louis noticed that platters of cheese, carrots, celery, apples, berries, wheat bread and a number of nuts were spread on the table near the door. Louis moved over and sat in the only chair and began devouring the food, one platter at a time. Moments later, the cheese, vegetables and half the nuts were gone; only then, did Louis look up at Marcel and Jean and ask, "Care to join me?"

"We've eaten Ambassador," Jean said.

"Excellent," Louis said. "What did you eat?"

"Eggs and milk," Jean said.

Louis stared for a moment, checked his anger, and then resumed his onslaught on the platters of food.

*   *   *   *

Sir Andrew, escorted by two Mastiffs instead of his customary Schnauzers, reached the door to Louis's guest room exactly a half an hour after the last attempt to retrieve the Ambassador. He was getting anxious for the summit to begin but had enjoyed being sent away each time by Marcel.

The two Mastiffs guarding the door stepped aside so that Sir Andrew's guard could continue to flank him. Sir Andrew tapped the door lightly and smiled down at the Mastiffs. The usually mute Mastiffs could not help but laugh at Sir Andrew's exaggerated attempt to be dainty. Marcel swung the door open quickly so that Sir Andrew caught Louis with his face covered in banana, flakes of nuts and cheese. Sir Andrew could not suppress his amusement.

"Quite sorry to interrupt your meal, Ambassador, but the representatives from Manor Farm and Knight Farm have been waiting for over two hours," Sir Andrew said softly. "May we escort you to the Great Hall?"

"My Poodles will escort me," Louis said testily. "You may show me the way."

"Of course Ambassador," Sir Andrew said tenderly. "Follow me, please."

Marcel and Jean were unable to keep the smiles off their faces. Sir Andrew was treating Louis like an elder statesman who could no longer hold his liquor and slept through meetings and it was clearly intended to outrage Louis. It was having the desired effect.

Sir Andrew turned quickly, neither Mastiff moved. They stood looking through their sad, brown eyes at Marcel and Jean. Once the Poodles followed Louis, the Mastiffs fell in behind them. Marcel and Jean knew that protocol required them to leave themselves and Louis vulnerable when visiting another farm but it was unsettling. They also knew that if a brawl broke out, the Mastiffs would simply engage with them until Sir Andrew could deliver a savage kick to their hind legs or head. The Mastiffs always conserved energy so that they could fight as long as

75

possible and allowed the Llamas to go in for the kill. Sir Andrew would love if such a brawl occurred as he still relished the blood of battle. Sir Andrew's willingness to enter the fray was what made the Dogs and Llamas of the Royal Guard remain loyal to the death.

"You smell fresh, Mr. Marcel," a voice said from behind Marcel. Marcel looked behind him and saw only one of the Mastiffs, outweighing him by at least one hundred pounds. He looked forward quickly to regain his bearings and then looked behind him again. "I beg your pardon, did you say something?"

"Yes," the Mastiff said with a large dog smile, "I said you smell very fresh."

"Thank you," Marcel said hesitantly. He knew that the Royal Guard could not speak when on duty but he also knew some of those of the higher ranks who did not guard the gates or doors ignored this rule. Sir Andrew did not mind as he believed escorts should be able to talk to the guests. However, no one having a designated post ever violated this rule as silence was necessary so that all unusual sounds could be heard and concentration was never broken.

Both Mastiffs laughed. "He thinks we are male," the one who had not paid Marcel the compliment said laughing. Marcel was so sure they were male because of their size he had not even bothered to check their scent.

Not a word was spoken after this as they covered the distance from the Administration building where the guests were staying to the Great Hall. When they reached the hall, a Mastiff, one hand taller than the two who made up Sir Andrew's escort, stood at the door. Marcel had never seen a Dog that large. Marcel halted for a moment and then pushed forward with the rest of the group. They stopped a couple of yards in front of the Mastiff. Sir Andrew turned to Louis and said, "A word please, Ambassador," and stepped a few feet away so that they would not be overheard.

"There are no guards inside," Sir Andrew said. "The Bull and Boar from Manor Farm are at the rear entrance with Henry's brother." When Sir Andrew said this, he nodded toward the Mastiff that seemed more of a bear than a Dog. "Some Schnauzers are also keeping them company. Your Poodles can stay with Henry and these two ladies here at the main entrance."

"Before I can agree to that . . ."

"I know," Sir Andrew said interrupting Louis, "you need to have your guards inspect the hall. As you wish. Henry will escort one of your Poodles so that he can conduct the inspection. Which one will go?"

"Marcel," Louis said. Jean was tougher but Marcel was smarter.

76

"Alright," Sir Andrew said.

Sir Andrew turned toward the group and said in a gentler tone than he had used with Louis, "Henry, please escort Mr. Marcel into the Great Hall so that he may take a look around."

"Yes, Sir Andrew," Henry said without hesitation.

Ten minutes later, Marcel and Henry emerged from the hall. Marcel stepped to the far side of the great marble entryway. Louis joined him.

"What do you think, Marcel?" Louis asked.

"I think with Sir Andrew in there along with the King and his brother, you are vulnerable," Marcel said. "However, as you know, we are vulnerable right here. I see no reason why they would harm you. It is a diplomatic mission and I recommend that you attend the meeting on King George's terms."

"Yes, of course," Louis said. "Thank you for your candor."

Louis moved quickly to the large wooden doors leading into the Great Hall and pushed them open himself. Henry bent his head toward Louis's haunches with an eye on Sir Andrew. Sir Andrew shook his head slightly and Henry pulled his head back just before his finger length incisors made contact with Louis's thigh. Henry smiled a Dog smile and Sir Andrew chuckled.

Sir Andrew followed Louis and left Henry and "The Ladies" to engage in idle chitchat with the Poodles.

*   *   *   *

Louis entered the Great Hall and paused to allow his eyes to adjust to the relative darkness. Compared to the festive atmosphere of the night before, Louis felt as if he was attending a funeral. Instead of hundreds of torches and a great fire in the hearth, there were only a score of candles on the large stone table at the end of the hall. Replacing the strings of the instruments, the singing of the birds and the drunken banter of the guests, were the whispers of the diplomatic envoys of Manor Farm and Knight Farm.

Louis walked confidently toward the table where Carter, Prince James and King George sat in what appeared to be silence. However, the whispers of Carter and Prince James bounced off the ceiling. When he was within twenty paces of the table, made from a single slab of granite, King George shifted his head and met Louis's eyes. Louis paused for a moment looking into the King's coal black eyes, regained his composure and then quickly covered the remaining distance to the table and took a seat next to Carter. The Animals of Knight Farm continued to stand.

After a few seconds of uncomfortable silence, King George turned his head slightly toward Louis. When the King made short, slow movements his monstrous, corkscrew horns seemed to be balanced there like some sort of ridiculous hat instead of part of King George's body. However, Louis knew from experience that when King George embraced his more animal nature in battle, his horns melded with his head and body to form a frightening battling ram.

"So nice of you to join the living Ambassador," King George said softly, his voice like a quiet foghorn.

"Yes," Prince James added, "we thought you decided our food and drink were not up to your standards and headed for home."

"Ah King George," Louis said, "I see your brother has not lost his ability to start off diplomatic talks on the wrong foot. However, my concern is for Manor Farm and my friends who rule that farm, Preston and Carter."

As always King George considered what Louis said before responding. "An interesting choice of words Ambassador," he finally said.

"How so, your Highness?" Louis asked because for once he had not made a calculated decision to use a particularly offensive word or combination of words.

"Well, I am a King and I lead the subjects of Knight Farm by their leave. It appears that Preston and Carter rule Manor Farm by their election. It is not a very progressive word that you used. I find it contrary to all I thought Snail Farm stood for but perhaps I am mistaken."

King George's large mouth turned up with a slight smile as he finished talking.

"Well, your Highness, I see your point but I don't think we came here to discuss the semantics appropriate for a discussion of political philosophy."

"You are quite right," King George said. "Carter, as the representative of the Farm that called this summit, I believe it is your right to set the stage for our discussion. I assume it is the unfortunate attack on Manor Farm that brings us together."

Carter cleared his throat and glanced at Louis before he began. "You are all aware of the brutal attack by Sabean in the dark of night but I don't believe you are aware of some specific facts relating to the attack that Manor Farm believe are relevant to the discussion of what course of action the united Farms should take under the terms of the accord."

"I beg your pardon, Mr. Carter," Prince James interrupted, "but the accord was agreed to in principle only. The details have not been written and nothing has been signed by my brother so under Animal Farm law there is no accord. With that said, I can assure you that Knight Farm will participate in the spirit of cooperation that is supported by the accord."

"My brother speaks plainly as usual," King George said. "He also accurately, if a little bluntly, states the position from which Knight Farm is approaching these talks."

"Thank you both for your candor," Carter said. He was proud that being interrupted before he had even begun had not thrown him off the mark. "Manor Farm expects nothing more than a discussion with the spirit of the accord considered.

"So," Carter continued, "what are the specifics that you should be aware of relating to the attack? First, the attack was coordinated in a way that is most unusual for rats. Instead of thirty to fifty rodents there were thousands. The rats attacked two sides of the Farm. They attacked first from the West to draw our defenses and then from the East with the main force to wreak havoc among our Chickens and Barn Animals."

"This is unusual, my friend," Louis said, "but not unheard of."

"True, Ambassador," Carter said with a polite nod, "but the decoy was an attack force and not just a diversion. Typically, a few rats will race through a farm, past the point of attack, for the purpose of drawing the guard in pursuit. In this case, the decoy was a major offensive on a wholly separate part of the Farm. An attack force of hundreds of rats descended on our Duck pond. We responded in force because of the carnage at the pond and only then did the second, much larger force, attack the coop."

"That is most unusual," Sir Andrew said slowly as he scratched the long hairs under his chin with a hoof.

King George tilted his head toward the giant Llama with surprise because in such diplomatic encounters Sir Andrew typically kept his own counsel until all the facts had been presented.

"But even more unusual were two things that even Frank and Jackson had never seen before," Carter said.

King George lifted his eyebrow toward one of his arm-sized horns indicating that Carter should continue.

"First, there was a weasel and a fox among the force that attacked the coop and barn. Second, there was a concerted effort to avoid engaging with the Dogs. All the other Animals were fair game. The rats even managed to kill a Cat. They attacked Pigs, Cows and Goats. The Horses were at the gate so we are not sure if they would have been off limits or not."

King George shook his head slowly. "That is an incredible tale," he said. "You were fortunate not to have lost more lives than you did."

"Yes," Carter said, "our defenses proved reliable as we have made protecting Manor Farm from the wilds one of our administration's main priorities."

"So Carter, how did Manor Farm respond to this cowardly attack?" King George asked knowing the answer. "Did Preston send out the Pack to wreak havoc on the stragglers?"

"Why no, your Highness," Carter responded a bit too quickly. "Preston and I are great believers in collective action in both our domestic programs and our farm relations. We wished to adhere to the spirit of the accord and form a united front with Knight and Snail Farms."

"I see," King George said. "Did it not occur to you that finding Sabean and his horde would be difficult without a fresh scent?"

"Yes your Highness, but we felt that in the long-term, the solidifying of the accord was much more important than retaliating quickly," Carter said.

"I must say," Louis interjected, "I believe that Preston and Carter made a wise decision. There are times when we must put satisfying our blood lust to the rear and use our more Animal nature by focusing on a long-term, inclusive resolution."

"I see," King George said calmly. He then turned his head slowly toward Carter and asked, "Do you and Preston have a proposed plan that will allow us to deal with Sabean?"

"We do . . ." Carter began.

"Excellent," Prince James interrupted. "Will it satisfy our blood lust as well?" he asked. His wry smile turned James's face into a more human profile.

Carter gave Prince James a blank stare and pressed onward. "Our proposal is simple and the tactics are ones that Ambassador Louis and the Premier used effectively against Poseidon a number of years ago."

After an uncomfortable silence, Prince James said, "Sadly Carter, we are not privy to what transpired between Snail Farm and Poseidon's pack of rats. We were only concerned with Snail Farm's blatant violation of a treaty that had been in place for hundreds of years."

Again, Carter remained calm and did not take the bait. "Well, I would defer to Louis as he and the Premier devised the strategy. Ambassador, would you mind sharing your tactics with the group as I don't know that I would do it justice?"

Louis lifted himself higher up on the magnificent stone stool. "I'd be honored to do so. But I'd like to set the scene, if I could."

"By all means," King George said, barely able to conceal his amusement with Louis's conceit.

80

"For a number of years we had been faced with a large number of raids by Poseidon's small band of rats. They were only a hundred or so strong. They would strike every few months; raiding the coop at Snail Farm or our stores of grain.

"We tried the usual means of retaliation by our packs of Poodles but they were never able to catch Poseidon's pack before they reached Beaver Creek. Once they reached the river, our Poodles did not stand a chance of catching them in the water."

"Perhaps having some Cats like Manor Farm might have helped the situation," Prince James said, ignoring the fact that no Cats lived on Knight Farm either.

"Perhaps so, Prince James," Louis said calmly, "but, as you know, Cats do not adhere to the political beliefs we cherish so deeply at Snail Farm. Cats have difficulty functioning in a society where all must contribute equally according to their abilities but all share in the fruits of the labor based on their needs."

"Indeed, Ambassador," Prince James said. "I simply made an observation related to protecting the citizens of Snail Farm. Keep in mind no Cats choose to live here either."

"Please continue, Ambassador," King George said with a shake of his head. He loved his brother but his combativeness was better utilized on the battlefield than in a political discussion.

"So the Premier, his top general and I devised a new plan of attack," Louis said. "We enlisted the Geese and Ravens to help the Dogs, Goats and Pigs rid the lands surrounding Snail Farm of rats. Early one morning, we sent half the force of Dogs, Goats, Pigs, Geese and Ravens along Beaver Creek three miles upstream from Snail Farm. We sent the other half of the force three miles downstream.

"We chose three miles because we didn't think that Sabean's force could be traveling from any farther than that to conduct their raid and then return to their base by daybreak. Our forces worked their way downstream and upstream on both sides of the bank. The Geese were in the water while the Ravens flew overhead. The Dogs, Pigs and Goats flushed out the wilds a half mile out in either direction from the river. Poodles would dig or bark when they caught a scent. It was time-consuming work but our force was two thousand strong so there were a thousand Animals moving in each direction. We put not only Poseidon's pack on the run but thousands of other rats as well. We killed hundreds that day but Poseidon and a small part of his pack managed to escape up a creek coming down from Pine Mountain that led into the river.

"I followed with my personal guard of twenty Poodles but we were unable to find Poseidon so we turned around as night fell. We were very successful that day and it is a tactic that I strongly recommend."

"But it ended up not being totally successful, correct?" Sir Andrew asked.

"True, but that was because of the intervention of Knight Farm," Louis said. "As a result we were unable to deal the final, triumphant blow."

"So this happened during the time of Snail Farm's attempt to push their territory to the banks of Beaver Creek," King George asked.

"Yes," Louis said. "After this tactic was exercised Poseidon unified the rats and tried to face us head on. It was then, as our Emissaries explained at the time, that we decided to push our boundaries so that we could patrol and defend Snail Farm from the rats. We planned to push Poseidon's army off the banks for good by claiming them as our own."

"In clear violation of the terms of the treaty," Prince James said cheerily as if he were commenting on someone's homemade apple pie.

"So what is the precise military response you propose Mr. Carter?" Sir Andrew asked clearly tiring of the Prince's shenanigans.

"What we propose is a variation on the tactics used so expertly by Louis and Snail Farm" Carter said. Each Farm's force will gather at day break. Half of Knight Farm's force will gather to the West with that of Manor Farm's and move east and the other half will join the forces of Snail Farm and move west along the river. We will flush out Sabean and his coconspirators just as we . . . I beg your pardon, just as Snail Farm did with Poseidon. This time there will be a big difference."

"What is the difference?" King George asked.

"This time we will have our Cats and Beagles and your Hawks and Owls to inflict casualties as we root them out," Carter said confidently. "Also we can hunt by night using the Cats and Owls, a luxury that Snail Farm did not have."

"I think it is a brilliant plan," Louis said. "We must bring the fight to the wilds." His voice echoed in the beams of the Great Hall.

"What about the impact on innocent wilds?" King George asked.

"There is no doubt that other wild animals will be disturbed and displaced and probably killed but we must react with unity and extreme force," Carter said forcefully.

"But your actions amount to a war on the forest instead of a war against Sabean and the rats," King George said calmly.

"Force must be targeted and swift not broad and slow," Sir Andrew said before Carter could respond.

"It is a different world, Sir Andrew," Louis said. "We must change our typical method of attack just as Sabean has changed the rats' standard method of attack. Rats have historically attacked in groups of twenty to fifty and without the support of other wilds. Now their forces number in the thousands with foxes and weasels among them. We must change our strategy."

King George looked first at Sir Andrew and then at Prince James. Neither of them responded to Louis. They kept their thoughts hidden behind their great eyes and stared blankly at Carter and Louis. A light wind made its way through the windows and into the rafters of the Great Hall pushing a warm noontime breeze onto the summit. The conversation carried on in this manner for some time.

Louis scanned the room. It remained dark despite the sun peering under the doors and through the windows on the East side of the hall. The candles had burned down over an inch and wax dripped to the stone table since Louis had arrived so he guessed he had been in the hall for at least two hours. He turned toward King George and waited.

"It is now past noon," King George said finally. "Perhaps we should break for lunch. I would like some time with Sir Andrew and Prince James. We have arranged for the two of you and your guard to lunch outside. Let's reconvene in two hours so that we can continue our discussion relating to our further course of action."

"Thank you, your Highness," Carter said.

King George nodded.

*   *   *   *

Louis and Carter made their way through the finely groomed rose garden of red, pink and white roses along a wide path of stones nearly small enough to be called pebbles. King George's servants had set out a feast on a white cloth on tables under a large maple tree on the north side of the Great Hall. The table sat on a lush expanse of manicured lawn looking east toward the majesty of the Pine Mountain range. On the far side of the range was Snail Farm.

Louis took a seat at one head of the table and Carter took the seat at the other. Marcel and Jean sat across from Alexander the Bull and Dutch. Across the vast expanse of Knight Farm, Louis could see apple orchards, rows of lettuce and carrots and glorious fields of golden wheat and green corn. The wealth of Knight Farm appeared to be never-ending and Louis tried not to feel envious.

"Well Ambassador, what do you think their response will be?" Carter said looking out at the rolling hills of Knight Farm and not at Louis.

"I am not sure. King George's instinct is to help and act in concert. He is a Ram after all. However, if presented with facts and arguments against your plan I think he can be swayed to deny your request."

"But there is no doubt the facts are on our side," Carter said a little too loudly.

Louis took a deep breath, trying to relax after the exchange in the Great Hall. He took a long drought from a bowl of water and a small sip of ale from another. Louis hoped that Carter would take a minute to calm down as well so that they could enjoy their lunch. Louis studied the Goat at the other end of the table. Carter had been one of his brightest students, in some ways brighter even than Preston, but he lacked Preston's ambition and uncanny ability to turn a phrase. Carter's bottom lip shook from the stress of the meeting with Knight Farm. The long, dark hairs on Carter's chin swayed back and forth to make sure his stress was obvious to all at the table.

When Carter's chin hair finally stopped swaying like the branches of a willow tree, Louis responded. "Well Carter," Louis said, "I, of course, agree with you. However, I start with the same basic political philosophy that you do; one based on collective action for the common good. King George starts from a different philosophical platform."

"Please, Ambassador," Carter said, "do not insult my intelligence. I understand we all approach this issue with differing basic assumptions."

Marcel and Jean looked at each other with looks of surprised amusement. Alexander and Dutch could only look down at their plates.

"You know I would never do such a thing," Louis said with a smile. "I hold your intellectual abilities in the highest regard."

Carter took a deep breath and sipped from his bowl of ale while keeping his eyes focused on the vase of flowers in the middle of the table. When he raised his eyes, his chin hair again twitched and moisture glistened in the ducts of his bulging, brown eyes. The water only accentuated his diamond shaped pupils.

"I know," Carter said, "I apologize for my rude behavior."

"Apology accepted," Louis said. "Now let's return to the business at hand. Two points besides the obvious one I already made. First, King George comes from a place we can understand as he thinks first of how he can best serve his subjects. However, Sir Andrew, and Lord Winston for that matter, approach issues in an entirely different way."

"How so?" Carter asked.

"Well, they look only at how they can protect Knight Farm and if necessary destroy any animal or Animal that poses a threat to the Farm. It is impossible for them to see beyond this basic objective. This is what makes them such a formidable enemy."

Carter sat silently chewing his food.

"Second," Louis continued, "Prince James, their wisest member . . ."

"You have got to be kidding me, Ambassador," Carter interrupted.

"Oh don't let his flippant attitude fool you. He is smart as a whip and knows other Animals better than they know themselves. Anyway, he thinks our philosophy and its resulting governments are ridiculous. As such, he thinks joint action of any kind is unlikely to be in the best interest of Knight Farm."

Louis stopped talking for a moment to shovel a pile of corn into his mouth. "So we start from a position where the facts are of very little importance," he said after he swallowed his corn.

"So are you telling me we have no chance?" Carter asked.

"No," Louis said in between bites, "I am telling you that success at this summit is highly unlikely. Success in obtaining an agreement for joint action will only come after another attack."

"But that could mean our Administration might lose the confidence of our citizens," Carter said. "It is not in our Farm's best interest to have to wait for another attack. We might be driven out of office. If that happens, we lose everything. We all finally have a real chance for equality."

"As you know, Carter, I agree that your political approach is the right one for Manor Farm," Louis said in a tone that might have been interpreted as condescending. "However, many others, including King George, do not share this sentiment and could care less whether you and Preston remain in power."

Carter looked out over the expanse of Knight Farm. His guard and Louis's guard were focused on their food and appeared to be paying little attention to his exchange with Louis. It seemed they all had already understood what he had not.

"I am blind or at least I was," Carter said still staring off into the distance. "They have no legal obligation to help. They have no love for our Administration. They despise Snail Farm and, with all due respect Ambassador, think even less of you."

Louis laughed loudly, his jowls shaking in hideous waves. "None taken my friend," Louis said. "I wear their disdain as a badge of honor." He smiled broadly, raised his cup of ale and drained what was left of it.

"So Preston sent me on a fool's errand," Carter said. "He knew I would fail but wanted my pleas to Knight Farm to be sincere."

"Yes," Louis said, "it appears so."

"But why?" Carter asked himself softly. "He has made me look like a fool."

"You can look at it that way," Louis said, "or you can consider the fact he has used your innocence to the advantage of Manor Farm."

"In what way?"

"For the future of course," Louis said as he refilled his bowl with ale.

Carter sat in silence. "I think I know what you mean but educate me," Carter finally said.

"If you walk away from here with no accord as we both think you will, you have an advantage."

"I don't see that."

"In negotiations on other issues with Knight Farm you can use their failure to help as leverage," Louis said. "More importantly, you can use their failure to help as a rallying point back at Manor Farm as long as you use it before another attack. It will allow you and Preston to discredit Frank and Cody as your citizens associate Knight Farm with the Pack."

"This is true," Carter said.

"On the first point, you will gain political clout with King George if you handle the rejection you will probably get with grace," Louis said. "When Preston sends you back to ask for something different, the King will be more inclined to say yes."

"What about the specter of a second attack?" Carter asked.

"Highly unlikely," Louis said confidently. "Rats have never managed to stay organized for a long period of time. They may strike again but now that all the farms are on alert it will not bear the same kind of fruit as it did last week. Yet, we may get concerted action out of it."

Carter sighed deeply, sipped his ale and then ate quietly for a few minutes. He looked like a goat in the human world with limited brainpower and no ability to talk.

"Preston knows you are a man of your word Carter, if you will pardon the expression," Louis said. "He also knows you expect the same of others. There are many ways to serve your Farm and here you did so nobly and I think you will continue to do so."

"I see that but I do not feel any better because serving one's party unknowingly is a bit idiotic."

"We have all been pawns at least once in our career," Louis said. "The key is what you learn from it."

They all passed the remainder of the meal in silence. The food, fresh and bountiful, and the rolling hills of Knight Farm made Carter forget his troubles until a Schnauzer and two Mastiffs notified them that the summit would recommence in fifteen minutes. After the messengers left, Carter asked Dutch, Alexander, Marcel and Jean to give him and Louis some privacy.

"So what should my end game be Ambassador?" Carter asked Louis.

"Tell them it is all or nothing and walk away with nothing."

"Those are Preston's orders but it is not what I would do," Carter said.

"You should follow Preston's orders," Louis said as he slid his bulk off the chair.

*   *   *   *

When Carter and Louis arrived back at the Great Hall it seemed much brighter than during the morning session. Somehow natural light permeated the hall but Carter was unable to identify its source. He studied the faces of King George, Prince James and Sir Andrew closely. He expected to see set chins and hardened eyes. Instead all three had softened in demeanor since the morning session.

After they had all taken their places around the stone table, Carter turned slowly toward King George on his left and said softly, "I think we left the ball in your court your Highness."

"Pun intended I presume," King George said with a smile.

"Yes, your Highness," Carter said.

Louis could not suppress a snort.

"We discussed your proposal at length, Carter," King George said. "Our general position is that we would like to honor the spirit of the accord we have yet to finalize but we propose an alternative course of action to your all-out offensive."

"I am anxious to hear your proposal, your Highness," Carter said. "However, if it is significantly different from our proposed course of action it will be difficult for Manor Farm to agree to it."

King George had trouble keeping the surprise from his face. His large eyes seem to grow in size and darkness while the rest of his face remained frozen like a statue.

"That is an interesting position to take given that Manor Farm has come here asking for assistance," Prince James said calmly as he put a hoof on Sir Andrew's long leg under the table.

"It may seem that way Prince James, but we are simply firm in our belief that the wilds must be dealt with swiftly and, more importantly, soundly and completely."

"Let us set forth our proposal as this conversation may be unnecessary," King George said.

"Agreed," Carter said a little too harshly.

King George glared at Carter for a moment then said calmly, "Here is what we propose. Knight Farm and Manor form an elite force to track down Sabean and his personal guard. Between Lord Winton's Schnauzers, our Owls and Hawks and Frank's Beagles and the Cats of Manor Farm this seems like a realistic and much more expeditious approach."

"First, the Beagles are not Frank's," Carter said. "Second, that is a temporary solution because another rat will rise up and take Sabean's place. Only complete annihilation of the local rat population will work. We must drive them back to the human lands."

"That plan harms innocent wilds," King George said, "and Knight Farm will not be a part of such a plan. In addition, my military advisors tell me this will work for only a short period of time and is unlikely to result in the death of Sabean."

"With all due respect," Louis said breaking his silence, "your advisors are wrong this time."

King George stared down at Louis. Sir Andrew straightened to his full height of nine feet and said as politely as he could manage, "You will include in your sentences the honorific, your Highness, Ambassador."

It was Louis's turn to stare, but after thirty seconds he again could no longer stare into the Llama's ice blue eyes. "My apologies your Highness," Louis said to King George.

"Apology accepted," King George said, clearly wanting to bring the meeting to an end. "Is my understanding correct that Manor Farm will only accept a full-scale offensive?"

"Yes, your Highness," Carter said.

"Then tell Preston that any political capital he may gain at Manor Farm from the failure of Knight Farm to support his plan he has lost twofold here in my realm," King George said with gravel in his baritone.

"I shall pass that message along, your Highness," Carter said, now anxious to get out of the Great Hall and away from the King's imposing presence.

"Thank you," King George said. "We will provide an escort home for both of you as there has been much strange movement in the forest over the last couple of days."

"I need no such escort, your Highness," Louis said.

"Nor do I, your Highness," Carter said before thinking the matter through.

King George smiled and his exasperation seemed to melt into the familiar, quiet resolve. "As you wish," he said. "May the man-God be with you."

Louis and Carter exited the Great Hall without responding.

CHAPTER EIGHT – DINNER IS SERVED

Carter headed toward the rear exit of the Great Hall, intending to tell his comrades what had happened. Instead, he became lost in thought. Carter walked briskly past Alexander and Dutch without saying a word. Dutch raised his eyebrows while looking at Alexander and lifted his head slightly. Alexander shook his head from side to side as he had no idea what had gotten into Carter either.

Louis exited the front entrance of the Great Hall and also rushed passed his escort. Marcel and Jean exchanged knowing Poodle smiles and padded after Louis with the smiles engraved on their powerful, black muzzles.

Alexander and Dutch hesitated, unsure what to do. After Carter had covered about ten yards, he realized he was alone and stopped. He looked back over his shoulder, beard quivering. "Are you two going to escort me to my room or am I to do that alone as well?" he asked.

Dutch took a deep breath and strode toward Carter. The muscle in Dutch's back rippled. No one at Knight Farm had ever seen a Pig like Dutch. He had spent his youth playing with the Dogs of the Pack and his body had developed lean muscle where the other Pigs of Manor Farm wore fat. His muscles relaxed when he was close enough to Carter to realize that Carter was not being rude. He was simply so flustered that he was overwhelmed by indecision.

"What happened in there, Carter?" Dutch asked. "Did they refuse to meet our demands?"

"Of course, I was sent on a fool's errand and advised by an even bigger one."

"What do you mean exactly?" Dutch asked.

"Let's wait to discuss it until we arrive back in our rooms," Carter said a little more calmly.

"Nice to see that you are once again speaking in the plural," Dutch said lightly.

Carter smiled, coming to grips with his inability to control the situation. "I know," Carter said, "I was acting ridiculous. Power is like ale. The more you have, the more you want."

Dutch nodded. By this time, Alexander had caught up, his huge frame dwarfing even Dutch. He did not say a word but nudged Carter with his nose in a show of support. When they arrived back at their rooms, Carter took a long drink of water. The door to their room was now guarded by two Schnauzers as well as the Mastiffs. King George was no longer concerned with creating the appearance that he was concerned with the safety and needs of his guests. It was clear that the Manor Farm contingent was not allowed to leave their room until they departed for Manor Farm or was beckoned by the King.

"Well, there is always an opportunity to make progress during tomorrow's talks," Alexander said.

"No, I'm afraid not," Carter said quickly. "As I started to tell Dutch, I gave them the ultimatum, they refused, and so now we leave at dawn."

Alexander and Dutch swiveled their large heads toward Carter in concurrent amazement. "What do you mean?" Dutch demanded. "I thought you were posturing."

"Yes," Alexander added, "we thought you were humoring Louis."

"No," Carter said with resignation. "Unfortunately, my orders from Preston were to come back with an all out attack or nothing at all."

"That is ridiculous," Dutch said heatedly. "I know you said those were your orders but I thought Preston gave you some semblance of authority if they refused. How could he instruct you that way?"

"I don't know," Carter said. "I thought we had already reached an accord with King George and that it would be easy to get Knight Farm in alignment. I knew Snail Farm would follow. But now, upon reflection, I think Preston knew I would fail and worse than that, it seems he probably wanted me to fail."

"But why?" Alexander asked.

"To unite Manor Farm behind him perhaps," Carter said mulling it over in his mind.

"I don't think it is that simple," Dutch said. "I don't think as highly of Preston as you do and I think his motivation may be even worse."

Before Carter could respond, they all heard Louis pontificating to Marcel and Jean as they walked past their room, on their way to their own. Carter couldn't hear the words through the mahogany door but there was something about the tone of Louis's voice that made him shutter.

"Dutch is right," Alexander said, interrupting Carter's panic attack.

"How so?" Carter asked.

Alexander chewed his cud as he formulated his words. "Well, if he wanted to rally the Farm in his favor all he had to do was to declare our own war on Sabean. Then we would not have lost the opportunity to find him. For some reason, he wanted to have Knight Farm reject our demands."

"Yes, I see your point," Carter said. "There were easier ways for him to unite the Farm behind him."

Carter continued to process all that had happened in a new light.

"We will leave first thing tomorrow and I will find out from Preston myself," Carter finally said. "He betrayed my trust and I have to believe there was a very good reason for doing so. He would not have sent me on this mission, in this manner, if it was not in the best interest of the Farm."

Dutch looked at Carter with what appeared to be one of his first lifelong attempts at sympathy. "In all honesty, I think he should expect to lose the loyalty of all three of us," Dutch said. "I am beginning to think that supporting you and Preston in the election was a mistake."

"How can you say that, Dutch?" Carter demanded. "The Pack has maintained the status quo for too long. There was no opportunity for others. You would never have been made put in charge of security if the Pack still ruled Manor Farm."

"Yes and no," Dutch said. "I was allowed to fight with the Pack and to even hold rank. I would not have been the lead on security because I was not the best Animal for the job. Cody was and is."

"But only because he is a Dog and that isn't fair to the rest of the Animals," Carter said a bit too loudly.

"I am not sure it should be about fairness if it isn't best for Manor Farm," Dutch said.

"Now you are starting to sound like a Dog. That is archaic thinking, designed for the days when we were under constant attack from both wilds and humans. It is not a progressive philosophy."

"But Carter, we are under attack," Alexander said. "And I have a feeling Sabean's attack on Manor Farm will not be the last. The issue will be the same tomorrow as it is today – not if we need to declare war on Sabean or any other wild that threatens our safety but how we wage that war."

"Perhaps, but I am still of the opinion that equality means we all participate in Farm activities equally," Carter said.

"It certainly sounded good in theory," Dutch said.

Carter smiled weakly. "Well, let's get as much rest as we can tonight so we can make good time getting home."

"Okay," Alexander said.

"Alright," Dutch said, seeing that Carter had had enough of the conversation and no longer wanted to argue with his friends.

They rested in the comfort of Knight Farm until dinner. Carter enjoyed the bed more than he thought he would. Now he understood why Preston had spent his first nights as leader in the bedroom of the farmhouse. They ate heartily of the meal of breads, fruit, and nuts that was brought by a couple of Ewes but they all refused the ale. After their meal, they went to sleep, just as the sun was setting.

＊　　　　＊　　　　＊　　　　＊

Carter woke with a start. He had been arguing with Preston in his dreams. However, the head on top of Preston's layers of fat was tiny and he appeared to have the teeth of a goat. The hair of the Preston of his dreams was black and gleamed in the moonlight as they exchanged insults. Carter closed his eyes and tried to pinpoint exactly what the Preston of his dreams had looked like. A moment or two later Carter said aloud, "a rat."

"I beg your pardon," Dutch said. "Are you awake?"

Carter opened his eyes and lifted his head out from between his front legs. He slept on the bed not based on rank but because he was the only one of the three who could put their full weight on it. If the Bull or the Boar had done so it would have collapsed. It was not nearly as sturdy as the bed provided to Louis.

Both Dutch and Alexander had slept on the soft carpets that covered most of the hardwood floor. Dutch sat wide awake, eyes wide open as if he had not closed his eyes since dinner had been served. Alexander breathed loudly, still sleeping soundly. Carter straightened his beard with his two front hooves.

"I'm sorry," Carter said. "Did I say something?"

"I think you said 'a rat,'" Dutch said.

"Yes, I think I did. I had the strangest dream."

"What was it?" Dutch asked.

"Well, I dreamed that I was arguing with Preston . . . "

"That doesn't surprise me," Dutch said interrupting.

"Are you mocking me?"

"Of course not," Dutch said with wide eyes.

Carter then realized that the Pack took dreams seriously, interpreting them and looking for omens. Dutch, practically a Dog, thought there might be something useful in Carter's dream.

"Right, of course," Carter said. "I was having an argument with Preston and . . . "

"About what?"

"About something awful he planned to do," Carter said. "It was in complete contrast to our philosophy."

"What did he plan to do?" Dutch demanded. "In what way was it in complete contrast to your philosophy?"

"He was planning something and had taken sides with someone who should have been our enemy." Carter paused.   "What or who that was I can't be sure."

93

"And he had the face of a rat?" Dutch asked, unable to conceal his concern.

"Yes, he did. Do you think that Preston could possibly be aligning himself with Sabean or some other rat?" Carter asked.

Dutch shook his giant head. "No. Most of the time the meaning of dreams is not quite that simple."

"Then what could it mean?" Carter asked.

"I don't know," Dutch said. "I wish Jackson was here."

"Why?" Carter asked.

"He reads dreams with uncanny precision. He read one of Frank's dreams and foretold Preston's victory in the election."

"Interesting," Carter said absently.

Noting that Carter wanted to mull the dream over himself, Dutch dropped the subject. "They left three packed meals for us to take on our journey," Dutch said.

"Good. Shall we wake Alexander?" Carter asked.

"What time is our escort due to pick us up?" Dutch asked.

"We do not have an escort," Carter said distractedly, still contemplating his dream.

"Why on earth not?" Dutch demanded, causing Carter to turn his head quickly. "Did the final talks go so badly that they refused to provide one?"

"No," Carter said with a slightly raised voice. "I refused an escort and so did Louis."

"But why? That makes no sense. According to Cody, Knight Farm always provides an escort for those leaving their farm. It is their way of ensuring they are not accused of attacking parties as they leave the farm."

"Louis felt it would be a show of strength for us to refuse," Carter said. He wished he could have grabbed the words and put them back into his uneven mouth immediately after he said them.

"Well, Louis is an idiot and he isn't your head of security. I am."

Carter took a deep breath. "Louis is not an idiot," he said. "He has decades of diplomatic experience and we have none. I thought it best to follow his advice."

"With all due respect, I disagree," Dutch said still managing to keep from yelling. "Louis's experience as a diplomat has led to two wars with Knight Farm. Both of which Snail Farm lost, I might add. As the Animal responsible for our safety, I must insist that we accept the escort."

"Why?" Carter asked mockingly. "What are you afraid of?"

94

"I sensed something following us on the way here," Dutch said. "I told you that and you followed my advice. There was something strange going on in the forest."

"I think you are starting to run scared, Dutch," Carter said curtly.

"Maybe, but I still want that escort," Dutch said softly. "There is no logical reason not to accept the offer."

"I can't ask for it now or I will lose face," Carter said regaining his composure and moderating the level of his voice.

"Then I will ask for it and say I am empowered by Preston to overrule you on matters of security," Dutch said.

"No you won't because then it will appear as if I have no real authority," Carter said.

"I suggest you let your ego take a back seat to our safety," Dutch said.

"That's enough," Carter said firmly. "We are not accepting the escort."

Dutch stared at Carter hard. "Fine," he finally said in as soft of a tone as he could muster.

"I have kept my counsel Carter but I agree with Dutch," Alexander, now awake, said as he rose to his feet. "With that said, it is clear that you have made your decision."

"I have," Carter said.

"Very well," Alexander said.

*   *   *   *

Fifteen minutes later, Carter, Alexander and Dutch made their way toward the main gate of Knight Farm with two Mastiffs and two Schnauzers behind them. Four Llamas pulled the massive wooden doors open as they approached. The doors, engraved with amazing detail in identical patterns, were two or three times higher than the tallest Llama pulling it open for them.

Two Mastiffs stood just outside the gate. Just ten yards from the gate was a bridge that spanned Beaver Creek from just beyond the walls of Knight Farm. On the other side began the road west. Two more Mastiffs stood on the far side of the bridge, staring off to the West. Carter knew that Sir Andrew's Royal Guard patrolled one mile around the perimeter of the Farm, and that Hawks or Owls, depending whether it was day or night, patrolled the sky in a ten mile radius. There would be little for him, Dutch and Alexander to worry about until nightfall.

Carter and Alexander walked side by side. Once they were beyond the mile of stone road leading away from Knight Farm, the dust painted Alexander's black hair beige. Carter's coat of black, grey and white remained the same. Nature had little effect on his coloring; Carter always appeared to be an ambiguous shade of grey. Dutch's coloring had not altered a bit either. However, his demeanor had turned black. He followed Carter and Alexander from ten paces behind and said even less than Alexander. His hooves didn't make a sound as he walked, even in the areas where the dirt road turned to grey gravel. At times, Carter looked over his shoulder to make sure that Dutch still followed. Each time Carter did so, Dutch appeared to be staring forward angrily but Dutch did not even see Carter look back at him. His eyes were on the forest.

They climbed down a small range of grassy hills around noon and dropped into the forest they would journey through for the next day and a half until they reached Manor Farm.

"Let's stop and eat," Dutch said. They had dropped down the last hill and were preparing to enter the forest.

Carter hesitated as he did not want to stop and then thought better of disagreeing with Dutch. "Alright," he said.

They made their way to the shade of some oak trees and dropped to the ground. If a human had seen this he would have seen what appeared to be three domesticated animals gathered together in the middle of the forest. It might strike the human as strange, but there would be no indication that these were Animals that matched his intelligence.

"Carter," Dutch said, "I am sorry I voiced my displeasure so vehemently. I could have made my point in a more sophisticated manner."

"It's alright," Carter said. "You were right, I realize upon reflection. There was no reason to risk our safety just to posture in front of King George. If we truly are going to act without the support of Knight Farm, we need not posture."

"Yes, well, here we are now," Dutch said. "I just want to make sure we are unified and share a common plan in case of trouble. In case of an attack of some sort we will all stay on the road and not move until I say otherwise. I will stand guard through the night and I suggest you both do the same."

"I agree an escort would have been a better option but isn't this overkill?" Carter asked.

"I don't think so," Dutch said shrugging his massive shoulders. "Plus, it is my job to be paranoid."

"That is very true," Alexander said joining the conversation. "But what could possibly harm a Bull, a Goat and a Boar that still inhabits this forest? The wolves are far to the East of Knight Farm near Snail Farm and the wild dogs are all on the Western plain that separates us from the human lands."

"I know but something was very strange in the forest the other night and I would just like us to be cautious," Dutch said.

"Very well," Carter said, "we will stick to the road unless you say otherwise."

"Yes," Dutch said with a quick nod.

They covered fifteen more miles before the sun no longer filtered through the outstretched arms of the giant oak trees. They could hear Beaver Creek in the distance as they ate their evening meal. But the Owls had just begun their shift in the night sky and the Hawks had returned to the aeries of Knight Farm for their evening meal. The closest Owls were ten miles to the East and could not see the contingent from Manor Farm. They were alone.

They made camp on a slight rise in the road so they could see down the road in either direction. The crickets and frogs broke the silence of dusk when the sun completely disappeared over the horizon. As night established itself firmly in the forest, they heard the occasional scream of a mouse as a snake stole him in the night. The only other sound was an occasional gust of wind blowing through the tops of the oak trees.

They did not speak. Each sat looking off in a different direction. Alexander looked north toward the human lands far off in the distance, Carter looked west toward Manor Farm and Dutch scanned both the South toward Beaver Creek and back east toward Knight Farm. Although they looked off in different directions, they all saw the same thing, a dense forest of oak and maples.

As the moon approached the middle of the night sky, its light was no longer blocked by the branches of the oaks and maples. This caused Carter to rest a little easier. He could now see fifty yards down the road. He began to resent Dutch for raising their fears. The chance of a real threat to the party from the animals in the forest was remote. Then he checked his emotions and realized that Dutch was just doing his job. Carter knew he should not punish him for doing so. As Carter chastised himself, there was a strange change in the voice of the night. Its croaks had broken off in mid-sentence. A silence fell over Beaver Creek while the crickets on the North side of the road continued their song. Dutch popped to his feet and silently made his way to the Southern edge of the road.

"What is it? Carter asked, also rising to his feet. Dutch looked at him quickly and shook his head to indicate he did not know. Thirty seconds later the crickets on the North side of the road fell silent.

"Remember to stick together and stay on the road," Dutch said. "We fight here and don't make a move unless I say otherwise."

"Alright," Alexander said calmly. "I smell something but can't identify the smell."

"Whatever is out there, I can tell that there are a lot of them," Dutch said.

"How in the hell would you know that?" Carter demanded. He had lost his patience with Dutch and his paranoid behavior.

"Because you can't hear a single frog or cricket."

"So?"

"If there were only a few animals on the side of the road the noise would pick up as soon as they passed a particular spot. But they don't pick up which means that whatever is out there is spread out over a wide area. Now, please be quiet – look and listen."

They backed toward each other until their tails nearly touched. Dutch faced Beaver Creek, Alexander faced the forest toward the north in the direction of the human lands and Carter faced west toward Manor Farm. Carter shook slightly.

After a couple of minutes passed, the frogs along Beaver Creek, a couple of hundred yards from the road, haltingly resumed their song. A minute or so later, they faintly heard the crickets' orchestra resume to the East and West. Carter looked at Dutch.

"Whatever it is they are now gathered close and on all sides of us," Dutch said.

"It is strange," Carter said softly, allowing himself to see reality. "Who could it be?"

"Sabean, I think," Dutch said. "I smell a rat."

"But what do they possibly think they can accomplish against us?" Carter asked.

"At the very least they can instill fear," Alexander said. "I am even feeling a bit uncomfortable."

"Remember . . ."

"Yes, we know," Carter said interrupting Dutch, "stay on the road together unless you say otherwise."

"Exactly," Dutch said, and took his eyes off the forest long enough to glare at Carter. "Now, please be quiet and listen for my command."

This time Carter fell into silent complicity.

One hundred yards down the road, four weasels and at least a few hundred rats materialized out of the forest and made their way quickly toward the three Animals of Manor Farm.

"Rats," Carter said with disgust.

Carter looked to the East toward Knight Farm. A dozen raccoons and another couple of hundred rats were racing toward them with eyes blazing blue and red in the moonlight.

98

"We have company from the East as well," Carter said. "Raccoons, at least ten, and a lot more rats."

"Raccoons?" Alexander asked.

"Alright, gentlemen," Dutch said calmly. "Hold your ground. We are going to have visitors from the North and South as well. We fight here."

"Why don't we run for it?" Carter asked.

"Because we will be playing into their hands," Dutch said.

"But we could . . . "

Before Carter could finish his hurried whisper, a thousand rats, blacker than the night sky flooded the dirt road. At first, they simply swirled around their legs just out of range. Carter attempted to stomp a few as they came close but they were far enough away that evasive action was easy. Dutch calmly conserved his energy and Alexander slowly swung his large tail back and forth. Dutch snorted softly, preparing for battle.

"Easy Carter," Dutch said.

Carter took a deep breath of the fresh night air and felt a little better. He checked the road from the West. The weasels and rats were only ten yards away. He turned quickly to the East, the raccoons were just five yards away and then they were on them. Carter watched as the weasels and nearly all of the rats, over a thousand, swarmed Dutch and Alexander. The rats were getting close enough so that Dutch and Alexander were able to stomp a few. Dutch also managed to crush two with his powerful jaws. Once Dutch and Alexander had killed about ten rats each, their momentum had carried them a couple of yards back down the road toward Knight Farm. Carter had not remembered to follow. He stood alone. Rats filled the space between Carter and his companions but they stayed far enough away so that Carter could not stomp on them.

Although more than a minute had passed, the raccoons had not entered the fray. They had left the road and passed by Alexander and Dutch while they were engaged with the rats and the weasels. Rats continued to run under Dutch's and Alexander's legs and bite at them. Neither panicked and they continued crushing them but it was now clear to Carter that the rats were moving Eastward intentionally in order to draw his friends in that direction. Now the rats closest to Carter moved toward him to drive him Westward.

Carter was pushed ten yards from his companions when he saw the eyes of the raccoons and their muscular bodies swaying in the moonlight. Six were on each side of the road and all twelve were bigger than the Beagles back home at Manor Farm.

"Dutch, it's a trap," Carter yelled out.

"What?" Dutch yelled, a little annoyed by the rats and Carter's interruption. But as soon as he turned toward Carter's voice, he saw it. He had not paid attention to where Carter was during the fighting.

The raccoons knew they could wait no longer. Three from each side of the road bounded toward Carter. The other six jumped into the middle of the road and turned toward Dutch and Alexander snarling. Clearly they meant to fight. Dutch would have laughed if he didn't see that Carter was in mortal danger. Carter saw it as well.

"Fight your way to us," Dutch bellowed as he frantically charged the raccoons with Alexander close behind.

Before Carter could jump off the ground and bound his way to Dutch, a raccoon tore a piece of his right rear leg down to the tendon. Carter turned his head quickly and butted a raccoon and crushed its skull. As Carter tried to jump again, another raccoon jumped on his back and ripped his flesh down to the ribs and bounded out of range. Carter kicked one coming for his left rear leg with both his hind legs and the sound of breaking bones gave Carter a brief feeling of confidence. But as he landed he realized that two raccoons had darted underneath him when he had kicked his legs out.

All of the rats had stayed out of the bloody fight between Carter and the raccoons. Instead, they had joined the weasels and the other six raccoons in trying to help slow down Dutch and Alexander. The rats were crawling all over the Boar and Bull as they engaged the raccoons. Hundreds of rats covered each of them as they charged toward Carter.

Three raccoons and four weasels along with hundreds of rats faced off against Dutch. The three raccoons and three of the weasels all snarling in fear and anger, met him head on while one of the weasels darted between his legs and sunk his teeth deep into Dutch's genitals. Dutch squealed in pain and rage and turned toward the weasel that had run out from under his legs. It was Willie. He had been too quick in moving to the East and scampered away. Two of the raccoons jumped on Dutch's back and it took him over thirty seconds to throw them off.

Alexander had rats moving all over his stomach and back and was forced to drop down and roll over at least thirty rats in the process.

The raccoons under Carter tore into his stomach and testicles with their claws. Carter managed to bounce away but was forced farther West and still had four raccoons surrounding him with Dutch and Alexander still over five yards away. Blood poured from his back, legs, stomach and testicles as he stood panting in the middle of the road.

"I'm making a run for it," Carter bellowed, his path back to Dutch and Alexander was blocked by four raccoons, three weasels and at least a thousand rats. The way west was blocked by only one raccoon.

"No," Dutch commanded. "We are almost there."

"I'm going," Carter said. "They will never stay with me."

"No, that is exactly what they want you to do," Dutch cried out in desperation.

Carter shook his head and bounded away. A raccoon slashed his side as he went by but he put five yards between himself and the raccoons in just a few seconds. He slowed his pace, and started to breathe a little easier, when he felt an excruciating pain. His left lower hind leg snapped in the jaws of the largest fox he had ever seen. Carter's scream was human as he tumbled off the road and down a small hill.

Rats and three more foxes were on him before he could get to his feet. A fox ripped off one of his ears and flung it on the wet grass. Carter heard the raccoons who had survived the earlier battle with him, snarling as they leapt from the road on to him before he could regain his feet. Carter was too weak to defend himself and four raccoons and three foxes were on him. One of the foxes now had time to get his relatively small jaws on his jugular. The fox growled and ripped a hole in Carter's throat. Blood pumped onto the wet, green grass turning it a deep purple in the moonlight.

Carter watched Dutch fly over the bank from the road. Carter was in awe that a Pig could move so quickly. Dutch had rats gnawing on his back as well as a lone raccoon ripping his shoulders but he did not seem to notice. The fox who had taken Carter's life turned his head toward the road and took off yelping, "Incoming." The foxes darted into the brush and found safety from the raging Boar.

Dutch leapt over Carter landing on the backs of two retreating raccoons. Even near death, Carter took satisfaction in their death cries. Dutch chased down one more raccoon and latched onto its tail before it could make it into the thick underbrush. Dutch broke one of the raccoon's hind legs with a vicious stomp from his front hoof. He broke the raccoon's other hind leg. Dutch dragged the raccoon back to the road where Alexander stood alone, among hundreds of dead rats and a couple of the eight dead raccoons. The massive Bull, his black hair covered with red dots, looked like a bovine pinprick. Dutch dropped the raccoon at Alexander's feet.

"Find out who is behind this attack although it is fairly obvious," Dutch said to Alexander.

Dutch, blood dripping quickly from his genitals and stomach, trotted back to Carter. Carter opened his eyes, sensing Dutch's presence.

"I'm sorry Dutch," Carter said. He was breathing quickly, the blood now pumping slowly from his neck. "You were right on all counts. I should have listened."

101

Dutch managed a smile. "You fought valiantly. Your name will forever be remembered in the annals of Manor Farm."

"We would have fared much better if Cody and the Beagles were here," Carter said, with short breaths in between each word.

Dutch did not respond. There was no satisfaction in Carter's admission. Dutch had seen what Carter now acknowledged only when they had reached Knight Farm. If he'd seen it before, he might have been able to convince Preston to allow the Dogs to escort them, Dutch thought bitterly to himself.

"I was a fool," Carter said.

"You were brave," Dutch responded.

Dutch took Carter up the embankment after he had drawn his last breath. He had said no more.

"Well?" Dutch asked Alexander.

"Sabean, now joined by Poseidon, a group of foxes, some weasels and a hundred or so raccoons," Alexander said.

Apparently, the raccoon had been slow to talk, because one of its front legs still resided beneath one of Alexander's massive hooves. Alexander crushed the raccoon's skull as they moved west a mile or so before dropping from exhaustion.

When dawn broke, Dutch managed to get Carter's body back on Alexander's back and they made their way the rest of the way home to Manor Farm. They arrived days before they were expected.

*   *   *   *

Louis, with Jean and Marcel on either side, stepped proudly through the rear gate of Knight Farm, a few hours after the contingent from Manor Farm had headed west. The journey East to Snail Farm would take a half a day more than the journey to Manor Farm. The first night would be spent in the mountains that separated Snail Farm from King George's domain.

They said little as they climbed the mountains. Jean and Marcel whispered to each other occasionally. Not wanting to inspire Louis's wrath, they did this only when out of earshot. In the early years, after Louis's heroic battle against the wolves that halted the decades of raids by One-eye and his forefathers, the relationship between Louis and the Poodles of Snail Farm had been different. Louis had had the loyalty of the Poodles, a couple of thousand strong, more so than any Pig before or after.

Now, as Louis's actions focused on the political rather than the military, in the minds of most Poodles, Louis had become fat in the head as well as the body. Jean looked at Louis's rolls of fat with disgust. The

102

Boar from Manor Farm who was named Dutch reminded Jean of the heroic Louis.

When Louis returned triumphant from the Battle of the Wolves, Jean watched in awe as his father, then the head of security for Snail Farm, pranced proudly at Louis's side. In those days, Louis trotted like a Poodle and had ten times the strength. When he entered the Farm that day, his pink body was rippled with muscle. A warrior first, Louis had said little to the public despite his advanced degree from the university in political philosophy. In the intervening years, Louis had let his ego rule his brain and the results were appalling to the Poodle population. Louis now spoke more than he thought.

Now, Jean and Marcel's loyalty was like that of a young man to his grandfather, accepting of his flaws while respecting his wisdom. Jean and Marcel bit their tongues in Louis's presence because of what he had been and what he stood for in the history of Snail Farm. As a pup, Jean never tired of hearing the story of the Battle of the Wolves as told by his father. A pack of a hundred Poodles, led by Louis, had pursued the dreaded wolf pack into the mountains. Louis and a team of the fastest Poodles was a mile ahead of the rest of the Dogs who were spread out wide to prevent the wolves from doubling back.

The plan was to keep a quarter of a mile between Louis's lead team of chasers and the main force, so that if the wolves turned to fight, the remaining ninety Poodles could converge in less than a couple of minutes. But as the climb into the mountains steepened, Louis's chase team increased their speed in order to close the distance on the wolves. The rest of the Poodles were forced to slow because they could not maintain their spacing over the rough terrain and also maintain the fast pace. This was because some were forced to move around hills that were too steep and boulders that were too big. They fell further and further behind the chase pack because the wolves were leading them up a cleared trail.

One-eye, then known only as Caesar, saw that the chase-pack was isolated. He halted his pack of forty wolves. They dissolved into the pine forest until Louis and his team reached their location. Then the wolves reappeared from the forest as if they were ghosts. They had Louis and his team of ten Poodles surrounded in a horseshoe and outnumbered four to one. The only opening was to retreat back down the mountain.

"Do we retreat?" Jean's father had asked Louis.

"No."

Both the wolves and the Poodles growled softly and shook slightly with blood lust.

"May I ask why not?" Jean's father had asked calmly.

"Because they will kill our slowest few before we make it ten yards and we will be lucky if more than half of us escape," Louis said as quietly as he could.

The wolves started to close the distance, forcing Louis's hand.

"We attack straight up the hill side by side," he said firmly. "Now," he bellowed, before any of the Poodles could question his plan.

Louis charged up the hill and aimed right at Caesar who stood in the middle of the horseshoe which was the highest spot held by the wolves. Caesar stood still for a moment, and then the surprised look on his faced turned to one of anger.

"Attack," the wolf howled.

Louis made it to Caesar before the sides of the horseshoe could collapse on his team. Louis veered away from Caesar who had charged right down the mountain at Louis as Louis charged up. As Louis veered, Caesar focused on Louis's rear legs. Caesar leapt toward Louis's haunches as Louis moved passed him but the moment he left the ground, Louis jumped and spun in mid-air. Louis swung his tusks at Caesar's head. Caesar's jaws snapped air as one of Louis's massive tusks ripped Caesar's right eye from the socket.

Louis and seven Poodles made it through the top of the horseshoe. The other three Poodles had been forced to engage and now had at least three wolves on them. The seven Poodles followed Louis as he turned and raced down the mountain at the wolves who were now concentrating on destroying the three Poodles who were unable to break the line.

One-eye had been struck by an uncontrollable rage when he lost his eye and had fallen on one of the unlucky Poodles and ripped its throat out. All the other wolves thought that Louis and the Poodles who had passed through the horseshoe had run for safety. The wolves that were not ripping the three Poodles to shreds were gathered around the carnage howling softly and deeply. Blood covered the white and grey fur of the wolves and ran in a steady stream from One-eye's socket.

The wolf pack turned as one when the charging Louis and Poodles were within a few yards. They froze momentarily as Louis led the charge toward the group that was furthest down the hill. One-eye watched as they flew past him but he now understood. He then watched Louis and the Poodles plough through five wolves that were finishing off a Poodle. Louis had managed to snap the spine of a wolf by jumping high in the air and landing on its back.

Jean's father had survived the charge up the mountain and at one hundred pounds was a good match for any wolf but One-eye. He had watched One-eye rip his brother's throat out and was wild with rage. He narrowly avoided the snapping jaws of a young wolf as he raced down the

104

mountain. After passing the wolf's head, he dropped low to the ground and managed to snap his jaws tight on the dark grey fur of one of the wolf's hind legs. The leg snapped but Jean's father did not let go. Instead, he pulled the wolf off balance, his speed creating incredible force. Ribs cracked on the rocky terrain as the wolf slammed to the ground. Jean's father continued the race down the mountain and did not release his hold on the wolf's leg.

The remainder of the wolf pack turned and pursued the Poodle's down the hill, hoping to repay Louis and his team for the outrage.

"No," One-eyed howled at the members of his pack who were lost in blood lust. "Back up the hill! Retreat!"

But only the group of eight that had gathered to watch One-eye rip the esophagus from Jean's uncle heard him. These eight halted. One-eye, and the eight wolves who had heard him, headed up the mountain, looking back only once as the remaining ninety Poodles of Snail Farm fell on the thirty members of One-eye's pack that had pursued Louis down the hill.

Trotting up the hill, One-eye knew it would be many years before he could rebuild his pack to its former strength. He was a wolf. He would be patient. One day he would exact his revenge on Snail Farm and Louis.

*   *   *   *

That story, and others told by his father about Louis, always came to his mind when he wanted to mock the Ambassador. This allowed him to hold his tongue. This was also true of Marcel who had heard the same stories from his uncle by Jean's side as a young pup. His father had lost his life that day, but he had fought to the death as One-eye ripped his flesh from the bone.

Louis and the Poodles spoke little as the sun crossed the sky and they continued to make their way over Pine Mountain. They stopped for the night as darkness fell. They ate in relative silence, Louis clearly so tired from the day's walk that he barely had the energy to chew. When they finished eating, Louis said, "We will guard our position in shifts."

"Alright Louis," Jean and Marcel said in unison.

"Jean will take the first watch. Marcel will take the second. I hate to admit it but I must sleep first or I will never stay awake during my watch."

Jean and Marcel did not say a word as Louis dropped his huge, pink head onto his fat front legs and closed his eyes. With total trust in the Poodles, he began snoring in minutes.

"I am assuming neither of us will sleep," Marcel said. Although Marcel was smarter, Jean ruled in combat situations. "It is only one night and I'd feel better if we each watched one side of the path."

"I was thinking the same thing," Jean said.

They dropped down side by side with their heads in opposite directions. Their black coats, covered in dust, were nearly invisible even with the full moon. Marcel faced north and Jean faced south. The terrain on either side was the same, tall pines yards apart with rock strewn across the barren earth. There were no pine needles on the ground this time of year. The view South sloped downward and the view North slightly up.

The sun broke through the clouds ten hours later and Louis finally stirred. Jean and Marcel had finished their breakfast of hard-boiled eggs, apples and bread that the cooks of Knight Farm had packed for them. A portion, big enough for two Poodles, was on a cloth that bore the emblem of Knight Farm. The morning air chilled their bones at this altitude despite the warming weather.

"You should not have let me sleep through my watch Marcel," Louis said as firmly as he could manage.

"We were both awake, Ambassador, and we saw no reason to wake you," Jean said before Marcel could say something sarcastic.

Louis grunted but did not have the energy to protest this explanation. Louis shook the stiffness out of his body and took his time eating the double portion that the Poodles had left him. An hour later, they were on the path making their way up a steep incline. Louis had already passed from stiff, to loose, to laboring as they made their way through the mountains. Unlike where they had camped, the trees were thick from hundreds of years of growth with no fires to clear out the dead or dying fir trees. The path narrowed to just twelve inches as it was mostly used by wild deer crossing from one side of the mountain to the other in spring and fall. The deer traveled in order to avoid the bitter cold of the East or the oppressive heat of the West. At this time of year, early spring, the weather was perfect on both sides of the mountain.

"Wait," Marcel said sharply.

"What is it?" Louis asked quietly.

Marcel did not answer. He sniffed the air as did Jean. Jean growled. Wolves appeared out of the forest, as if by magic, and surrounded them. There were twelve in sight and Jean could smell more in the forest. One-eye stepped silently onto the path, ten yards ahead of the three from Snail Farm.

"Good morning, Ambassador," One-eye said.

Louis recognized him immediately as he looked much the same as the day he had poked his eye out with his tusk. Louis flashed to his own

106

reflection he'd seen the morning before they had left Knight Farm. He wondered why his body had turned to fat and folds and One-eye looked leaner and more muscular than he had ten years earlier. One-eye, his muzzle of white contrasting sharply with his coat of grey, stepped within six feet of Louis. The Poodles growled deeply as the wolves growled and yelped.

"We do not want you two," One-eye said dismissively to Jean and Marcel, training his good eye on first one and then the other. "It is the Pig I want. You may go."

"Can't do that, I'm afraid," Jean said with an unsettling calm.

"As you wish," One-eye said. "I have longed for this day for ten years," One-eye continued after redirecting his attention to Louis. "Yes, you took my eye. This is not a big deal to me. But you also destroyed most of my family and that is an awfully big deal."

Louis and the Poodles did not respond. One-eye lifted his left paw and two wolves were on each of them in seconds. They nipped at Louis, drawing blood but never staying close enough for Louis to strike them with his now dull and brittle tusks. Jean and Marcel fought valiantly but a third wolf fell on each of them as they started to tire and they took their last breath five minutes after they were ambushed.

Louis now stood alone, bleeding and snorting with rage as he no longer had the quickness to catch up with a wolf in battle.

"You have slowed down, Ambassador," One-eye said. He stated it as fact and not as an insult. One-eye had splattered patterns of blood on his muzzle from nipping at Louis.

"Finish it," Louis said. "Your pack is doomed in any case."

"Perhaps you're right, perhaps not," One-eye said to Louis. "Let's eat," he sang with glee to the pack. A wolf grabbed each of Louis's legs and they pulled him off balance. He ended up on his side, rolls of fat hanging over the large rocks scattered on the ground. One-eye ripped at Louis's jugular and the pack yelped in excitement as they lapped up the thick blood.

When the meal was over and night fell hours later, One-eye made his way to the rock he had sat on when he met Sabean. One-eye howled, as if the world had magically righted itself.

CHAPTER NINE – ALLIANCE

While Carter was away, the Pack continued to spend their nights guarding the perimeter Farm consistent with Preston's orders. During the day they found shade as far from the farmhouse and barn as possible; this was the giant oak the Pack called home. They said very little because Frank did not speak, unless spoken to, when he was angry or concerned.

Cody couldn't stand the tension of keeping his thoughts to himself any longer. His large body, taut with stress, shook despite the heat. He padded over to Frank and sat down slowly, giving Frank time to tell him, "Not now." Frank did not say a word. Cody took this as assent to his presence. Cody couldn't believe he could feel so terrible on such a beautiful spring day.

"I am sending the Beagles to Knight Farm tonight," Cody said. "I want them to figure out what is happening. It is strange not knowing. Preston must know something but he never comes out of the farmhouse. He keeps all the information to himself."

Cody paused between sentences and waited for Frank to respond. Frank continued to stare down the road toward the farmhouse.

"Unless you tell me otherwise, I will send them," Cody said giving Frank an opportunity to disclaim responsibility for Cody's actions.

"I'd like you to honor Preston's request or I should say orders," Frank said so softly that Cody strained to make out the words.

"Why?" Cody asked.

"Because what's done is done; I can feel it in my bones," Frank said, now speaking in a more regular tone and volume. "It is too late to change the course of events relating to Carter's diplomatic mission. Our contingents' wellbeing is out of our hands."

Cody knew that the old Labrador had a keen sense of what was happening to the citizens of Manor Farm even when they were far away. What Frank said concerned him. "Are you sure?" Cody asked.

Frank looked over the farmhouse to the wheat fields in the distance, and then back at the farmhouse, as he focused his thoughts. Cody gave him time as he had seen Frank sit like this for hours waiting for a vision. Cody scanned the Pack, just fifty or so strong. He wondered in amazement how it was that the Pack had been elected so many times to rule over the thousands of Pigs, Cows and other Animals when there were over a thousand Pigs on the Farm. He knew it was because of Dogs like Frank. The Animals, Pigs included, entrusted their lives to his judgment.

Yet, in fewer than six months, the members of the Pack had been excluded from all levels of Preston's administration. The Cats had also been left out of the decision- making process. However, being solitary

Animals, Cats spent their days and nights much as before. They simply did what they did when Frank led the Farm because they believed that the strategy was sound. However, they did not have the political interest to push to have the Dogs where they belonged. On the other hand, Preston was practical and did not try to change the role the Cats played.

A breeze briefly pushed through the branches of the oak tree and provided momentary relief from the heat. When the wheat stopped swaying, Frank responded. "Yes," he said. "There is nothing for us to do. It is done."

"Okay," Cody said. "I will hold off on taking any action until you give me the go ahead."

"I say now," Frank said.

"I don't follow you Frank. Speak plainly."

"Send the Beagles off toward Knight Farm now."

"As you wish," Cody said as he popped to his feet.

"Cody," Frank said as Cody padded away. Cody stopped. "Go with the Beagles and bring Maggie. Something isn't right and I feel it very strongly now. There is nothing we can do but we must go to help anyway."

Cody nodded. Cody hoped that Frank was now going to move into a more active role in Farm politics. Cody could not stand waiting around for something bad to happen. The vision had brought Frank back to the present, Cody hoped Frank would stay there.

*   *   *   *

Cody and Maggie, huge tongues hanging from the side of their mouths, struggled to keep up with Paulie, Pete and Patrick. Despite the heat, the Beagles couldn't help but move down the dirt road quickly with their noses to the ground. As Cody watched this, he thought he'd never be able to tell the three Beagles apart if he couldn't pick up their scent. They were all tall and wide for Beagles and had nearly identical tri-color coats.

Cody and Maggie would let the Beagles get twenty or so yards ahead and then pick up their pace to catch up with their tireless companions. The Beagles would smell danger long before it came upon them; so all of them battled only heat, not fear.

After they had been gone from Manor Farm for less than two hours, Patrick stopped, lifted a paw and howled. This was much to the disappointment of Paulie and Pete. He had struck the scent before they had. For Beagles, life was a competition. Before Cody could get a word out, the Beagles were on the run. He and Maggie gave chase.

A minute later Pete let out a howl which meant he had found the source of the scent that Patrick had discovered. Cody and Maggie rounded a bend in the road, tall oaks and an assortment of local fauna made seeing through the forest to the road spot in the road Patrick had identified impossible. The path straightened and an eighth of a mile ahead they saw the Beagles greeting Dutch and Alexander. Alexander appeared to have a large pack on his massive, black back.

As they closed the distance, Cody saw that both Dutch and Alexander were covered in blood. Carter had been placed on Alexander's back, either severely injured or worse.

"Is he dead?" Maggie asked between pants.

"Not sure," Cody said as he picked up the pace.

As they drew closer, turning up the dry dirt as morning turned to noon, it became clear that the second-in-command at Manor Farm was dead. Cody let out a cry, more snarl than howl. He stopped directly in front of Dutch and, trying to keep the anger out of his voice, asked, "Who did this, my friend?"

"Sabean," Dutch said.

"Of course," Cody said. "He has declared war. That was not an isolated raid."

"Yes," Dutch said as he moved to the side of the road and found some shade. "He is not alone though, Cody."

"The fox and the weasel again?" Maggie asked.

"Yes, but at least four weasels and at least three foxes, also raccoons."

"Raccoons," Cody said. "This is unbelievable. Why would the raccoons even bother? They have no problem getting food."

"I don't know," Dutch said. "But there were water rats with Sabean's band. They were larger and darker than those that attacked the Farm. Somehow, Sabean has managed to continue to unite different packs of rats just like Poseidon did years ago."

Cody, Maggie and the Beagles didn't respond for a number of seconds.

"This isn't just random wild animal attacks," Cody finally said. "We have an all-out war on our hands."

"Seems that way," Dutch said, no longer laboring to breath. "Can we get back to the Farm now? We need food and water, and we need our wounds tended to."

Cody sighed with self-loathing. "Of course," he said. "I'm sorry, I'm not thinking."

The seven of them made their way back to Manor Farm. When they arrived, Alexander still had not said a word.

110

After Dutch and Alexander had their wounds tended to, and drank and ate, they related the entire story to the Pack. They were under the shade of the giant oak near the main gate. They had sat in silence for some time after Dutch told the story. Frank stared and his black fur stood so quickly it appeared to have responded to a command.

"What is it?" Cody asked.

"They've been back for over an hour and no one has told Preston," Frank said. "Paulie, run over to the farmhouse and alert Preston that they've returned. Tell Preston that there has been another tragedy."

"Alright," Paulie said.

She bounded down the gravel road and told the guard at the porch. She returned to her spot in the shade of the oak tree between Pete and Patrick in less than five minutes. Cody looked in amazement as she barely panted. Sometimes he wondered if Beagles were an entirely different species. They ate anything and appeared to never get tired.

Cody expected to see Preston marching down the path with one of his college cronies in toe. Cody assumed it would be Isaac, his best friend from childhood who had gone with Preston to Snail University. Cody believed that Preston would first react angrily to the news and then, immediately after, complain to Frank that he should have escorted Dutch and Alexander directly to the farmhouse. Frank thought Preston would tell him that letting them eat and drink could have waited and so could have tending to their wounds.

Instead, Isaac waddled down the path alone. He had left the farmhouse a little later than seemed acceptable. The delay seemed disrespectful. Isaac was taller than Dutch and even Preston and thus stood taller than any Pig at Manor Farm. But instead of layers of muscle like Dutch, Isaac had thick plates of fat. Instead of dark hair, Isaac was Pig of the pink variety. After Cody had watched Paulie cover the distance from the farmhouse and back, it seemed to take Isaac an eternity to make his way down the gravel drive.

It took Isaac thirty seconds in the shade of the oak tree before he could speak clearly. "Preston would like to see you both at the farmhouse," Isaac demanded.

"Aren't you curious as to why Carter isn't with them?" Cody asked.

"Yes," Isaac said matter-of-factly, "but my orders are to bring them directly to Preston and it's pretty clear to me that the Goat is not here."

"Ah," Cody said, and just stared at the deep folds of fat in the Pig's neck.

"If you please," Isaac said to Dutch and Alexander.

Dutch rose to his feet, he and Alexander looked at Frank. Frank nodded.

"I am quite sure Leader Frank has no say in whether you obey Preston's directives," Isaac said boldly.

The Pack burst into howls of laughter. Dutch and Alexander could not suppress grins. Isaac turned a darker shade of pink in his face and around his neck. He turned and began walking toward the farmhouse. Dutch and Alexander followed, the gravel crunching under their feet heavily as they were still barely able to walk.

"Those Dogs are very strange creatures," Isaac said when they were out of earshot from the Pack. "They seem to be having trouble adjusting to the fact that they lost the election."

Neither Dutch nor Alexander responded. They continued to move slowly down the road, each step opening up a scab that had started to form over the hundreds of rat bites covering their bodies.

"Well, they better get used to it," Isaac said, oblivious to his audience's reaction or lack thereof. "Preston will be our leader for many years seeing how Frank failed to take any action to rid the forest of vicious wilds."

"That's ridiculous," Dutch said sharply.

They passed the remainder of the walk in silence. They entered the main room in the farmhouse. Preston sat alone with a pile of scrambled eggs and a tankard of ale in front of him. Dutch and Alexander relayed the tale to Preston and Isaac as soon as they entered the room.

"That is awful," Preston said. "It is an outrage. We must strike back."

Although he seemed slightly angry, he showed no sorrow at the loss of his first advisor who was also one of his closest friends. He had appeared angrier when Frank had questioned his tactics in the aftermath of Sabean's attack on Manor Farm.

Isaac escorted Dutch and Alexander back to the shaded oak near the front gate.

"In addition to the terrible news of Carter's death, we have received a message from Snail Farm," Isaac told the Pack. "Just this morning, their Ambassador and his escort were attacked and killed in the mountains by One-eye's pack. Snail Farm is sending an emissary to discuss a united front in the face of these outrageous attacks."

"Of course they are," Cody said.

112

Isaac ignored him. "I will meet the emissary a mile from the Farm with Preston's personal guard. We will escort them through the rear gate. Preston would like the Pack to maintain security on this side of the Farm."

"I see," Cody said. "It's a Pig only discussion. How inclusive this new administration is. It's very refreshing."

Again, Isaac's rolls of fat around his cheeks and neck turned a dark pink. This time the color was nearly red.

*   *   *   *

Percy and Sammy dropped from a branch in the large oak tree. They landed right in front of Frank and Cody, who lay in silence. Cody gave a start and glared at the Cats. Frank chuckled. Cody's irritation vanished at the sound of Frank's laughter. Frank had decided that hope remained. It was twenty-four hours since Dutch and Alexander had returned to Manor Farm. Percy licked his black fur distractedly while Sammy stared at Frank. Sammy's orange tail, mottled with black stripes, swayed slowly back and forth.

"Well?" Frank asked, amused.

"Pigs, ten of them besides Preston's guard, entered last night around midnight."

"We figured out that much with our noses," Cody said with a smile.

"I didn't think you could count them with your nose," Percy replied sarcastically.

"I can't," Cody said seriously, "but Patrick can."

"So tell us what you've seen," Frank said, tired of the showmanship.

"Well," Percy said, "even in the dark it was obvious that there was a high ranking official visiting from Snail Farm. The guards were Boars, large and muscular like Dutch."

"Yes," Sammy said. "The guards were not flabby and grotesque like Isaac."

Like all Cats, Percy and Sammy were disgusted by fat Animals. Frank raised his eyebrows at Sammy, as if to say "Are you through yet?"

"Right," Percy said. "In addition to that, one of our Cats outside the perimeter of the Farm spotted a pack of twenty Poodles. They were camped two miles downwind, apparently so the Beagles wouldn't smell them."

"Interesting," Frank said. "We know it wasn't Ambassador Louis."

"We saw who it was when the party made their way out of the Farm this morning," Percy said. "It was the Premier of Snail Farm."

Neither Frank nor Cody said a word. Finally, Sammy broke the silence. "What do you think it means?" he asked.

"I'm not sure," Frank said. "Something is happening that we don't know about. I am sure the Premier is not overly concerned about Carter's death. I'd also be surprised if he was that upset about Louis's demise. Let's all take some time to think about this and we will meet back here at sunset. Maybe we will hear from Preston by then and he will provide some clarity."

*   *   *   *

They didn't have to wait long to hear from him, but the clarity would come another day. An hour after Percy and Sammy informed them of the Premier's visit, the Crows were circling the Farm informing all the Animals that Preston would address the Farm in two hours from the porch of the farmhouse.

"Perhaps Preston is going to demonstrate some leadership," Cody said.

"We'll see," Frank said.

Two hours and ten minutes later, Preston stepped out from the front door of the farmhouse, closely followed by Isaac. Preston, the second tallest Pig at Manor Farm, looked short compared to his new second-in-command. Isaac was followed by eight Boars who made up the rest of Preston's inner circle, and two muscular Boars who served as Preston's personal guard. They had replaced Dutch, who was both injured and disenchanted.

Preston scanned the Animals, but did not smile at individuals as he had during his campaign and his first couple of speeches as the leader of Manor Farm. Over a thousand Pigs, hundreds of Goats, Sheep and Cows, thousands of Chickens and Ducks and the fifty or so Cats, and fifty members of the Pack surrounded the porch. The Ducks and Chickens were closest. The Pigs, Goats and Sheep were spread along the gravel road that led in from the front gate and were in what had been the corral hundreds of years ago. The Cows stood behind the Pigs, Goats and Sheep. The corral was now the location for all Farm assemblies and celebrations. The Pack and the Cats stood way to the back, in the wild bush to the East of the corral.

Silence fell over the Farm when Preston stepped to the edge of the porch. The Pigs had covered the porch with a fresh layer of red paint a

114

couple of days before. The color contrasted sharply with the white paint of the farmhouse.

"My fellow Animals and Comrades," Preston began. "We have again been beset by tragedy."

Many Animals muttered among themselves. It was only when they stopped and all eyes had turned back toward Preston that he continued.

"Our second-in-command was murdered the night before last while making the return journey from Knight Farm."

Gasps of surprise filled the audience of Animals.

"How could they not know?" Cody asked Frank quietly.

"It is amazing," Frank said. "We truly are out of touch with the other Animals on the Farm. Preston managed to use our isolation to keep the news a secret for an entire day."

"But why?"

"I have no idea," Frank said. "Now listen, we can discuss it later."

"The wilds of the forest have again united in a terrible act of war. Sabean and his rats were again joined by other wild animals just as he was on the night he attacked our Farm. However, this time more than one fox and one weasel were by his side. There were at least four of each. But two nights ago he had two more allies to help him perpetrate his heinous crimes. He was joined by a band of raccoons and also by Poseidon and his band of rats."

This time the Animals of Manor Farm did not say a word. Their shock slowly turned to fear. Even Dogs hated the thought of battling with raccoons. They were vicious, fearless warriors.

"Carter, Dutch and Alexander fought valiantly – killing hundreds of rats and more than half of the raccoons involved in the murder. This was clearly an assassination. Carter was separated from his guard and savagely murdered."

Preston allowed the crowd to regain its composure. "But the tragic news does not end there. Around the time that Carter lost his life, the life of Ambassador Louis from Snail Farm and his personal guard was savagely ended by One-eye and his pack of wolves."

The Pigs snorted in anger. They were no longer scared. That the wilds had dare attack such an icon of Pig history sent them into frenzy.

"In hearing the details of the attack," Preston continued, "it appears it was a synchronized effort to disrupt our diplomatic attempts to build a consensus.

Last night, under cover of darkness, the Premier of Snail Farm, through the stealth and the protection of his personal guard, arrived here on an emergency diplomatic mission. Upon hearing of the death of Louis, the Premier immediately made his way to Manor Farm.

After serious consultation and deliberation, we have decided, with much regret, to fight Sabean and One-eye with a united, all-out offensive. At dawn tomorrow, we will move out from Manor Farm in force. Only a skeleton crew will remain behind to protect the chickens and the elderly. We will make our way East, through the forest, destroying every rat, fox, weasel and raccoon we encounter."

The Pigs snorted in delight. The Goats and Sheep bobbed their heads in approval. The Cows did not respond. They never found conflict appealing. The Pack, the Cats, and the Horses who stood among them, shook their heads collectively in disbelief.

"Something strange is going on here," Cody said quietly.

"Wait," Frank said.

"We will give more details relating to the plan of attack in the morning," Preston said a little too loudly. "We will send a Crow to Knight Farm to determine the final results of the talks between Carter and King George. We have been informed by Dutch that an accord could not be reached. Knight Farm refused to join us in unity against the wilds. Carter and Louis left in protest to make their fateful journeys home. We will confirm that this is still King George's position.

"We gather back here at dawn. United we shall rein the land."

This final slogan sent the Pigs into frenzy once again. The Pack quickly dispersed and reconvened at the oak tree. Despite some initial protest, Frank made it clear that the Pack would follow Preston's leadership until there was a concrete reason not to do so.

CHAPTER TEN – BATTLE

That night, the Pack roamed out into the forest and killed a deer. They ate it raw. This custom had been in place for centuries. A meal of a wild was served before all important battles. The fresh blood pushed their killer instinct to the surface. The next day, there would be no hesitation during the battle. After the meal, they swam in the pond and slept soundly under the giant oak tree.

The sun woke Cody just as it peered over the Eastern horizon. The Beagles slept so soundly they had to be nudged with significant force to get them to stir. Fifteen minutes later, the Pack, Dutch, Alexander and the Horses made their way to the corral. All the other Animals had arrived early. The Pigs because they were filled with bloodlust, and the Goats, Sheep and Cows because they had barely slept during the night for fear of the coming day.

Cody scanned the gathered force. The Crows lined the barn and what was left of the fence that once encircled the corral. The Pigs were all outside the perimeter of the corral. They stood on the gravel road and in the tall grass lining the dirt of the corral. The Cats were in the grass behind the Pigs, barely visible. Cody was surprised to find that the Ducks appeared to be part of the attack force.

"What are you doing here?" Cody asked the head Drake.

"Not sure," he said with obvious trepidation. "Isaac asked us to show up this morning, so we did."

A short time later, Preston, Isaac and the other top advisors stepped from the farmhouse. The smell of fresh bread drifted out of the green front door. Preston looked different to Cody. With his head held high, Preston scanned the herd Animals in the corral and made eye contact with many of the thousand Pigs who circled the corral. He nodded to at least twenty of them, in special recognition, when he found their eyes. His pink skin still glistened from his morning bath.

"Good morning warriors of Manor Farm," Preston said. "I do not have words to inspire you. Carter's death should be inspiration enough. Each of you has an important role to play in exacting revenge in the name of justice.

I am asking the Horses and Cows to remain behind at Manor Farm to protect the Farm in the event that our assault is somehow evaded by the wilds. Twenty Pigs shall remain behind to lead the defense of the Farm. This will include Dutch, so that he can tend to his wounds."

"What?" Dutch said to Alexander in a violent whisper. "That is ridiculous."

He did not make a scene but felt betrayed.

117

"I ask that Percy leave behind five Cats to guard the coop but mobilize the reminder of the Cats, forty-five I believe, to participate in the attack," Preston continued.

Preston nodded in the direction of the Cats in the grass even though he could not make out Percy's exact location.

"Our plan is simple," Preston continued a bit louder. "The Beagles and Pigs will form a line spreading a mile across – a half of mile on either side of Beaver Creek. They will maintain as tight a line as possible and drive all the wild animals east. As the wilds break for freedom from the line, the Pack, Cats, Goats and Sheep shall pass through the line in waves destroying any rats, weasels, raccoons and foxes that they can catch up with."

At this, the Pigs let out snorts of support.

"Our allies from Snail Farm shall be exacting the same revenge heading east. We shall meet our comrades tomorrow morning and all wilds will be caught in the cross-fire as the humans used to say."

The snorts from the Pigs were so loud the members of the Pack were momentarily deafened.

"I will lead the front line and Frank shall lead the assaults through the line," Preston said.

"Did you know that?" Cody whispered in Frank's ear. Frank shook his head.

"We will gather outside the East gate. Paulie will give a signal when we are nearly ready to set out for battle. I will then form you into a line and Frank will divide his troops into attack teams. Today will go down as one of the greatest days in the history of Manor Farm."

By now, Preston's voice was a mixture of a bellow and violent snort. Spittle covered the lower portion of his snout. After the few minutes of frenzy wore off, the Pigs and the herd Animals dispersed. By this time, the Pack, followed by Dutch and Alexander, were half way to the giant oak tree.

"Well?" Cody asked when they were out of earshot. Paulie, Pete and Patrick were to one side of Cody. Frank and Maggie were on the other. Maggie made her husband look like a medium-sized Dog even though they were the same height. She was a hand wider on each side and in the haunches, and it was solid muscle, not Pig fat.

"Well what?" Frank gently answered Cody's question with a question.

"Well, what are we going to do?" Cody asked.

"We are going to meet at the main gate and follow the plan," Frank said, as if there had never been any question.

118

"But why, Frank?" Paulie asked. "We have forever adhered to the philosophy that innocent wild animals must not be killed except for food. Why the change?"

Paulie looked at him with searching Beagle eyes as she waited for an answer. Seldom did any of the Beagles question him, so Frank considered his words carefully.

"Because this plan of attack is better than no plan at all," Frank said. "It may be more full scale than you or I would implement but it will resolve the issue and protect Manor Farm. At the end of the day, that is the most important thing and we need to remember that."

The Dogs walked in silence to the oak tree. No one raised a further objection. Frank and Cody settled under the oak for a five minute rest in the shade while the other Animals gathered.

"Don't you think it's strange that the Premier arrived so quickly?" Cody asked. "The timing is impossible unless he was already traveling somewhere close to Manor Farm when he received the news."

"I suppose," Frank said absently.

"Don't you think it is strange that Preston and the Premier came to an agreement so quickly and were able to devise a plan so rapidly?"

"I suppose," Frank said. "But we should commend Preston for acting so decisively."

"I suppose," Cody said, not trying to be funny.

*   *   *   *

At the East gate of Manor Farm, the dust had been kicked up by thousands of hooves, paws and feet so that the Labradors of the Pack looked grey. Frank divided the troops assigned to him into ten teams. Each had two Dogs, two Cats and approximately fifty Goats and Sheep.

His teams arranged, Frank sat with Cody on one side and Maggie on the other. Cody watched as Preston waddled toward Frank in the hot sun. His layers of fat contrasted sharply with the ripple of Maggie's black muscle. Cody couldn't keep the disgust from his muzzle. When Preston arrived, he was greeted by a cold silence.

"Are you ready?" Preston asked.

Beads of sweat dripped from Preston's face. Cody had seen humans sweat as a Pup, before he fled for the Animal Lands. Seeing the beads glimmer in the morning sun made Preston seem more human than Animal.

"We are ready," Frank said.

"How many teams did you divide them into?" Preston asked.

119

"Ten," Frank said.

"Do you think that is enough teams?"

Frank thought about this question for a moment. "Not sure," he finally said.

Preston turned red, took a deep breath and let ten seconds pass. "It is very important that we have enough teams, sufficient to cover the length of the line," Preston said. "If we don't have enough coverage, then the rats and other wilds will turn and try to fight through the line."

"I understand the plan, Preston," Frank said calmly. "However, it is much easier to divide forces than to join forces. I am erring on the side of teams that are too big instead of too small. I can always divide the groups. They are structured the way they are so I can do just that."

"Why didn't you just say so?" Preston asked sharply.

"To be honest with you, I didn't think I would have to explain it," Frank said, cocking his head to the side.

Cody and Maggie smiled but held their laughter in check.

"I see," Preston said. "Well, let's win the battle and then we can resume our rivalry. How does that sound to you?" Preston asked, a little too loudly with a tight mouth.

"I don't consider you a rival," Frank said. "Rivalries are for politicians and lovers. I am not a politician and I don't believe we have the same taste in females."

Preston turned the color of a radish but did not say a word. He stared at Frank with his large, brown eyes for a few seconds and then returned to the front of the army.

*   *   *   *

It took Preston another hour to spread the Pigs across the mile of varied terrain. Once the Pigs had been spread out on either side of Beaver Creek, Frank's teams took up positions behind the line. Finally, Preston ordered the Ducks to the sky so they could drop into the water and force the rats downstream or drown them if they opted to turn and fight.

Preston led the line down the North shore and Isaac led them down the South shore. Frank's group followed directly behind Preston on the North shore. Cody's group followed behind Isaac on the South shore.

For the first mile out from Manor Farm, the Pigs only rooted out the occasional quail and sent frogs leaping into Beaver Creek. The Pigs circled around a number of rattlesnakes who announced their presence with a rapid shake of their tails. Because a lot of traffic circled its way around the perimeter of Manor Farm, no one was surprised that few wild animals were encountered as the shrubby terrain of Manor Farm slowly gave way to the cool green of the forest. Oaks were replaced by maples and buckeyes.

Once they entered the forest, they drove foxes, weasels, and mice ahead of them. Isaac's group hit pay dirt at the bottom of Mist Falls. Rats began running for the water in front of the line of Pigs. The Pigs snorted the alarm. "Rats on the run," Isaac bellowed, "hundreds of them."

"Now," Cody snarled.

He and Jackson, followed by the two Cats on their team, led the charge through the line of Pigs and began killing scores of rats before the rats could make it to the creek. As planned, the Goats and Sheep ran ahead of the Dogs and stomped rats as they fled the Dogs.

Soon, rats, foxes, raccoons and weasels were fleeing the line of Pigs. The other teams then charged through the line to destroy the wilds. Cats killed the rats with a vengeance. They had not forgotten their fallen comrade. The Beagles and Pigs dug rats and weasels from their hiding places with a furious passion. The Dogs tried to isolate the raccoons and foxes.

Within two hours there were hundreds of rats in the creek, thinking they had made it to safety.

The Ducks dropped from the sky and exacted a fierce revenge for the lost eggs and murdered Ducklings. They used their beaks to drown the rats or drive them to shore where the Cats and Dogs waited. In spots, the river had a copper hue from the blood of rats.

While the carnage took place, the Beagles gathered out of sight of Preston and Isaac. Frank had previously instructed them to gather when rats were spotted. They found a hedge of wild roses that served the purpose of cover.

"Do you have Sabean's scent?" Paulie asked.

"I think I picked it up back at Mist Falls when we first spotted all the rats," Patrick said.

"Let's go," Paulie said.

"First we have to get the Cats," Pete said.

"You going?" Patrick said, knowing his brother was the fastest.

"Yep." Pete said.

He darted away, through boulders and tree trunks, until he found Percy at the bank of Beaver Creek, his fur matted with rat blood.

"We think we picked up Sabean's scent back at Mist Falls," Pete said.

"Excellent," Percy said calmly.

Percy's calm made Pete uncomfortable, given the number of rats Percy had killed that day. But Pete could never understand Cats, as much as he loved Percy.

121

"Buster, Buddy," Percy screeched, losing his calm instantly. "The Beagles have Sabean's scent."

Two Tabby Cats, the size of Pete, appeared less than a minute later. Pete's eyes grew a half size when he saw the blood on the Cats paws and muzzles.

"It is a bad day to be a rat," Pete said with a smile.

The three Beagles and three Cats made their way through the line of Pigs that were still driving the wilds eastward. Less than half an hour later, the Dogs and Cats were taking a long drink of water and cooling themselves in the spray of Mist Falls.

*   *   *   *

"Ready?" Paulie asked, once they had caught their breath and had their fill of water. All five nodded in unison.

"Lead the way, Patrick," Paulie said. "Then Buster, Buddy and Me and then Percy and Pete will bring up the rear."

Patrick went under the waterfall and entered a small cave hidden behind the falls. Patrick always felt confident when Paulie took charge. They all understood Patrick led because his nose would take them directly to Sabean. Paulie, Buster and Buddy followed because the rats would have little chance of fighting off their unified assault. Pete and Percy brought up the rear. They were the fastest and could either dart to the front to fight, or retreat to bring back reinforcements if things went terribly wrong. Only the other Dogs and Cats knew they had backtracked. Frank had told the Cats and Dogs as they moved through the forest of his plan. This was the only liberty Frank agreed to take in his discussions with Cody the night before, while the others slept. Other than this assault on Sabean, Frank insisted that the Pack follow Preston's orders.

The cave opening was the height of a small human. The grey stone, smooth and sharp like obsidian, shimmered with light at the entrance but turned black when the cave dropped a couple of feet and turned a sharp left. Patrick followed Sabean's scent, nose to the ground, with Paulie and the twin Tabbies padding along just behind him. As they made their way deeper into the cave, Sabean's scent permeated the air, mixed with that of thousands of other rats. Patrick let out a slight whimper. He would have felt ashamed if he couldn't smell the others' fear. Patrick, now soaked from the moisture dripping from the roof of the cave, expected to feel the wet walls push in on him as he made his way deeper underground. Instead, after what seemed like an hour but was only five minutes, the cave widened and grew in height so that Bart the Horse could have walked through comfortably.

Patrick stopped suddenly, and lifted his nose. The others froze. They had worked as a team hunting wilds a score of times before and trained thousands of hours together. None moved a muscle as they waited for Patrick to speak.

"Fifty yards ahead," he said. "At least a hundred rats and Sabean are among them. I don't smell their fear so I don't think they have caught our scent yet."

"How come you can't do that Pete?" Percy asked with a smirk.

"Cute," Pete said softly. "Can you murder rats like the twins?"

Paulie looked back over her shoulder at Percy and her brother. "Don't you two ever get tired of the same routine?" she asked pleasantly.

Percy and Pete looked at each other and shook their heads.

"Okay," Paulie said, her tone changing from one of light amusement to heavy seriousness. "On a three count, we attack. Me and the twins first, followed by you three."

Paulie darted past Patrick, down the smooth wet rock, turned a hard right and in an instant she could see twice as far in front of her as before. There was a faint light shining from above, magically bringing daylight into the cavern. What Paulie saw amazed and disgusted her. A hundred rats fed on the corpse of a fawn. The biggest rat she had ever seen turned and looked at her. The fawn's brown eyeball hung from the rat's mouth. The rat snarled. Paulie growled and the twins hissed in response.

"How dare you?" Sabean snarled. "Attack!"

The rat pack seemed to move as one as they scurried off the corpse. It was clear they were Sabean's personal warriors. They broke into six teams of about twenty, defined attack squads with a lot of fighting experience. Paulie slowed to allow Pete, Percy and Patrick to catch up with her and the twins. All six had the fur on their backs pointing toward the ceiling. Paulie looked to her left and her right and quickly behind her.

"That big black thing might be the biggest rat we have ever seen, but they've never seen Cats as big as the twins," Paulie said calmly. "Don't let them isolate us. Stay together. Everybody follow me, I'm heading straight for Sabean."

Paulie took off across the wet stone, trying to spread her paws to keep traction. There was one squad between their position and the squad of twenty rats that included Sabean. There were two squads on each side of these squads. The cave echoed with snarls and squeals. Paulie had no idea that rats could be so loud.

Just before she made it to the first rats she said, "Bust through, don't kill any rats until I am engaged with Sabean."

Rats trying to stop Paulie's progress were bulled out of the way by her muscular chest, or swatted out of the way by the twins. Pete and Patrick flanked Percy, behind Paulie and the twins. Patrick bulled rats over. Percy swatted at the rats' head and took out their eyes. Pete bit the head off any rat that made the mistake of getting too close to him. Paulie smiled to herself as she looked back over her shoulder and took this in. She had held out no real hope that Pete and Percy would follow her orders not to kill the rats yet.

Paulie bounded over the last five or six rats between her and Sabean and landed directly in front of him. Sabean's red eyes glimmered in the glowing light from above. His personal bodyguards, two brown rats nearly as big as Sabean, scurried in front of their master. They were trapped against a wall.

"Just the three of you?" Paulie asked with genuine curiosity in her voice.

"You are an amusing dog," Sabean said in a guttural voice. "I look forward to eating you. Perhaps your cells will improve my demeanor."

Paulie now had her brothers and the three cats guarding her back. They were turned in the opposite direction so that they could fight the remaining hundred rats that encircled them while Paulie took care of Sabean.

"You can start killing these disgusting rodents," Paulie said.

She darted toward Sabean and his guards. She veered left just before she reached them. She snapped her jaws on one of the bodyguards who had jumped toward her. The rat had expected to land on Paulie's back as she attacked Sabean but he landed in her mouth. Paulie snapped its neck as the other bodyguard landed on her back. This must be what it feels like when Percy jumps on Maggie's back for fun, Paulie thought to herself. The bodyguard bit deeply into her back but that was all the damage the rat could inflict. Paulie quickly rolled over onto the hard, slippery stone, crushing the rat's hind legs with her weight and the speed with which she flipped herself.

Sabean jumped onto Paulie's head and tried to bite her eyeball, missed and took a chunk out of Paulie's eyebrow. Blood streamed down over the white and light brown fur of Paulie's muzzle. She snapped her head upward and Sabean was airborne. Although huge for a rat he was only half Paulie's weight. Sabean snarled in midair as he righted himself and prepared to land on all four paws. His red eyes gleamed with fear when he realized he would never touch the ground. Paulie snagged his hind legs out of the air, clamped her jaws violently until her teeth met and then shook her head viciously. Sabean slammed against the wet wall of the cave. His legs were still in Paulie's mouth.

Paulie turned to watch the battle. The twins were killing rats the way a farmer swats flies. The rats on the outside of the fighting began to retreat. Patrick, Pete and Percy followed in pursuit. Pete overtook them and turned them back toward Patrick and Percy, who killed them quickly. Paulie and the twins finished off the rats that choose to stay and fight.

Less than twenty minutes after they had entered the cave all of its inhabitants had been destroyed. The mission accomplished, the team of six returned to the front line of the battle. Preston and the other Pigs had not even noticed their absence.

*   *   *   *   *

Near mid-afternoon of the following day, the forces of Manor Farm heard the forces of Snail Farm in the distance. The night had gone much as the day, killing many wilds but most of them fleeing in the wake of the forces of Manor Farm. Snail Farm was also driving thousands of wilds in front of them. Although still miles apart, the Pigs of Snail Farm snorted and squealed and the Poodles barked and growled so loud that an Animal with less discriminating hearing would have assumed that they would meet around the next bend in Beaver Creek.

In the sector of the battle controlled by Manor Farm, some rats and raccoons took to the trees. The rats were knocked from the branches by Cats, Crows and even Ducks. The raccoons posed a larger problem. Dogs and Pigs would keep the raccoons at bay until a large enough force of Cats and Crows could be gathered to simply overwhelm the savage fighters and knock them to the ground and certain death.

Preston's army had yet to engage with a single fox or weasel. They were much better at avoiding the danger and could cover ground much quicker than the other wilds.

The battle raged on through the afternoon. In the early evening, Frank heard the death screams of rats and other wilds mixed in with the ferocious growls of the giant Poodles of Snail Farm. The Crows reported that Snail Farm's front line was less than a half a mile away.

"Paulie and Pete, to me please," Frank barked over the chaos.

A minute later they appeared in front of Frank. Cody bounded over as well. Cody looked like himself for the first time in months. His grey, brown and black fur glistened with river water and the bright red blood of the wilds he had killed. His paws were purple and covered with the innards of rats and raccoons.

"As the lines converge, the foxes and the weasels are going to be forced to head North or South to avoid the armies," Frank said. "Reform into the battle groups and assume your original positions. As wilds appear,

125

let the Cats and others attack through the lines of Pigs. If a fox shows himself, tell the group leaders to sound the alarm. Paulie, Maggie and I will be the fox pursuit team. If a weasel is spotted, Cody, Patrick and Pete are the attack team. The remaining Dogs are to stay behind the line and destroy anything that breaks through. Got it?"

"Got it," Paulie and Pete said in unison.

"Good. Now go spread the order and tell the teams to form quickly. Let their current targets go into the forces of Snail Farm. I want to catch some foxes and weasels."

Paulie headed north and Pete headed south. Within five minutes the orders were spread across the line and the attack squads were reforming behind the line of Pigs. Preston had given an order to reform the line and this happened nearly as quickly.

"Maybe that Pig isn't as dumb as we thought," Cody said to Frank when he saw the line reforming.

Cody was feeling camaraderie toward the Pigs that could have only been developed in battle.

"Much smarter, and I am thinking much more dangerous," Frank said.

"How so?" Cody asked. His euphoria was suddenly extinguished.

"Not sure," Frank said quickly. "You'd better get back to your squad."

Cody bounded across the river and didn't give Frank's comment another thought that day. Cody reveled in the pace of the bloody battle once again.

The troops of Manor Farm were driving down a gentle slope and the terrain had opened up into a meadow a half a mile long and a quarter of a mile wide on either side of the river. Although Frank initially doubted this was an agreed upon meeting place, he thought differently when he saw the army of Snail Farm.

Two thousand Pigs were standing in a perfect line across the edge of the forest of liquid ambers on the far side of the meadow. They had intentionally waited to press on into the meadow. The Premier of Snail Farm stood alone on the bank of Beaver Creek, in the middle of the meadow.

Every couple of seconds, a Poodle, either jet black or snow white but in all cases covered with blood, would dart out from the forest. A couple of seconds later, a wild would shriek in fear and pain as the Poodle finally closed the gap.

Frank scanned both the North and the South bank of Beaver Creek. To the North and South, the line of Pigs from Snail Farm had situated themselves a little farther West so that the army formed a crescent.

126

This was clearly done to prevent too many wilds from escaping. As soon as the Premier saw the troops of Manor Farm emerge from the forest, he ordered an advance into the tall, green grass of the meadow. The grass stood taller than the Beagles but just a bit shorter than the larger Dogs. The Poodles waited until they saw the grass move and then bolted to the spot to kill the wild trying to make a break for safety.

Frank's squad had an advantage over the Poodles for this type of fighting. He could send the Beagles and the Cats in. The Beagles would sniff them out and the Cats could follow in the cover of the grass. Frank ordered the attack team of six into the grass, Patrick followed by Paulie, Pete, Percy and the twins flew into the meadow ahead of Preston's line of Pigs that were making their way triumphantly toward the Premier. Surprisingly, Preston did not bat an eye. He just continued to press his troops forward when he saw the attack team forge ahead.

Less than a minute later, Percy let out a cry, "Weasels."

Cody bounded over a couple of Pigs that were pushing wilds toward Snail Farm's troops and followed Percy's voice. Cody, joined by Pete and Patrick, overtook Percy. Five weasels darted through the grass, no longer carrying their trademark smirks. Cody nearly snapped one up, but they managed to change direction and head back the way they had come so that Cody overshot them. However, the Beagles were too quick and they waited for the five weasels as they tried to make it to the river. They darted left to avoid Patrick and Pete and this slowed their progress. Cody crushed two of them before they realized they had turned the wrong way. The Beagles caught the other three as they tried to avoid Cody's wrath. They were killed quickly.

Just seconds later, both armies spotted Alvarez and the other foxes bounding toward the South. Paulie and a Poodle from Snail Farm were in hot pursuit. Frank scanned the meadow and watched two more Poodles hop out of the liquid ambers of the forest and cut off the foxes' escape routes. The foxes now had no choice but to head toward Manor Farm's army and Frank.

Frank headed toward Beaver Creek as Alvarez and the other four foxes headed away from it. The foxes had given up hiding and now used their speed and quickness to create distance from the Dogs. Nearly exhausted, the foxes' tongues dangled from their mouths as ten Poodles, Frank and Paulie all converged on them. All five stopped and headed toward Paulie. Frank and the Poodles jumped on them and broke their backs before they could reach her. The Dogs mercifully ripped the foxes' throats to stop their suffering.

CHAPTER ELEVEN – OUR CROWNING ACHIEVEMENT

Ten minutes after the armies converged on the meadow, most of the carnage was over. The Poodles and members of the Pack had entered Beaver Creek and, along with the Ducks in the water and the Crows of both Farms in the air, destroyed the rats that had taken refuge in the water. Blood washed along the banks of the river. Frank stood watching the last of the rats as they shrieked more in anger than in fear. They awaited their execution with fury, reacting in a way that only rats were capable of. In the distance, Frank heard the Poodles growling and barking – they had cornered another family of raccoons. The mother pled for the lives of her children. Frank heard more growls and shrieks and then silence.

Cody, exhausted from battle, waded into the river with Maggie. Blood drifted from their coats and they gently licked each others' wounds.

"Cody?" Frank called.

Cody turned his head toward Frank. Blood was smeared on the large boulder Frank sat on. There were red paw prints leading along the rock from the grassy shore.

"Could you come here, please?" Frank asked.

"Of course," Cody said, already concerned by Frank's tone. Cody swam across the river, his long fur leaning downstream as he made his way slowly to Frank. Cody pulled himself onto a boulder near the middle of the river and then jumped from one boulder to another until he bounded to Frank's side. Drops of water hung from Cody's coat. The water began to dilute and smear the pool of blood surrounding Frank.

"What is it?" Cody asked, unable to hide the concern in his voice.

"Have you any word about Poseidon and his rats?" Frank asked.

"No," Cody said slowly. "As a matter of fact, I haven't."

"There aren't any large, grey rats among the dead," Frank said, as he tossed his head toward the bank where hundreds of rats had washed ashore at a sharp bend in Beaver Creek.

"What did Preston say to the Premier?" Cody asked. "Did he ask about Poseidon?"

"No," Frank said. "But the Premier did ask about Sabean."

"Was Preston mad that you had the Beagles and the Cats double-back?" Cody asked.

"No, he was ecstatic."

"Perhaps the Premier already told Preston that Poseidon had avoided the onslaught," Cody said, still not sure what Frank was getting at.

"No," Frank said. "I was there when they first met. It was as if they knew Poseidon's pack of rats would not be found."

"So what?" Cody said, tired of trying to guess at what Frank's concern was. "We accomplished a lot today regardless of whether Poseidon was allowed to live."

"True," Frank said, "but for what purpose? The Premier and Preston acted as if they had accomplished only a part of what they had set out to do."

Frank looked old. The grey on his muzzle seemed to be spreading before Cody's eyes. "Gather the Pack," Frank said. "I want us all together."

"As you wish," Cody said.

A short time later, Preston spread the word that provisions would arrive before nightfall and that the armies would spend the night on the meadow. The night passed peacefully and, at dawn, word spread that Preston would address Manor Farm on the West side of the meadow while the Premier addressed Snail Farm on the East side.

The members of the Pack had eaten well the night before and slept from dusk until dawn. As they made their way toward the West end of the meadow, Cody studied Frank. Frank pretended not to notice.

"You didn't sleep at all did you?" Cody asked.

Frank smiled a large Dog smile. "No, I didn't."

Frank padded along, head held high but his steps slow. He stopped. Cody looked at him with a raised eyebrow. "Wait here with me," Frank said.

"As you wish," Cody said.

When the rest of the Pack had moved past them, Frank sat down and looked at Cody.

"What?" Cody asked.

""You know you will make a fine leader of the Pack someday," Frank said proudly.

"Yes Frank, you have told me so before and I appreciate it."

"You don't have the vision but your decisiveness will make up for that," Frank said, ignoring Cody's obvious desire to drop the subject.

"Perhaps," Cody said. "What are you getting at Frank?"

"Last night, the vision was telling me to send the attack team to look for Poseidon and his pack," Frank paused and took a deep breath. His eyes were slightly glazed over from lack of sleep. "But I ignored it. Now I wish I had sent them."

"Why?"

"Because I don't believe that they just got away."

"What is the big deal about Poseidon?" Cody asked. "It was Sabean who led the wilds in the war."

"I don't know" Frank said. "I know it makes no logical sense, but the vision tells me something is wrong about his escape. Something just doesn't feel right."

"Do you think Poseidon is attacking one of the Farms while we are all here?" Cody asked. He was now starting to feel concerned.

"I just don't know," Frank said.

Cody stared at Frank. Frank just looked out into the distance toward Manor Farm. Frank was lost in his world of visions. Frank stood and they made their way through the flattened, bloodstained grass of the meadow. They took their place in the front row, next to Maggie, to listen to Preston's speech. The other members of the Pack circled behind them.

A thousand Pigs surrounded the Pack from behind. The Pigs were trapped in by a slightly lesser numbers of Sheep and Goats. The Cats and Crows had the spots in the oak trees lining the meadow. Preston stepped out from the forest, surrounded by his personal guard of now twenty Boars. They were nearly as tall and wide as Isaac but made of muscle. Isaac stood at the far end of one side of the guard. Preston had decided that brawn was a more important criterion than brains in choosing an advisor.

"My fellow warriors," Preston began forcefully. "Let me first thank you for your courageous contribution to the safety and glory of Manor Farm."

The Pigs, Goats and Sheep released a chorus of sounds, joined by the Crows and Ducks from the tree tops.

"That's a bit of an exaggeration," Maggie said under her breath. Cody nodded.

"When I asked for your vote, so that I could lead Manor Farm, I did so in partnership with my friend, Carter," Preston continued.

A hush fell over the meadow. Even Cody maintained a respectful silence.

"We both believed that by uniting with other Farms we could strike fear into the hearts of the wild animals," Preston said. "We also believed that by uniting with the other major Farms, peace would be the first word on each of our lips throughout the world of Animals.

Today, we have demonstrated the power of combining the strength of Manor Farm with that of Snail Farm. Today," Preston's voice was now reaching a bellow, "we have demonstrated that Animals besides Dogs can lead a force from Manor Farm."

"What the hell is he talking about?" Cody asked Frank.

"Not sure," Frank said with a slow shake of his head.

Frank's level of intensity rose with each word. When Preston began speaking, Frank had been laying down. First, he had raised his

131

head, and then he had sat up with one hind leg tucked under his body. Now he sat at full attention. Cody thought Frank was tying to melt Preston he stared at him with such fire.

Preston, spittle now on the edge of his mouth, continued his tirade. "Pigs, Goats and Sheep made up the majority of the attack force and the leadership. But I would be remiss if I did not thank Frank and the members of the Pack for their efforts. The Pack played a pivotal role in the destruction of Sabean, the foxes and the weasels. For this, we are grateful and I honor them for continuing to provide outstanding support to my Administration."

Preston let this last statement hang in the air, signaling the troops to provide a roar of support for the Pack. Once the snorts and others sounds died down, Cody nudged Frank out of his stupor.

"What was that all about?" Cody asked. "Support for his Administration? First he hates us and now he loves us. I am very confused."

"Just listen," Frank said patiently. His calm had miraculously returned.

"But my friends, something is not right among the Farms," Preston continued in a more somber tone. "We believed in unification. Our friends from Snail Farm also believe in unity and equality. They demonstrated this over the course of the last week. Remember friends, Snail Farm was willing to come to our aid against Sabean before Ambassador Louis was destroyed by One-eye's pack. They offered to join us because of a passion for justice, not a thirst for revenge."

Preston scanned the crowd and took a couple of deep breaths. "What do our friends from Knight Farm believe? They refused to come to our aide when our Farm was attacked in the dark of night. They sent our emissaries home and let them leave without an escort."

The Pigs snorted in disgust. The Sheep and Goats did not react. For generations, Knight Farm had been held up as the model of a fair and just administration. Knight Farm was the symbol for progress because they had running water and hundreds of acres of unique fruits and vegetables that no other farms were able to grow. This was the first time a leader of Manor Farm had verbally attacked Knight Farm. It took the Goats and Sheep by surprise. Preston was not done.

"But my friends, there is something even more disturbing about Knight Farm," Preston said with more passion. "We can excuse their unwillingness to help. Perhaps they believed an all-out assault was not warranted. But why do they continue to believe that an Animal is only as good as the species he or she is born into? Why does King George believe he should rule because his father ruled before him? Why can't the Llamas rule? Why can't the other Sheep families rule? Why can't the Cows of Knight Farm rule? Why can't their Owls rule? Is a Pig unqualified to rule Knight Farm? Is a Poodle?"

Preston no longer had spittle on the sides of his mouth. He had yelled so loud that he could not say another word without a drink. He dropped his snout into a bucket of water one his guards had laid in front of him. The Pigs of Manor Farm were in frenzy.

"My friends," Preston continued after his long drink, "King George does not believe in equality. King George does not believe in alliances. King George is an elitist, like his forefathers before him. Only Snail Farm has dared to stand against the obscene monarchy of Knight Farm. Today, that all changes."

"You have to say something," Cody said to Frank urgently. "This is getting out of hand."

"Too late," Frank said. "Let's let him finish. Tell the others to follow my lead."

The Pigs were snorting and squealing so loudly that the Cats began to stand in the branches of the trees. Some of them followed Percy's lead and moved higher and hid among the leaves. Percy, like Frank, had already decided the Cats would have no part in whatever it was that Preston was about to propose.

"Tomorrow, we march on Knight Farm," Preston said. "Not to enslave it, but to liberate it. Its citizens will no longer live under the rule of one family. Its citizens will no longer be unable to participate in democracy. They will vote as all Animals should be entitled to do. Mark my words, when the citizens of Knight Farm see an opportunity for freedom, many will join us. Some time in the coming days, the citizens of Knight Farm shall share the same rights as those of Manor Farm and Snail Farm. We shall be brothers in liberation. Tomorrow we take on this great task. It will not be easy, but we shall be righteous. It will be our crowning achievement. Are you with me my fellow citizens?"

The Pigs' snorts sounded like human shouts. They foamed at the mouth with excitement.

Frank leaned into to Cody and said, "Spread the word through the Pack that we are making a break for it."

The tension and anger directed toward the Pack pushed the Pack together. Frank had always been a staunch ally of King George. The Pack all understood that to object to the war would mean certain death. The options were to fight with Manor Farm or die here in the meadow.

Preston continued to his speech by slamming the door. "You are either with us or against us." Preston glared at Frank. "Any Animal who will not support our cause will be considered a traitor."

Frank met Preston's gaze. The Pigs, now being pushed in by the Goats and Sheep behind them, closed ranks. The Pack's view east was black and pink Pigs for a hundred yards. Beyond this was a mixture of dusty white, brown, black and grey Goat and Sheep. Cody and Maggie and the others members of the Pack formed a barrier between the Pigs and Frank. The three Beagles were at Frank's back and remained facing Preston as did Frank. Preston stared at Frank until his survival instinct forced him to turn his eyes away.

"We are breaking through Preston's guard to the West. I am going to attack Preston. The rest of you continue to push through right behind me," Frank said to the Beagles. "Tell Cody no argument. Tell him that he and Maggie must make it through. Tell Jackson to come and join me. He is old and wise, and will understand the plan."

The Beagles saw immediately that this was the only way to escape and preserve the Pack.

"Come back here and confirm the message has been heard," Frank said. "Hurry now."

The Beagles darted through the legs of the larger Dogs spreading Frank's command. In less than a minute the word had been spread.

*   *   *   *

Jackson, his muzzle and legs covered with grey fur, popped up like he was a six-month old Pup when the Beagles told him the plan. He had killed dozens of rats the day before and fell asleep by Beaver Creek at dusk. He awoke only to eat and then slept until Paulie had nudged him awake to come hear Preston's speech.

He had grown old in the way all Dogs dream. He slowed down only a little over the years. The difference was that, except for his shift on the watch back at Manor Farm, he was rarely awake. He knew he would soon be unable to stay awake during his watch and would be of no use to the Pack. His spirits soared, and he felt profound joy and fondness for Frank, for allowing an old soldier to go this way. He strutted over to Frank and sat next to him, his back straight and head held high.

"What do you think of my plan?" Frank asked Jackson.

"Good, but I think the two of us should attack Isaac instead," Jackson said.

"Why?"

"We will get to him because Preston's guard is focused on Preston as they should be," Jackson said. "It still serves the same purpose of creating a distraction so the rest of the Pack escapes but we may be able to inflict some serious harm. It will also create an opening on the exterior of Preston's guard instead of the right in the middle."

Frank scanned the ten yards of meadow between the Pack and Preston, Isaac and the Guard. As Jackson had observed, they could get to Isaac as he stood at the edge of the Guard whereas Preston had ten Boars on either side of him.

"You're right," Frank said quickly. "Still teaching an old Dog new tricks after all these years."

"And you are still teaching me about leadership by making this proposal," Jackson said. "May we attack now?" Jackson asked with exaggerated formality.

"Not yet," Frank said. "I want to interrupt Preston's speech so let's wait for him to start talking again."

Jackson smiled. Interrupting Preston's speech would make him angrier than if they attacked him. When the Pigs were drawn in close around the backside of the Pack with the Guards on the other, Preston returned to his oratory.

"So I ask, Pigs, are you with me?" Preston bellowed.

The Pigs snorted and squealed with fervor.

"So I ask, Goats, are you with me?"

The Goats let out a loud, rattled yes. Many of the Animals were in such frenzy they began relieving themselves.

"So I ask, Sheep, are you with . . . ."

"Now," Frank howled to the Pack, stopping Preston in mid-sentence. Frank covered the ten yards of lush, green grass with Jackson on his tail before Preston's Guard could react. Preston watched the rest of the Pack wait a three count, turn away from the Pigs that surrounded them and follow the two old Labradors into the fray.

Preston's Guard initially fell inward, in front of and toward Preston, as Dutch had trained them to do. Isaac, who had no military training, simply froze. The member of the Guard closest to him was five yards away when Frank and Jackson veered off and fell on him. Isaac instinctively dropped his head so his tusks could provide a minimal level of protection, making it difficult to get to his neck or underbelly.

This did not surprise either Frank or Jackson. Frank darted past Isaac's flailing tusks and snapped his jaws onto one of his fat, hind haunches. Frank rolled his ninety pound frame to the ground while holding fast with his now locked jaws. Isaac had two choices, hold his ground and have his leg broken or roll with Frank. A Boar who was a seasoned fighter would have accepted a broken leg and then gored Frank with his tusks. Instead, Isaac followed his instinct and rolled.

Jackson was on his genitals before Isaac's back hit the ground. He ripped the sack off with expertise gained only from his early years fighting for Knight Farm against Snail Farm, when the Knight Farm/Manor Farm alliance was strong.

Cody, Maggie, the Beagles and the rest of the Pack tore past Frank and Jackson before Preston's Guard could close ranks. The Pigs, Sheep and Goat's station behind the Pack half-heartedly gave chase. But they knew they couldn't catch them, and knew that if they did, certain death awaited them.

Jackson bit hard into Isaac's layered belly, trying to dig deep enough to get to the Pig's intestines. Isaac kicked with all four legs. Blood flew from the hole where Frank had taken a piece out of one of his haunches. Isaac caught Jackson with one of his hind legs in the ribs and two cracked loudly. Jackson muffled a yelp as he was pushed backward three feet.

Frank regained his balance, popped up, and checked the location of the Boars. Frank pounced on Isaac just as Jackson was thrown off in the direction of the Boars. Frank knew he had just a couple of seconds before the Boars had him surrounded. Isaac started to his feet as quickly as he could, his torn leg barely functioning, but only made it to his forelegs when Frank snapped down on his snout and again rolled his body. This time there was no bone or cartilage to slow Frank's progress. The last two inches of Isaac's snout ripped off and blood gushed out like a bursting balloon.

As Frank tore Isaac's nose he heard Jackson yelp as a Boar came down on his back and snapped it. Frank knew this would be his fate. He did not bother trying to regain his feet. He closed his eyes. Two Boars landed on his back and neck, breaking them both simultaneously. Frank heard the Beagles howl in sorrow like a chorus. Their pain hurt more than death.

CHAPTER TWELVE – FLIGHT

The Pack flew west on tired legs and bleeding paws. The larger Dogs found it difficult to keep up with the Beagles. When the tri-colored triplets had covered five miles from the meadow, they stopped and waited for the rest of the Pack to catch up. They had run along the main dirt road, on a parallel course to Beaver Creek.

When the rest of the Pack caught up, they all dropped off the road and plunged into the water. They drank deeply and soaked their burning bodies. Cody padded out of the water, shook himself briskly, and worked his way through the thick brush back onto the road. He dropped down onto the dust and rock under a large maple tree.

The forty-eight members of the Pack followed him to the road and plopped down around him. They waited for Cody to speak. He stared off to the East until Maggie gave him a gentle lick on the snout. A human would have found such a display between a German Sheppard and a Rottweiler in some way amusing. The Pack simply watched.

Cody stood to address the Pack as their leader for the first time. The muscles on his hind legs twitched from the long run. His long fur dripped with water from Beaver Creek, but Cody had managed to finally stop panting.

"Frank was a magnificent leader of our Pack," Cody said, his voice choked with a whimper. "His bravery was only surpassed by his intelligence and Cat-like intuition. He was like a father to me, and all I can promise is that I will honor his memory by always thinking of the long-term interests of the Pack. I will never put the life of one Dog, even Maggie's, over the life of the Pack."

While Cody regained his composure, the Pack contemplated his words. The Pack understood this would be the last time that Cody would speak of Frank until the war was over. Frank had ingrained into all of their heads that the past was the past when there was work to be done. Learn from it, but do not dwell on it. When your days are numbered and the present has a plan for your death, only then, in those final days, should a Dog reflect on his life.

"Paulie," Cody said.

"Yes, Cody," Paulie said sharply.

"Make your way to Knight Farm and warn them of the impending attack," Cody said.

"What about letting us go with her?" Patrick said with Pete at his side.

"Not this time Patrick," Cody said with a smile. "I need you to go to Manor Farm and tell Dutch, Alexander and Bart all that has happened. Tell them to join us if they would like, but the odds are not in our favor."

Cody looked at Pete and knew he was sending him on a very dangerous mission. "Pete, I need you to go back to the East and find Percy and the other Cats. It is my guess that they bolted right after we did. Once you find them, tell Percy that none of Poseidon's rats were found on the battleground. Ask her and the other Cats to help you find Poseidon, find out why they all escaped. Destroy them, if necessary."

"Do you really think Percy will help us?" Paulie asked.

"Don't you?" Cody said.

Paulie thought about this for a moment or two. "Yes, I suppose I do," she finally said.

"Patrick and Pete, return as fast as you can to Sabean's cave. Patrick, tell Dutch and the others to do the same if they wish to join us. Paulie you stay at Knight Farm. We will rendezvous with you on the battlefield, if Knight Farm makes it long enough for us to help them. Any of the rest of us will slow you down so I am asking each of you three to do this alone."

The Beagles nodded. Without another word, Patrick took off West and Paulie and Pete headed off together in the direction of the meadow. They looked as if they had enjoyed a full meal and a good night's sleep despite the events of the morning. Cody shook his head in wonder.

*　　　　　*　　　　　*　　　　　*

Patrick covered the remaining distance to Manor Farm in less than three hours. He made a stop at Bart's drinking trough, and found Dutch, Alexander, Bart and Bart's wife and son, under the giant oak where the Pack had left them just two days before. All but Dutch stood in the shade, silently swinging their tails at horse flies. They nibbled the yellow-green grass growing in the shade under what the humans used to call the Manor Oak. Dutch was on his stomach on the opposite side of the giant trunk, snoring loudly. Despite his anger at being excluded from the fighting, exhaustion had finally taken control of his wounded body.

Patrick, covered in dust so that he appeared grey, approached Alexander and the horses. Patrick's tongue flopped wildly on the side of his face. Alexander smiled down at Patrick. He favored only Cats and Beagles with a smile.

"Been running, Patrick?" Alexander asked.

Patrick smiled. "Just a little bit," Patrick said, between deep breaths.

"What happened?" Bart asked, as he high-stepped over to Alexander's side. His voice was so deep it sounded like a hum, making it difficult to decipher his words. Even though one was a Stallion and one was a Bull, Alexander and Bart seemed to be related, their coats were the same shiny black. Bart stood two heads taller but Alexander was nearly twice as wide. Despite this, there was an eerie family resemblance for Animals of a different species. Their eyes were the same dark brown that appeared both absent and intelligent.

"Where is Dutch?" Patrick asked. "I'd rather tell you all at once."

"Around the other side of the tree sleeping," Alexander said.

Bart sent his son trotting around the tree to Dutch. A few moments later, Dutch ambled over to them. Patrick told the story as quickly as he could and relayed Cody's request that they join him at Sabean's rock as soon as possible.

Just as Patrick was finishing, three Pigs and four Cows appeared on the gravel drive, heading toward the oak tree from the farmhouse. Patrick darted through Bart's legs, hoping he had not been spotted.

The three Pigs were joined by a couple more who had been following from behind and the Cows now numbered six. The five Pigs and six Cows were breathing a little too hard considering the time it took them to cover the distance on the dusty, gravel road from the farmhouse to Manor Oak.

"Who was that?" one of the Boars asked.

"Patrick the Beagle," Dutch answered quickly, before the others could respond.

"What did he want?" the same Boar asked.

"Not sure he wanted anything, Barry," Dutch said. "He saw you all and took off before he made any type of request."

"What did he say?" Barry asked.

"That the wilds had been defeated yesterday and that Preston gave a speech this morning," Dutch said. Dutch paused and stared at Barry for a moment to see if there was any surprise on his face. "Then he saw you all coming and darted off, saying he would be back when it was safe."

"Why wouldn't he feel safe here, I wonder?" Barry asked no one in particular.

"Not sure," Dutch said. "I was hoping you might be able to tell us."

Dutch scanned the line of Pigs and Cows in front of him. "Quite a few of you came out to greet Patrick," Dutch said glaring at Barry's fat face. "Why such a heightened interest?"

"We were hoping for news from the battlefield," Barry said quickly.

139

"I saw a number of Crows fly in last night," Dutch said. "Didn't they bring any news?"

"Those were patrols, not messengers," Barry said.

Dutch grinned at Barry but did not say a word. "Let's go," Barry said to the other Pigs and Cows. Dutch watched them rush back to the farmhouse. A minute later, a Crow headed out the window and headed east.

"Well," Bart asked, "what do you two recommend?"

"We join them at Sabean's rock," Alexander said, as if there were no other option.

"I agree," Dutch said.

"It is unanimous," Bart said as he trotted over to tell his wife and son.

*   *   *   *

Pete and Paulie worked their way cautiously back toward the meadow where the wilds had been crushed and Preston had declared war on Knight Farm. This time, they made their way along the bank of Beaver Creek, in order to stay out of sight of the Crows who circled the skies trying to find the Pack. It was near nightfall as they approached the meadow. A couple of miles before they reached the gathered troops, Pete picked up Percy's scent along with that of the fifty or so other Cats.

The Cats had headed North, in the direction of the human lands. Paulie and Pete parted ways with a quick lick. Pete followed Percy's scent to the North. Paulie headed south so that she could swing wide of the armies of Knight and Manor Farms that were still gathered at the meadow for another night of rest. She hoped she could circle around and still warn Knight Farm in time for them to prepare for the attack. Both Paulie and Pete picked up the pace significantly.

The Cats had a three or four hour head start on their journey north. Pete darted through the thick forest of oaks, which gave way to pines after about five miles. The air cooled as night fell completely over the forest. With each panting breath, Pete created a stream of mist larger than his head.

A couple of hours deeper into the night, Pete knew by the strength of the Cats' scent that he knew he was close as he trotted over a small hill, nose to the ground. When he reached the top, he lifted his head and saw a small field, the size of the corral at Manor Farm. The field was surrounded by boulders and pines that reached hundreds of feet into the night sky.

The nearly full moon provided enough light for Pete to see the Cats spread out on the boulders. He watched for a couple of minutes from the cover of the pines. When he saw a Cat leap from a boulder and then heard the agonizing scream of a field mouse, he knew what the Cats were up to. He bounded down to the boulders, found Percy and pulled her to a private location.

"What is it you want?" Percy asked, trying to hide her irritation at having their solitude interrupted.

"I have a message from Cody," Pete said.

"Yes," Percy said a little more congenially.

"He is asking two things," Pete said quickly. "First, he would like us to track and interrogate Poseidon. It seems he survived the attack by the Farms and neither Preston nor the Premier has said 'boo' about it."

"So?"

"Well, not only did Poseidon survive but none of his rats seemed to have been killed either."

Percy did not respond. Pete, impatient, continued, "Second, he asks that you come and meet him at Sabean's rock after we accomplish this mission."

"For what purpose?" Percy asked.

"To plan a course of action in light of yesterday's events, I presume," Pete said. It was now Pete who was irritated with his friend.

"I am not sure the Cats have any interest in living with other Animals any longer," Percy said in a distracted Cat manner.

Pete let out a deep sigh, mixed with a growl. His patience with Percy's attitude was starting to wear very thin.

"Look Percy, that is up to you," Pete said. "I fully understand your opinion. I am not sure Cats living alone is the wrong course of action. But what Preston is doing is wrong. You know it and so do I. If you don't want to help, then that is your prerogative. If you want to help and then move on with the other Cats, that is okay too. I am simply conveying a message from the new leader of the Pack." Pete paused and glared at Percy. "I think I deserve a little more courtesy in light of our friendship."

Percy stared at his Cats as they leapt off boulders and killed their dinner. He turned toward Pete. "I'm sorry," Percy said. "You and the Pack have always acted honorably. Cats are simply not cut out for democracy of Preston's kind. We may not be cut out for the Pack's kind of democracy either."

"I understand but that does not mean we are not friends and allies," Pete said. "Unfortunately, I need an answer of yes or no shortly if we are to catch Poseidon. If we're to be of any help to Knight Farm, we need to make it back to Sabean's rock quickly."

Percy tossed Pete a mouse which Pete swallowed whole. "Wait here while I talk to the other Cats," Percy said.

Ten minutes later, Percy returned to where Pete was sprawled on a boulder.

"Get up," Percy said. "We need to hurry if we are going to get Poseidon and get back to Sabean's rock by the end of the day." Percy's impish smile reflected the moonlight.

*   *   *   *

Pete and the Cats headed straight toward Beaver Creek and then headed east as fast as they could. They finally picked up the scent of water rats that Pete had picked up off Carter's body. They were about a mile east of the meadow. They followed the scent south, up a fairly large stream that ran down the mountains to Beaver Creek.

"This way," he said to Percy, who managed to stay with Pete while the other Cats fell behind.

Pete led them up the steep slope along the rushing water. The scent was strong as the rats would have needed to run up the banks as opposed to swim against such a strong current. About a mile South of Beaver Creek, the scent became overpowering just as they approached a waterfall. A large, grey rat on a boulder, at the top of the waterfall, let out a shriek. He had spotted the Dog and the Cats making their way up the mountain toward their swimming hole.

"Let's go," Percy shouted at the Cats.

They scrambled up the hill. Pete was a full ten yards ahead when they reached the twenty feet by twenty feet span of water that the rats were using as a base. Unfortunately for the rats, there were no good hiding places and they knew they could not outrun Pete and the Cats. There were over two hundred rats. Instead of spreading out and running, so that some of their members could live, Poseidon ordered them to turn to fight.

"We are victorious together or we die together," Poseidon shouted over the snarls, hissing and Pete's growl.

Pete stopped at the bank of the pool of water, allowing the Cats time to catch up. Once they were behind him, he looked at the snarling rats on the far side of the pool.

"What a noble thing for you to do," Pete said sarcastically. "Is it because you are the slowest?"

Poseidon glared at Pete, his eyes red in the moonlight.

"I have a proposal," Pete said. "Tell me how it is you escaped the clutches of the forces from Snail Farm and we will be on our way."

142

Poseidon considered this statement for a moment and this caused the other rats to quiet down to allow the conversation to follow its natural progression.

"I don't know what you are talking about," Poseidon said. "And it would be short-sighted of me to alienate Snail Farm anymore than I have over the last fifteen years."

"My orders are to find out this information or destroy you and your pack," Pete said matter-of-factly.

"Or die trying," Poseidon said with a smile that made Pete's skin crawl. A part of him wished that Paulie was with him.

"I'm glad the twins are here," Percy said, as if reading Pete's mind.

"Me too," Pete said, looking over his shoulder at the giant tabby Cats. "Let's go," Pete said.

He bounded upstream to where the pool became a stream again and darted across, followed by fifty snarling Cats. The rats put up a hard fight for the first couple of minutes and managed to kill one Cat by pushing her over the waterfall. Their resistance was short-lived once the twins had ensconced themselves in the middle of Poseidon's forces. They killed two rats at a time with their Dog-sized paws and the battle was quickly over.

Percy and Pete pursued Poseidon to the edge of the waterfall. He had ten rats with him. They hopped on the boulders so that they were in the middle of the falls. There were five Cats waiting for them on the other side.

"You are trapped," Pete observed, as he licked the rat blood from his muzzle.

"It seems that way," Poseidon said. "I am ready for death."

"I understand," Percy said, taking over for Pete. "You are old and tired. But can that be said for the rats that are with you?"

To Pete's surprise, Poseidon took a look at who was with him. They were scared but, like all rats in such situations, angry as well. Rats, especially those of Poseidon's ilk, were never simply frightened.

"What are the terms?" Poseidon asked.

"Same as before," Percy said. "You tell us what we want to know and we let you go."

"For how long?"

"Forever unless you cross the Pack, us Cats or Manor Farm," Percy said.

"Done," Poseidon said, seeing this bargain was better than dying a now certain death and taking two of his sons with him.

"Tell us the deal you had with the Premier," Pete said.

"He approached us after the election at Manor Farm and basically said that if we did not support him in the coming days we would be destroyed," Poseidon said with venom. "Apparently some sore of alliance was already in place with Preston. I had to agree as we had already been driven West by Snail Farm twice before."

"And then what?" Pete asked.

"Then, after the attack on Manor Farm he asked me to approach Sabean and ask to join his forces. He wanted me to make sure that the Goat from Manor Farm did not make it back from the mission he had been sent on. In exchange, we become part of the Farm's economy by being given their trash and, on occasion, eggs and other fresh food."

"But why?" Pete asked, unable to hide the shock in his voice.

"It appears Preston and the Premier have their eyes on uniting the farms and most of the wilds while they are at it," Poseidon said with amusement. "They think that the way of the Pig is the way of the wild. Apparently, they think the way of the Pig is the way of the Animal also. Anyway, I knew I couldn't beat them."

"So you joined them and helped murder Carter," Pete said. "I ought to renege on the deal and kill you all right here."

"But you won't," Poseidon said. "The way of the Dog is your way; as it should be."

They all stood staring at each other for thirty seconds. The tension was thick as the Cats were inclined to kill Poseidon and his rats, regardless of any role they had played in Carter's death.

"Let them pass please," Pete finally said. The five Cats on the far side of the falls moved away. Poseidon and the rats scurried past into the dark of the forest.

*   *   *   *

Paulie set a steady pace but conserved her energy in case she ran into trouble. She now moved North over the dry fields and into the lands that, in theory, were still controlled by humans. She had circled South around the meadow. She moved north for some miles until she met up with a seldom used dirt road that intersected the vast fields. The nearest human settlement was hundreds of miles away and there was little chance of running into one of those amazing two-legged creatures she had only heard about from Cody. In fact, she could not even smell a human, so none had been in these parts for years. It was still dark but there was a glimmer of sunlight on the Eastern horizon.

In the early years of the Animal Farms, men had often strayed into Animal territory to spy on the farms. Before the great wars that the humans fought among themselves, the men had had time for such adventures and to make half-hearted attempts to retake the land. Now, with no machines to aid them, and little government over their own affairs, they left this land alone. Over the generations, humans had begun to believe that the land was haunted and inhabited by strange creatures. Their fear and own struggle for survival kept them away.

Although Paulie picked up the scent of mice, rats, birds, coyotes and other wilds, she did not see another mammal during her hours in the human lands. When she was five miles east of Knight Farm she headed west. She knew she had circled around the main armies of Snail and Manor Farms.

She knew there would be scouts from Snail Farm near Knight Farm in the South-Eastern frontier of the Animal lands. The scouts would be as close as they could get without the Hawks and Owls who patrolled the skies in a ten mile radius around Knight Farm spotting them. The Snail Farm scouts would need to find cover under the trees. To Paulie this made the road the safest bet. She found the road leading directly to the rear entrance of Knight Farm and decided this was as quick and safe as she was going to find. She hoped an Owl would see her long before she was within howling distance of Knight Farm.

She moved at a quicker pace but still conserved energy as it appeared she still had at least five miles to go. The first mile was in high grassland. Then she reached a high bluff looking to the West. Off in the distance, around the time that Pete and the Cats were fighting Poseidon, she saw the fires of Knight Farm. If she hurried she could still make it before dawn and the exposure of daylight.

If she reached the King before dawn, it would give Knight Farm a couple of hours to prepare for the assault. Now time was more important than conserving her energy. The rest of the journey was downhill into the lush valley of Knight Farm and its legendary crops. She began running, only dropping her nose occasionally to check for threatening scents.

She covered the road with fields of tall, yellow grass on either side with little worry of danger. The grasslands gave way to a forest of tall buckeyes, their husks dotting the dirt road. There were patches of grass and shrubs growing within the seldom used road. Animals rarely ventured into no man's land except for security patrols and the occasional exploration by Knight Farm to get an update on the status of the humans and their crumbling society.

The forest thickened as Paulie closed within a couple of miles of Knight Farm. A variety of trees, oaks and maples, now mingled with the buckeyes. Blackberry bushes pushed out of the forest onto the dirt road. Paulie dropped her nose to the ground more frequently now as her line of sight was limited in the dense forest. A short distance later and she would be in the Knight Farm crops that grew outside the walls.

A half an hour after she entered the forest, she froze. Poodles, at least five of them, were nearby. She could not hear them but the scent was coming from the direction of Knight Farm. She had no choice but to continue on. The scent grew stronger and she heard them just as they finally picked up her scent.

They were about fifty yards to the West in the forest. She heard their growls and knew she still had over three miles to go before she reached the walls of Knight Farm and safety.

Paulie listened as they made their way toward her through the thick blackberry bushes. She sprinted forward so that they would overshoot her position. Now she saw it was six large, black Poodles, and she had managed to put them behind her. She also noticed that they had their tongues hanging from their black muzzles. They were already tired from a night on the move. Paulie hoped this would give her a few more minutes before she would be forced to dart into the forest to evade them.

Paulie let out a howl, the loudest she could muster on a dead run. She turned her head every thirty seconds to see how much ground the Poodles had gained on her. They were faster and, in this race, endurance meant little, if anything. By the time a few minutes had passed the lead Poodle was only five yards behind her. Paulie darted into the blackberry bushes.

The Poodles would never be able to stay with her in the bushes, but she would never make it to Knight Farm in time if she was forced to pick her way through the thick forest. After moving about fifty yards into the forest, she turned toward Knight Farm. She could hear the Poodles making slow progress behind her, but soon the noises became faint and, shortly after, she could not hear them at all. Only their strong, sweaty scents let her know they were still near.

After twenty minutes of picking her way through the blackberry bushes, ferns and ivy that covered the floor of the forest around the trunks of the closely growing trees, Paulie turned back toward the road.

Paulie hesitated before she pushed through an opening that would let her back onto the dirt road. She popped her head out and smelled the air. The scent of the Poodles filled the air from all directions. "Not good," Paulie thought to herself. She looked down the road but didn't see any movement in the fading moonlight. She bolted onto the road and ran as fast as she could West, in the direction of Knight Farm.

A Poodle yelped behind her, obviously picking up her scent. Two Poodles gave a response from the blackberry bushes. These two had trailed her in the forest. A minute later, the one behind her had closed the

146

distance to less than fifty yards. Paulie began looking for an opening in the thick patch of blackberry bushes so she could make her escape into the forest for a second time. As she did so, she ran right past a shadow that did not reflect the moonlight like the leaves. A Poodle darted after her but stayed close to the edge of the road. Paulie looked to the other side of the road and a Poodle ran parallel to her here as well, just a few yards behind. There was no way to get back into the forest without having to evade a Poodle.

In desperation, Paulie howled her most urgent howl. The Poodles growled and she could now hear their paws falling behind her as they closed the gap. She planned on stopping just when the Poodles on the rear caught up, in the hope that they would overshoot her.

As she prepared to put this hopeless plan into place, she was caught, before she thought a Poodle had closed the distance. The pain was excruciating as teeth, large even for a Poodle, dug into the skin of her back. She was lifted off the ground as if the Poodle had tossed her into the air.

Paulie looked down so that she could land on her feet and it was only then that she realized she was flying ten feet off the dirt road, and rising at an alarming rate.

*   *   *   *

"Hello Paulie," a calm, deep voice said from just above her head. Paulie would have thought the Man God had decided to save her and speak to her, if she hadn't recognized the voice.

"Hello Waterhouse," Paulie said gleefully. "It's about time."

"Yes," Waterhouse replied. "You did seem to be in a bit of trouble. Say, do you have any idea what those Poodles are doing so close to Knight Farm?"

"Oh yeah, but I think you better get us to King George and I will tell you as much as I can on the way."

"As you wish," Waterhouse said.

The Owl flapped his great wings to reach a stronger wind current and they road it to King George's castle in less than five minutes. Waterhouse dove through a large window into the Great Hall and dropped Paulie to the stone floor.

Two Mastiffs guarded the hallway from the Great Hall into the living quarters of King George and his family. Candles burnt in the windows of the Hall and on either side of the great doors that led to the courtyard. On the other side of these doors, stood two Mastiffs nearly as

147

large as those Paulie currently stared at. There was no fire in the two-story hearth tonight.

Dim candle light glimmered behind the Mastiffs. Paulie stared in admiration mixed with fear. They were a male and a female as was the custom for the personal guard of the King. Upon entering the King's Guard, and immediately after marriage, the Dogs swore allegiance to the King. Unlike the members of the Royal Guard, who were commanded by Sir Andrew and numbered in the hundreds, the King's Guard was commanded directly by the King and numbered about twenty. The King's Guard guarded the King's living quarters and escorted him on all journeys outside the castle.

The female's coat was such a light tan she appeared to be white. Despite the flaps of skin characteristic of a Mastiff, her muscle created wide contours on her chest and thighs. Her dark brown eyes reflected the candlelight. Her expression made it clear she would swallow Paulie whole if she tried to enter the hallway to the King's quarters without permission.

She had not moved since turning her head slightly to watch Waterhouse glide through the window. Waterhouse had given a quick "hoot, hoot," as they approached the Hall. Paulie figured this must be protocol, but she now understood it might have been self-preservation on the part of Waterhouse. Paulie sensed that the two Mastiffs did not respond favorably to surprises.

The male had layers of fat covering his muscle and stood half a head higher than the female. His fur darker and eyes lighter than his wife's, he stood with his slab of a tongue hanging from his mouth. His size and the dangling tongue made him appear calmer than his spouse, as if he understood no creature within a thousand miles would think of crossing him. Paulie eyed one of his huge front paws. It was the size of Paulie's head. He probably outweighed Maggie, the heaviest Dog at Manor Farm, by one hundred pounds.

"Good evening, Sir Nelson," Waterhouse said in his soothing baritone. "Lady Eliza, always a pleasure."

"Good evening, Waterhouse," Lady Eliza said. "Is this Beagle expected by the Royal Family?"

"No," Waterhouse said. "This is Paulie from Manor Farm. She has urgent news and has requested an emergency meeting with King George."

"What is the topic of this emergency meeting?" Sir Nelson asked with a raised eyebrow, but no other movement of his giant body or face.

"A pending attack by the combined forces of Snail Farm and Manor Farm," Paulie said a bit louder than she had intended.

Eliza turned and headed into the living quarters of King George without saying a word.

"She will be right back," Sir Nelson said, without taking his egg-sized eyes off of Paulie.

"I need to get back into the sky and expand the radius of my flight pattern," Waterhouse said. "I will come visit you when I can Paulie."

"Okay," Paulie said. "Their forces are gathered on the large meadow running parallel to Beaver Creek. You will see I am speaking the truth."

"Thank you," Waterhouse said. "Why are you doing this?"

"They killed Frank," Paulie said, choking back a whine.

Eliza padded silently back down the hallway, as silently as Percy on the hunt. Paulie's senses were honed from adrenaline so she could smell Eliza's clean, healthy fur and gland excretions. All she could hear was the rhythmic panting of Sir Nelson. His tongue continued to bob up and down but no other muscle on his body moved. Eliza arrived at her post but did not say a word.

Paulie started to speak but she stopped short when four Schnauzers, nearly as large as the Poodles from Snail Farm, came into view at the end of the hallway. Paulie had been so focused on Eliza, she didn't notice the new smells coming into the background. The events of the last few days were starting to take a toll even on her amazing Beagle energy.

When they reached Paulie, a female with light grey fur and slightly darker patches around her eyes and muzzle stepped forward.

"If you will follow us, Miss Paulie," the female said.

All four of the Schnauzer's turned in unison. Two of them allowed Paulie to get in front of them so she was surrounded as they made their way into the private quarters of King George and his family. They made their way along torch-lit hallways. There were human objects – weapons, coats of arms, portraits of humans from many centuries ago – covering the stone walls. Mixed with these relics were paintings created by Animals and the broken stick that started the Rebellion of the Animals so many years before.

Paulie felt as if the Animals of Knight Farm were in some way superior as she looked at this history. They had managed to take the best of what the humans had – fire, running water, spreading the written word, crops and orchards – while doing away with unnecessary things like an overabundance of leisure goods and distracting information.

Paulie followed the two Schnauzers ahead of her into a large room. A large stone table, bowls of water and plates with bread, fruits and vegetables were the only items that she could see. This was clearly a room where decisions were made. So many torches were lit that they created the feel of a summer day.

King George stood at one head of the table and Prince James at the other. Lord Winston was at the side of the table closest to Paulie and Sir Andrew was at the far side.

"You may leave us," King George said to the Schnauzers. They turned and exited like ghosts.

"Very nice to see you again, Paulie," Lord Winston said. "Your Highness, Prince James, Sir Andrew," Lord Winston said with a nod, "may I present Paulie from Manor Farm. The finest rat killer I have ever seen."

"A pleasure," they said in unison.

"Please have a seat," King George said, gesturing to the seat next to Lord Winston, the only other Animal in attendance on a stool. Paulie hopped up on the stool. She and Lord Winston were still a head below the King and the Prince, and two heads below Sir Andrew.

It took just a few moments to see that all four leaders of Knight Farm were formulating how to respond to the pending attack and the purpose of the meeting was to garner as many facts from Paulie as possible.

"Please tell us everything you know," King George said kindly.

Paulie told the story of the destruction of Sabean and Preston's subsequent speech as quickly as she could, without omitting any relevant facts. When she finished, King George shook his head sadly.

"I am so sorry for the loss of Frank," King George said. "He was my close friend and one of the finest leaders in Animal history. Knight Farm offers our thanks to you, Cody and the other members of the Pack for warning us of the pending attack. Now, if you will pardon us, we must prepare for war."

King George stomped his hoof and his faced changed from the opened kindness he was showing Paulie to firm resolve. The four Schnauzers reentered the room in response to King George's massive hoof hitting the stone.

"Please escort Paulie to my guest quarters and provide her with food, water and a warm bath, if she would like one. Her leader, Cody, has requested that we provide her protection during the war and this we will do."

"As you wish, your Highness," said the grey female, who clearly was the leader of his bodyguards.

The Schnauzers led Paulie to her quarters. There was a stone bath dug into the bottom of the floor and a large, human bed for her to sleep on. The stone floors had a lush rug on them and there were a couple of chairs in addition to more food set out on a table with a huge jug of water. She ate all the cheese and eggs and most of the fruit they had left for her, stepped into the clean water long enough for all the dirt to wash away and then dropped down onto the human bed. She was asleep as soon as she dropped her head onto her forepaws.

CHAPTER THIRTEEN – WAR

The scouts from Snail Farm reported back to the Premier just as the Manor Farm and Snail Farm armies were preparing to depart the meadow; after a short hike, the armies would descend on Knight Farm. The scouts told the Premier of their failed attempt to capture Paulie.

The Premier made his way down the front line, in order to strategize with Preston and share the news from his scouts. The Animals were already tense with anticipation for the coming battle. The Premier could tell because it was uncommonly quiet, and those who tried to hide their tension spoke too loudly.

"Hello Comrade Preston," the Premier said brightly. "Our scouts returned a few minutes ago. They bring news."

"They do?" Preston asked a bit too loudly.

"Yes," the Premier said with amusement. "It appears one of your Beagles took it upon herself to warn Knight Farm of our attack."

"Why didn't your Poodles prevent this from happening?" Preston asked, his words coming out staccato.

"They attempted to do just that. Sadly, an Owl intervened and rescued the Beagle in the nick of time. No matter. We outnumber the forces of Knight Farm two to one. A few hours of preparation will make no difference. Let's march."

Preston stared for a brief moment at the Premier. He was as fat as Isaac had been but covered with course, black hair. He carried his weight more naturally than Isaac had. Despite his girth, he appeared threatening and dangerous.

"Yes," Preston said. "I suppose you are right. No turning back now. Let's march."

"We shall finalize the details of the attack when we gather on the hill before the Western gate of Knight Farm," the Premier said. He turned and rejoined his advisors.

The armies moved unopposed to the crest that rose up about a half of a mile West of Knight Farm. No one in either army was surprised by the lack of opposition. The advance scouts had not spotted a single Knight Farm soldier on the ground.

The sky overhead was a different story. Fifty hawks circled in the sky, watching the amassing armies. Preston and the Premier kept their two hundred Crows near the army and lower to the ground. Occasionally, the Premier directed his one hundred Crows to fly over Knight Farm to gather intelligence. The Hawks of Knight Farm drifted eerily away, higher up in the sky, and watched.

Preston made his way to the Premier. They both stood in the middle of the road looking down on Knight Farm's high walls. Preston's ten Boars stood in a semi-circle on the North side of the road and five large, battle-tested Poodles watched the Premier's every move.

"What news do the Crows bring?" Preston asked in a clear, confident voice.

"They are gathering at the gate and outside the walls to the North and the South," the Premier said.

"Are they in any particular formation?" Preston asked.

The Premier chuckled. "I see you have continued your study of military tactics. It appears they have mixed the three groups. There are Mastiffs, Schnauzers, Rams and Llamas in each."

"Do you have any idea what that means?" Preston asked.

"I believe they plan on waiting for us to get within a hundred yards of the wall and then they will engage us." The Premier said this in a matter-of-fact way, with little confidence that he was right.

"What do you suggest?"

"We stick with our plan," the Premier said. "We send in the Goats and the Sheep to force their troops to engage, we send in the Pigs in a second wave to push their troops to the wall and then have the Poodles follow behind and try to scale the wall."

Preston nodded, went back to his personal guards, and conferred quietly for a couple of minutes. He returned to the Premier. "We are in agreement."

"Excellent," the Premier said, unable to hide his sarcasm. "Let's give the order to form the lines accordingly. Once this is done, I will give the order to attack."

Preston overlooked this slight, nodded and returned to the Boars so he could have them circulate the plan through the troops of Manor Farm.

*   *   *   *

It took the thousands of Animals from Snail and Manor Farms over an hour to properly align for the attack. During this time, the Pigs and Poodles had worked themselves into a mouth-foaming frenzy. The Goats and Rams dropped pellets from terror.

The Generals spread the word through the ranks that the Poodles would hang back until the troops were engaged and the army of Knight Farm had been spread thin. The front line of Goats and Rams spread out over a half of a mile. Twenty Boar-lengths behind them were the Pigs of both Farms. This line measured nearly three-fourths of a mile. Fifty Boar-lengths behind the Pigs were the line of Poodles a quarter of mile long.

The Rams and Goats rolled their heads nervously in expectation of absorbing the defenses of Knight Farm. They expected Mastiff jaws and Schnauzer team attacks, and knew their best chance was to drive forward quickly and help push the Knight Farm army backwards. This would allow the Poodles to scale the walls and end the carnage. If not, the battle would be long and bloody and the Goats and Rams would be the first to die.

Preston and the Premier, now silent, marched in the middle of the line of Pigs. The forces of Manor Farm were to one side and the forces of Snail Farm to the other side. The Hawks of Knight Farm dropped down closed to the line and then darted back to the great gates of Knight Farm. The Crows tried to pursue them in bunches but the Hawks were much too fast for them to catch.

Fifty Crows would fly over to gather intelligence and try to determine the location of the defenses of Knight Farm. It appeared that the Knight Farm Animals remained in three groups of about five hundred each. However, the Hawks were now attacking the Crows as they tried to get a closer look at their defenses. The air resonated with the grating screams of the Crows. The Hawks managed to rip the wings off a couple of Crows in flight before the other members of the flock of Crows could repel them. The Poodles of Snail Farm howled in rage.

When the armies of Manor and Snail Farms were within five hundred yards of Knight Farm, Animals – Mastiffs, Rams and Llamas – poured out of the great gates that had stood ajar. At the same time, the group to the South and the group to the North of the gate dispatched to form a line of defense. Yet, there was something strange about the formation.

"What are they doing?" Preston asked.

"Not sure," the Premier said. "I thought for sure that the Dogs would be their first line of defense in order to instill fear."

They watched for another couple of minutes trying to figure out what the Knight Farm strategy might be for the battle.

"It appears as if the Schnauzers are on the wall to repel any of our Poodles trying to leap the wall," the Premier said.

"Why is King George in the middle of the front line with his brother right behind him?" Preston asked.

"Don't know the answer to that, Comrade," the Premier said.

"Sir Andrew is right behind them with Llamas and Mastiffs."

"No matter," the Premier said. "We will overwhelm them with sheer numbers regardless of the strategy they adopt."

"Perhaps," Preston said. He was growing tired of deferring to the older Pig.

Preston conferred with his advisors who were also his personal guard for a few moments. He returned quickly to the Premier's side. The Premier's big black eyes reflected the mid-morning sun. With his coarse black hair hiding his pink skin, the Premier looked more like a member of the Rodentia order than the Suidae Family. A shiver went down Preston's back as he considered his ally.

"We are in agreement," Preston said when it became clear that the Premier did not intend to look at Preston but preferred to keep his eye on the movements of the Knight Farm defenses.

"Of course," the Premier said softly. "First line attacks. Lines two and three keep at their assigned distances until my signal." Both the Snail Farm and the Manor Farm generals nodded. Preston passed command on to his personal guard even though they had already nodded at the Premier.

With no additional ceremony, the Premier bellowed, "First line! Attack!"

Thousands of Rams and Goats barreled down the hill toward Knight Farm. Grass, dirt and snapped branches of the occasional bush flew in their wake. The thousands of Pigs followed at a slobbering, grunting walk allowing the first line to put a hundred yards between them.

* * * *

"They are extremely brave," Sir Andrew said to no one in particular. To his surprise someone responded.

"What makes you say so?"

It was Sir Nelson who stood quietly at his side. Sir Nelson's wife, Lady Eliza, stood on the other side of her husband. Sir Andrew's white coat glistened with water. He had drenched himself to keep cooler during battle as had the Mastiffs on either side of him. The three of them stood directly behind Prince James who stood behind King George.

"Because King George and the other Rams of Knight Farm are a hundred pounds heavier than the Rams and Goats flying down the hill right now. I am larger still." Sir Andrew said as they watched the enemy close to within two hundred yards.

Rams and Llamas from Knight Farm formed a long line of defense, as long as the line of Pigs making their way down the hill. All of them breathed deeply but kept silent. Their training taught the soldiers to hold their tongues until given the order to attack. Only their twitching

155

muscles revealed their anticipation and anxiety. Overhead, the Hawks were chasing the Crows from the battlefield with cold precision.

"Attack," Sir Andrew said loudly and firmly.

King George roared, more like a lion than a Ram. The other Rams did the same and, with most of the Llamas by their side, loped up the hill. Each one looked for their first victim and communicated their intended target to the soldier next to them. The kills needed to be quick and calculated given the two to one advantage of the enemy.

Sir Andrew, his elite force of Llamas and Mastiffs numbering forty, twenty of each, and Sir Nelson's King's Guard adding another ten Mastiffs, now stood alone at the main gate. The rest of Mastiffs and some Llamas were now spread in a line along the wall. The fifteen-foot-high oak doors had been shut and the board dropped across so there was no where to run. Of course, the thought of running would never enter Sir Andrew's mind.

When the armies' first lines clashed, the sound of shrieking Animals, butting horns and stomping hooves rebounded off the rocky walls of Knight Farm. Sir Andrew watched the battle taking place on the grassy knoll, a hundred yards from the gate. The battle-tested Rams and Llamas of King George were leaving broken bones and crushed skulls in their wake. Legs snapped, blood rushed from head wounds and vertebrae separated as the Rams butted and kicked the smaller Rams and Goats of Manor and Snail Farms. The Llamas raised their forelegs high in the air and crushed the smaller, less experienced enemy.

Seeing the carnage, the Premier did not hesitate. "Attack," he yelled.

The Boars of Snail Farm and Knight Farm barreled down the hill and aimed straight for the legs of the Rams and Llamas. The Premier engaged his bloodlust by taking the lead. Preston stayed back and watched the battle with the ten members of his personal guard.

Now both armies' soldiers fell to the ground by the dozen. King George and Prince James, keeping their heads low, began crushing the skulls of the oncoming Boars. The Boars had trouble slowing down as gravity forced them to pick up speed as they raced down the hill. Brains, blood, urine and foam from the Animals' mouths made the formerly dry grass more like mud. The sound of injured Animals crying and bellowing now drowned out the cracking of bones and the deep thud of the Boars' small horns penetrating the bellies of the Knight Farm Llamas and Rams.

Sir Andrew watched the battle intently. Outnumbered as they were, the Knight Farm army could only battle head-on for a short period of time. When the Rams and Llamas began to tire, Sir Andrew shouted

156

forcefully, "Fall back and reform." King George led his troops' quick return to the wall.

The Premier, gore dangling from his tusks and blood splattered over his dark hair, did not wait. "Poodles over the wall," he commanded. The Poodles were the true warriors of Snail Farm and they fought in well-trained attack forces of twenty Dogs each. Bounding down the hill, they divided up into their fifty groups of twenty. They formed two lines of twenty-five groups each. If the group in the first line was repelled, the second would immediately follow and overwhelm the Schnauzers on the wall.

*   *   *   *

The Poodles darted past Preston's position and he squealed with delight; "Now we will show them," he cried.

The members of his guard did not say anything in response; a few even rolled their eyes. Preston had not moved from his position behind the battle lines. His personal guard, ten large Boars, each longed to join the battle. Preston stood shifting his weight from one side of his body to the other while looking down on the battle in front of the walls of Knight Farm, a hundred yards away.

Lord Winston's Schnauzers growled and barked ferociously at the Poodles bounding down the hill toward them. The other Animals from all threes farms shuddered at the sound. They knew that with the Dogs entering the battle, the intensity of the fighting would increase tenfold and make the initial stages seem like sparring.

One thousand Poodles, an even mixture of black and white, passed into the line expecting the Mastiffs and Sir Andrew's Llamas to spread out and engage them. The Premier believed they would attack as the Poodles attempted to leap to the top of the rock wall. Instead they remained perfectly still.

"What are they doing?" Preston asked the Boar next to him.

"I'm not sure," the Boar said. "Perhaps they are waiting until the Poodles start trying to leap up the wall."

A Hawk soared out of nowhere over Preston's head and like a missile sped toward Sir Andrew and somehow managed to land on his back. A moment later, the Hawk was in the air racing away from a small flock of Crows in hot pursuit. The air battle was loud but only a couple of Crows and one Hawk had lost their lives. The Hawks continued to fly high above the battle field. King George's troops had reformed at the wall with the Pigs, Goats and Rams of Manor and Snail Farm right behind them. The teams of Poodles were twenty yards from Sir Andrew when he took off running at a group of Poodles directly in front of him.

The leader of the pack of Poodles had his group split up and run along the battle line north to South, in order to avoid complete destruction. The elite squad of Mastiffs and Llamas were now running behind Sir Andrew. Instead of engaging, Sir Andrew ran straight through the Snail Farm and Manor Farm forces.

The Premier spotted Sir Andrew and his team and roared, "Pigs from Snail Farm turn and form a defensive line. They are trying to box us in."

The well-trained troops of Snail Farm turned as directed while the Animals from Manor Farm battled with King George's Rams and Llamas.

Preston watched Sir Andrew's force break through the line and waited for them to turn back toward the fighting and engage with the Premier's Boars. Instead, Sir Andrew led a charge up what just ten minutes before had been a perfectly manicured lawn, but had been transformed into a dark and rugged terrain.

When Sir Andrew and the twenty Llamas and thirty Mastiffs were within fifty yards of Preston's position, one of the Boars in Preston's guard said calmly, "I think we better take evasive action."

Preston's eyes bulged as the reality of war finally set in. There was a chance he could die, and this did not feel very good.

"Yes," Preston said quickly. "Lead the way."

The Sergeant was only too happy to take control of the other Boars. "Follow me," he screamed.

The Sergeant bolted along the ridge of the hill. It was slow going as they were running at an angle, with one side of their bodies a foot higher up the hill than the other. The Llamas and Mastiffs closed fast. Sir Andrew and the Llamas were twenty-five yards ahead of the Mastiffs. The Sergeant said softly so that just Preston could hear, "Preston, run for the line."

Preston nodded and did not break stride but altered his course so that he was now running diagonally down the hill toward the main battle, in an attempt to evade the Llamas' pursuit.

"Guards halt and attack," the Sergeant said in a loud, calm voice.

Dutch had trained this Boar a year before and it was paying off for Preston. The Boars turned to intercept the Llamas. They moved in force down the hill to cross paths with the Llamas before they reached Preston.

Sir Andrew ran easily up the hill and then changed his course to run slightly downhill in order to meet Preston before he could lose himself among his troops. The Premier watched from the front line and contemplated his next move. It was unlikely that Preston would make it even close to his Boars who watched the scene stoically. The Rams, Goats and Pigs of Manor Farm continued to fight with the Llamas and Rams of Manor Farm a short distance from the wall. Poodles continued to scale the wall.

The Llamas did not slow as the Boars began snorting in anticipation of the fight. At the meeting point, Sir Andrew's Llamas leapt high over the rushing Boars of Manor Farm. All but one made it past and continued in hot pursuit of Preston.

Preston slowed as his lungs refused to expand, so that he could take in the necessary oxygen. Mucus dripped thickly from his snout. Despite his brain instructing him not to, he shouted out, "Help me please." He saw that his guard had failed to slow down Sir Andrew and the remaining nineteen Llamas.

"Fourth and Third Company," the Premier shouted, "to the leader of Manor Farm."

The order made its way down the line. By the time they left their positions on the line, the Mastiffs in Sir Andrew's attack force, led by Sir Nelson, were getting ready to tear the throats of the members of Preston's personal guard. Outnumbered three to one, the Boars knew that the only consolation is that they might take a few of the enemy with them.

But the Mastiffs of Knight Farm were too well-trained. They attacked in pairs, with each rapping their huge mouths around the leg of a Boar. Then a third Mastiff would move in for the kill.

Preston saw the fifty Boars of Snail Farm making their way up the hill. He felt a glimmer of hope and managed to pick up his pace just a little, despite his exhaustion. He thought he might make it, as the Boars were only fifty yards away. He turned again to check how much ground Sir Andrew had gained over the last few seconds.

Looking over his shoulder as he ran, the only thing Preston could see was a giant Llama body. It appeared to be headless. Then a split second before it happened, clarity. Sir Andrew swept Preston's hind legs out from under him with his huge head. Preston's rear end went up the hill as he took a step down the hill with his front legs. He flew in the air with his back to the ground. His ribs cracked loudly as he hit the muddy grass.

Preston rolled three times downhill – at least I am still moving in the right direction, he thought as he tumbled in what felt like slow motion. As he regained his feet, he was facing downhill. He saw Sir Andrew alter his course to head up the hill to avoid the Boars of Snail Farm, who were closing ground quickly.

Preston looked back toward the direction that Sir Andrew had come from. Two Llamas stood over Preston with their front legs dangling over him. Their hooves raised ominously, directly over his head, Preston

159

could see their stomachs were pressed tightly against their ribs as they inhaled. Preston did not see the Llamas exhale. Instead, he watched the hooves of one come crashing down on his snout while the hooves of the other slammed his vertebrae. For a brief moment his skull burned and then there was nothing. The morning sun gone from sight, he was only aware of the blood dripping over his eyelids.

The Mastiffs had made quick work of Preston's personal guard, and were reformed in tight formation as they padded down the hill to engage with the Premier's Third and Fourth Companies. After eliminating Preston, Sir Andrew and the other nineteen Llamas had run up the hill and taken a position behind the thirty snarling Mastiffs.

"Third and Fourth Companies back to the line," the Premier shouted from the battle at the wall.

The Boars of Third and Fourth Company breathed a sigh of relief and made their way back to the line of Boars. The complete line was reformed by the time the Mastiffs were fifty yards away. The Mastiffs stopped and sat down in the muddy, bloody grass and stared at the Boars.

*   *   *   *

Paulie had been allowed to watch the battle from the wall, as long as she did not try to assist. Although King George did not believe there was a chance that she was a spy, Sir Andrew had insisted that she be kept from the fighting. "Just to be overly cautious of her safety and ours," Sir Andrew had said, despite having total confidence that Paulie was their ally. He simply followed his own protocol.

To Paulie's surprise, not an inkling of sorrow passed over her heart when the Llamas descended on Preston on the hill just a hundred yards in front of her on the wall. The noon sky was covered in clouds, as if the Man God knew that it was a day of sorrow. Up on the wall, she felt as safe as if she were back at Manor Farm.

She watched in fascination as Lord Winton's Schnauzers defended the walls. The pattern became clear to Paulie after just a couple minute of careful observation. If only one defender could greet a Poodle, as the Poodle leapt to the top of the wall, then the forces allowed the Poodle to drop down into Knight Farm. If a team of two Schnauzers was within striking distance as the Poodle scaled the wall, then the Poodle would be torn at until he or she jumped back into the battle outside the wall or was killed.

Paulie scanned the defenses of Knight Farm. She was surprised by the minimum force gathered behind the massive front gate. It was now closed but only twenty very large Rams stood guard inside with the idea that they could prevent the Manor Farm and Snail Farm forces from opening it. But once enough Poodles made it over the wall and into Knight Farm, the Rams would not be able to hold them off and the gates would be opened by the enemy from the inside. There were already twenty Poodles inside, forming into an attack team to engage with the Rams.

Initially, Paulie couldn't understand the Knight Farm strategy. She knew that something unusual had been proposed by Lord Winston, but couldn't figure it out. However, when she heard Sir Andrew's voice loud over the battlefield she finally understood.

"To me," Sir Andrew shouted over the chaos. Word spread down the line. A hundred Llamas broke from the battle taking place along the wall. Black, white and brown Llamas, and those with a mix of colors, made their way over the line of Boars and to Sir Andrew who still stood with the Llamas of the Royal Guard behind the Mastiffs of that team and ten members of the King's Guard. Most of the Llamas ran toward Sir Andrew as if they had just woke to a brilliant sun. The training they endured was so intense that they were able to fight for a couple of hours, while most Animals exhausted their energy in less than half an hour. A few, bleeding and wounded, made their way more slowly up the hill.

At the same time, twenty additional Mastiffs who had not yet joined the fighting left their positions along the wall, burst through the line of Boars and away from Knight Farm, and joined Sir Nelson to form a force of a hundred.

Sir Andrew didn't say a word until the Llamas were gathered around him. Sir Andrew's large, blue eyes scanned his Llamas. He paused at the five or six Llamas who had trouble making it up the hill in turn. Then he finally spoke. "Can everyone make it?"

The Llamas said "Yes, Sir Andrew," in unison, firmly and quietly. The injured had given a firm nod of the head to confirm their resolve. Sir Andrew, his legs now covered in mud, turned downhill and faced Sir Nelson and the other Mastiffs, who sat patiently, catching their breath. No amount of training can prevent a Mastiff from panting at even the smallest exertion.

"Sir Nelson," Sir Andrew said, "are you and your team ready, my friend?"

"Yes, Sir Andrew," the giant Dog said. "We are locked and loaded as the humans used to say."

Sir Nelson's muzzle was smeared with Pig's blood. His friendly eyes danced from the joy of battle.

"Then we shall await your combat before we charge," Sir Andrew said with a smile.

"Mastiffs, into position," Sir Nelson said with a growl, as he stood up. The Mastiffs rose in unison and formed into two lines of fifty. Sir Nelson led them loping the fifty yards down the hill to the Premier's Boars.

*   *   *   *

The Premier watched the Mastiffs making their way downhill directly to his position in the front of the main gate. The fighting between the remaining Llamas and Rams of Knight Farm and the Goats, Rams and Boars of Manor Farm carried on behind him.

"Twenty-first and thirteenth Companies fall in," the Premier shouted.

Boars from farther down the line moved over toward the Premier's position in front of the gate, and filled the gaps on either side of the Boars already prepared to face the onslaught. The Boars now outnumbered the Mastiffs and Llamas by more than three to one in front of the gate. Still, the coming Mastiff onslaught turned the Premier's stomach.

The Mastiffs barked loudly, from the bottom of their chests, while the Boars snorted and waived their large, black heads in response. The Premier watched the Dogs and when they were within five yards he shuddered involuntarily. The Dogs were nearly as large as the Boars. He lowered his head, snarled and charged the closest Mastiff.

The battlefield resonated with new sounds: the deep growls and gravelly yelps of the Mastiffs, mixed with the terrified squeals of the Boars whose legs the Mastiffs were snapping in two like they were mere twigs. The Mastiffs were not bothering to kill the Boars. Their strategy was to put them out of commission, so that they could no longer fight. Sir Nelson and the Mastiffs left scores of fallen Boars in their wake.

"Attack," Sir Andrew commanded his Llamas, as he leapt high in the air before breaking into a dead run toward the ten foot high walls of Knight Farm. The other Llamas mimicked his behavior; they each jumped up into the air so that their immense size sent a message to the enemy before they sprinted after Sir Andrew. Clods of dirt and grass flew in all directions as the herd rumbled toward the Premier.

"Incoming," the Premier said, just as he drove his tusks into the exposed ribs of a Mastiff who had been dragging one of the Snail Farm Boars by a hind leg. "Thirty-second and Thirty-eighth Companies fall in," he bellowed over the carnage.

Again more Boars filled gaps in front of the gate in preparation for the one hundred charging Llamas.

162

Sir Andrew, his blue eyes wild and his white fur dry and bouncing in the morning sunlight, veered right toward the location where the Thirty-second Company of Snail Farm had been positioned just moments before. The Premier watched Sir Andrew jump a Boar trying to intercept him and then bound over the ten foot wall like it was a white picket fence. A hundred Llamas followed Sir Andrew over the wall and into Knight Farm. In some cases, the Llamas jumped right next to a Snail Farm Poodle who was trying to scale the wall.

By the time Sir Andrew landed on the far side of the wall, there were over fifty Poodles gathered inside preparing to attack the Rams that guarded the massive, wooden gate. The Poodles looked up in surprise as the Llamas glided over the wall one after the other. Their grace did not fool the Poodles who had fought the Llamas in prior wars. Llamas kicked as hard as Mules, with twice the quickness.

"Poodles back over the wall," the Premier shouted. "All Animals, Retreat!"

The Boars, Rams, Goats and Poodles outside the walls followed his orders immediately and moved up the hill a couple of hundred yards. King George and the Rams and Llamas still fighting along side of him, and the Mastiffs fighting with Sir Nelson, stopped and did not pursue them. Instead, they fell back to the wall in a defensive position.

Inside Knight Farm, Sir Andrew's Llamas circled around the Poodles, and now that the fighting had stopped along the walls, five hundred of the thousand Schnauzers dropped from the wall, and made their way through the legs of the Llamas to get close to the Poodles. Lord Winston hobbled on ancient legs to Sir Andrew's side.

"Would you like honor, Sir Andrew?" Lord Winston asked. "You have most certainly earned it."

"It would be my pleasure," Sir Andrew said.

Sir Andrew moved forward and glared at the Poodles. "You may choose to live or die," he offered.

The Poodles did not need any more urging, as they knew that fighting would be useless. They dropped to their bellies and rolled over, in a symbol emblematic of dropping one's weapon or waiving a white flag. A roar went up from the Rams, Llamas and Schnauzers inside the walls of Knight Farm. This was echoed by the Knight Farm forces on the other side.

*   *   *   *

A couple of hours later, Sir Andrew, Lord Winston, Sir Nelson and Prince James joined King George in the Great Hall. Outside, a scattering of Mastiffs and Schnauzers patrolled the walls while ten Hawks roamed the sky. The remainder of the Knight Farm army rested just inside the gates, eating fresh food and drinking gallons of water brought by the Animals who were not part of the Knight Farm army. The Dogs on the wall watched the combined armies of Snail and Manor Farms form a large encampment on the ridge above Knight Farm, less than a half a mile up the hill.

Back inside the Great Hall, the leaders of Knight Farm let out a collective sigh of relief. "Your troops fought bravely today," King George said. All four said "Thank you your Highness" in unison.

"And Lord Winston, your plan worked perfectly," King George said.

The other three nodded their heads in agreement. King George took a long drink of water from a bowl sitting in front of him on the large stone table. Then he lapped a little ale from the stein next to the bowl of water. The afternoon sun penetrated the inherent darkness of the Hall, creating the illusion of dusk. They all waited patiently, sipping their ale. Lord Winston was already on his second stein full of ale and he attacked it with relish. His bowl of water was untouched.

"Tomorrow will be a different story," King George said. "They still outnumber us two to one, even with all the casualties we inflicted today. The Premier has no qualms about losing his own life in battle and this makes his troops fiercely loyal and obscenely brave. Killing the Premier will only make his Boars and the Poodles more ferocious. Any suggestions on a strategy as we move forward Lord Winston?"

Lord Winston looked up from his ale and fixed his good eye on King George. Lord Winston took a long drink of ale. Although they were all used to the old Schnauzer's slow speech patterns, it could be frustrating in times of great stress such as these. But they held their tongues and lapped their ale as patiently as they could manage because, in this instance, Lord Winston's opinion carried the most weight. Lord Winston inhaled deeply and then violently coughed up blood-filled mucus. It dribbled slowly over the white fur around his muzzle. The other Animals pretended not to notice. His death was near and there was no need to discuss it.

"I don't believe you will like what I have to say, your Highness," Lord Winston said slowly.

"I will hear it anyway," King George said with an amused smile.

"I say we defend the walls," Lord Winston said.

"Are you being serious Lord Winston," Sir Andrew said as politely as he could manage.

"Please Sir Andrew, let him finish," King George said.

164

Lord Winston had not taken his eye off of King George. "From sheer numbers alone, we will eventually be overrun if we go out and do battle. If not tomorrow, then some time in the coming weeks."

"My Llamas and the Mastiffs will wreak havoc among them," Sir Andrew said confidently.

"Sir Andrew, please show Lord Winston the deference his position as General of the Army, and his twenty years of battle experience, have earned for him and let him finish," King George said more sharply than he had intended.

"There are Llamas in the army and the Royal Guard and Schnauzers in both as well," Sir Andrew said. "It was not meant as a slight to Schnauzers."

Again, Lord Winston did not turn toward Sir Andrew to meet his cold, blue gaze.

"It is an old military tactic used by humans; defend the walls in the hope that the enemy will lose the will to fight or run out of food. I suggest we put all the Dogs on the walls day and night. Let them sleep and eat up there. If a Poodle tries to come over the wall we fall on him or her, kill them or push them into Knight Farm where the Llamas and Rams will be waiting."

Again, the Great Hall magnified the long silence. "Alright," King George said. "Does anyone have a plan other than to meet their force out in the battlefield as we did today or to defend the walls as Lord Winston suggests?"

Sir Andrew, Prince James and Sir Nelson all shook their heads slowly. Sir Andrew's inability to come up with something creative caused him to soften a bit toward Lord Winston.

"Before we discuss whether we would like to die valiantly or live sheepishly, let's eat lunch and then I will hear from each of you."

*   *   *   *

After a lunch of bread and fruit for all of them, and also pork for the Dogs, Lord Winston, Sir Andrew, Sir Nelson and Prince James gathered around the stone table. Its formerly rough surface had grown smooth from centuries of friction caused by bowls, plates, mugs, claws, hooves and nails. Ale spilled from mugs over the many centuries gave the table a sticky texture in spots that no amount of cleaning could erase. The sun struggled to penetrate the vast man-made cave, so servants had lit the torches hours in advance of the setting sun.

King George arrived last, walking slowly from his chambers where he had dined alone. The others sat quietly with their opinions hidden behind weary eyes. King George nodded to each of them as he stepped up to the head of the table. His eyes gleamed with the same resolve, but his body clearly needed rest.

"Your Highness," Lord Winston, Sir Andrew and Sir Nelson said in unison.

"Sir Nelson, let's begin with you," King George said. It was protocol when making a decision of importance to have the junior member of the group voice their opinion first.

"With all due respect to Lord Winston," Sir Nelson began, "I believe we must meet them outside the walls."

Sir Nelson waited so long to say anything further that King George asked, "Do you wish to share your reasoning?"

Sir Nelson stared at the King with his golf-ball-sized eyes for a moment and said, "Yes, I do. First, I believe we will show weakness and a lack of resolve if we do not meet them on the battlefield tomorrow. This is especially the case given our victory today. Second, I believe they will try to wait us out if we adopt this plan instead of continuing to attack. We know that the farms affiliated with Snail Farm could send an additional thousand to two thousand Boars and then the odds against victory would be even greater."

All four of the other Animals stared at Sir Nelson. None of them had ever heard him string more than two sentences together at one time before this afternoon. Sir Nelson started panting, as if speaking were more laborious than fighting Boars.

"Thank you," King George said. "Prince James?"

"My brother," Prince James said with a tilt of the head, "I agree with Sir Nelson for the reasons he so eloquently stated. He should do a little more talking, as it suits him."

The other Animals laughed at this. "In addition, I believe we will win if we fight now," Prince James said. "Let's bring the battle to them early tomorrow morning and drive them from our Kingdom."

Lord Winston let out an audible sigh and shook his head in amusement and worry at the younger Animals' bravado.

"Sir Andrew, I am guessing your position is in accordance with Sir Nelson and Prince James," King George said.

"Actually, no it is not," Sir Andrew said.

King George looked at Sir Andrew with raised eyebrows. Lord Winston had known the King since the King's birth, and this was the first time he had ever seen the King's face belie his emotions.

"I have considered Lord Winston's words carefully and believe his proposed strategy is the correct one. Their numbers are too large to fight without some sort of plan besides trying to beat them on the battle lines."

Lord Winston turned his good eye from King George to Sir Andrew. The Prince and Sir Nelson tilted their heads in confusion. Had Sir Andrew lost his nerve?

"Do you have a suggestion for a plan if we simply hold the walls?" King George asked, he was clearly taken off guard and slightly agitated by Sir Andrew's change of heart.

"Yes, your Highness," Sir Andrew said, "I think I do."

"Please share it with us," King George directed.

"It is more of a strategy than a plan your Highness," Sir Andrew was back to addressing the King formally in light of his clear agitation.

"Fine," King George said, "let's hear it."

"As you know, your Highness," Sir Andrew said, "the Pack from Manor Farm and some other Animals may join our cause if Paulie is to be believed. This could provide us with an opportunity to again surprise the armies of Snail Farm and Manor Farm."

"How so?" King George asked, now more curious than agitated.

"I don't know for sure but if our Hawks can find them we could try to devise some sort of coordinated attack," Sir Andrew said with more confidence than he felt. He looked down at King George with a curious blue eye.

King George nodded his head. The other four Animals knew in matters of war, King George was decisive. "We will remain behind the walls for at least a day and rest. The day after tomorrow I may change my mind. Go tell the troops to get some rest tonight and tomorrow."

CHAPTER FOURTEEN – TERROR FOR JUSTICE

Cody waited until late in the afternoon to convene the meeting at Sabean's rock. It was shortly after King George met with his advisors the second time, and decided to defend the walls. Cody stepped out from the shadows of the cave to address those who had responded to his summons. He and the Pack had taken shelter in the cave, in order to escape the afternoon heat.

Along the banks of Beaver Creek stood Dutch, Alexander, Bart, and Bart's wife and son. They stared intently at Cody. They looked slightly out of place in the thick brush of the forest. They dwarfed their surroundings, as if a child had mismatched two sets of toys by putting farm animals that were much too large for his toy, plastic forest.

Sunlight fought its way through branches of oak and maple to touch the river water. On both sides of the shore, members of the Pack took up defensive positions. Percy's Cats had arrived moments earlier. Paulie had arrived just ahead of the Cats, to announce their presence. This had driven Cody from his self-imposed silence.

Percy's Cats climbed the trees surrounding Sabean's rock. They assumed positions over the Dogs that just a few days before had been occupied by rats and raccoons. Just as Cody was about to speak, Rocky, the largest of the black Labradors, let a booming bark followed by the word, "Wolves." He was at the position furthest East and closest to Pine Mountain.

Maggie, Cody and the other members of the Pack bounded down the shoreline on both sides of the river. They followed the sound of Rocky's deep, baritone bark; each one ended with a rumbling growl.

"Stay here," Cody said to the other Animals as he took off. "We will call you if we need you."

"But . . .," Dutch tried to object.

"I don't want to force a fight with the wolves and you all will scare them into an attack," Cody said. "And I don't want to risk one of you being isolated."

Cody said all this over his shoulder as he made his way through the forest toward Rocky. Cody could tell that Rocky had moved East to investigate the scent before he spotted the wolves, as Rocky was fairly deep into the forest. Rocky stood on a fallen log more than five football fields from Sabean's rock.

Cody bounded up onto the log, right behind Maggie. It was only then that Cody could see One-eye and his pack. One-eye had come forward, within ten yards of Rocky. One-eye stood in a small clearing of tall grass. To Cody's surprise, One-eye was lying down. One-eye's pack was about twenty feet behind him, spread out in a semi-circle. They, too, were lying on the ground. Cody gave Rocky a gentle nudge with his wet nose. Rocky finally fell silent. Cody took a deep breath to relax and to catch his breath from the five hundred yard dash.

"What are you doing this far West, One-eye?" Cody asked as civilly as he could manage given the natural animosity.

"I will get to that Cody," One-eye said. "But first let me pass on my condolences regarding Frank. The wilds respected him and feared him as well."

Cody nodded. "Thank you," he finally managed. "And what is it you want?"

"The vultures bring news of the destruction of Sabean's forces," One –eye said. "But that is not all. They say you and the Pack have separated from Manor Farm and this was the cause of Frank's death."

Cody knew there was no reason to hide this obvious truth. "Yes, we have parted from Preston and this was the cause of Frank's death."

One-eye smiled. "I see. It is difficult to understand the motives of Pigs isn't it?" One-eye asked.

Cody didn't respond.

"My vulture friends have also seen the forces of Manor Farm and Snail Farm marching as one toward Knight Farm."

When Cody again did not respond, One-eye asked, "Do you know why they march?"

"I have an opinion but not a definitive answer," Cody said.

"Will you share your opinion with us?" One-eye said, nodding his head left and right at the other members of his pack who remained silent on the grass behind him.

"I believe that Preston is a pawn of the Premier and does his bidding. Preston's actions are based on a warped adherence to a political philosophy. He does not act because of his loyalty to Manor Farm," Cody said.

"You are sounding like more than a warrior, Leader Cody," One-eye said, without sarcasm. One-eye looked at Cody, his eye sparkling in the sunlight that pushed through the dense tree leaves overhead.

"You see my friend, on at least this point we wolves are much smarter than the members of your Pack," One-eye said. "No other Animals' loyalty can match that of us canines. It is in our nature to have obsessive loyalty to our packs. Pigs have no such instinct, nor do Cats for that matter."

As he finished this sentence, One-eye nodded up at the branches over his head. Percy had assumed a position in the trees above One-eye, despite Cody's directive to stay at Sabean's rock. If Percy heard what

169

One-eye said, he gave no indication. He waved his tail slowly back and forth and continued to stare into One-eye's good eye.

"What is your point One-eye?" Cody asked.

"A treaty. And it would give me great pleasure if you could address me as Caesar, at least to my face," One-eye said with amusement, as he turned his attention back toward Cody. "What you call me when I am absent is not my concern."

One-eye smiled, but this simply made Cody more aware of the differences between Dogs and wolves. One-eye looked more savage when he smiled. Dog softened.

"Unfortunately," Cody said, "I have trouble believing you and your pack would adhere to any agreement we might come up with."

"With good reason Cody," One-eye said. "It is not in a wolf's nature to form a pact with any animal except another wolf. However, I have never broken a pact and, in this case, I see a great opportunity for my pack."

"What opportunity do you see?" Percy asked from overhead. "Would you like to pick off stragglers during the battle for an easy meal?"

"Very clever, Mr. Cat, but no," One-eye said. "If I may continue?" One-eye said to Percy. Percy nodded. One-eye turned his attention back toward Cody.

"The wolf pack would like an agreement that you will not come to the defense of Snail Farm in the event that we attack them for food or any other reason," One-eye said.

"But I do not control Manor Farm," Cody said.

"But your word on behalf of the Pack is all I need. Don't you see?"

Cody pondered this for a minute. "Yes, I suppose you are right. What do we receive in return?"

"That is up to you," One-eye said.

Cody paused and then whispered first to Maggie and then to Rocky.

"There is something we would like," Cody said. "If you can agree, we have a deal as long as you never venture this far West again. Follow me so we can speak alone," Cody said.

*   *   *   *

The following morning, Lord Winston patrolled the walls of Knight Farm as the sun peeked over the mountains. Sunlight first touched the gathering forces of Snail Farm and Manor Farm on the hillside west of the gate. As the minutes passed, it moved down the hill toward the walls of Knight Farm. Mist drifted off the mud, blood and grass. Lord Winston watched the heads of Poodles, Pigs, Goats and Rams pop out of the mist. They appeared to be swimming instead of walking into formation.

An hour later, Lord Winston had a clear view of the opposing forces gathering a half a mile away. The morning chill started to resign itself to the power of the sun. The armies of the enemy appeared to be broken into attack groups in a circle, as if they were being given instructions for the coming battle. It wasn't until he heard the baleful voice of the Rams and the Goats that he understood what was happening. They were paying their respects to Preston. Lord Winston shook his head in disdain at this false hero's burial.

*   *   *   *

The Premier stood before the combined forces of Snail Farm and Manor Farm. None of the Animals from Manor Farm had stepped forward to lead Manor Farm, so the Premier had assumed full responsibility for the armies. The Pigs of Manor Farm did not object and, for the most part, seemed relieved. The Premier looked at the armies for nearly a minute before he spoke in the silence of early morning.

"Our enemies are cowards my friends," the Premier began quietly. "They understand they are no match for our collective might. They understand that fighting for equality cannot be matched by an illogical loyalty to royalty. So instead of fighting, they turned to a cowardly assassination."

The Premier paused. The Animals closest to him nodded and murmured their approval. The Premier shook his giant head swiftly, as if shaking off a swarm of flies.

"But what they do not understand is that killing a leader of our cause only makes us stronger. Because they believe that Animals should be led by a King, they think that without a leader Animals will lose their way. But we know differently. We know that for right-thinking Animals, this is not the way of the world. We believe that a leader follows the Animals. I assure you that I, as your leader, do your bidding."

The Animals, thousands strong, roared their approval. It could be heard on the far side of Knight Farm, miles away.

"Let us honor Preston and all the other brave Animals who fell yesterday. But we honor all our warriors equally. Preston's loss is a tragedy. But it is no more of a tragedy than the loss of any of our other fallen Comrades.

"Today, we will scales those walls," the Premier shouted as he tossed his head in the direction of Knight Farm. "Today, we bring equality to Knight Farm. Today, we will sweep away centuries of oppression. Today, we shall not stop until King George's head has lost its horns. Join me in avenging the death of all our brothers."

*   *   *   *

Lord Winston found the roars of anger coming from the hill unusual for a memorial service. It was a brief service, which Lord Winston thought appropriate for a politician. He still believed that the service was for Preston alone. He watched the army on the hill break into battle lines. This time, the Boars were interspersed with the Rams and Goats in the front line, with the Poodles in a line behind them.

"Soldiers, assume your positions," Lord Winston bellowed.

The volume of his voice surprised Sir Andrew, who stood inside the walls, just below Lord Winston. It amazed him that an old Dog could still manage such a menacing tone. Mastiffs and Schnauzers from inside Knight Farm made their way quickly up stone steps to the top of the Western wall. They joined the guard of Schnauzers already in position. A skeleton crew of Schnauzers, with Hawks as their lookouts, patrolled the East, South and North walls in case the enemy tried to attack at multiple locations. Rams and Llamas patrolled just inside the West wall. The Ewes patrolled the inside of the East, North and South walls.

King George, Sir Andrew and Prince James moved quickly to join Lord Winston at the top of the wall. Lord Winston looked at them disapprovingly.

"Back down, your Highness," Lord Winston said, as if his orders would be followed. "It would be much too easy for a couple of Poodles to drag you over the edge."

King George looked at Lord Winston with surprise and, a moment later, a huge smile broke over his face. "Alright, Lord Winston," King George said. "That is logical."

As quickly as they had arrived, they headed back down, inside of Knight Farm. Lord Winston turned his attention back toward the armies of Snail Farm and Manor Farm.

The front line of the Premier's forces had reached the wall. The Boars had formed a long line, just a few feet from the wall. The Goats and Rams held back and joined the Poodles in a line fifty yards from the wall.

"They plan to use the Boars as a platform to scale the walls," Lord Winston yelled over the snorts and grunts of the angry Boars. "Look sharp now."

Lord Winston paced back and forth and rotated his head in a small circle as he shouted out his orders.

There were nearly a thousand Poodles. Lord Winston knew he was outnumbered in total Animals at the point of attack by at least two to one. His troops understood that some of the enemy would make it over but their goal was to prevent a break in the defense along the wall. If the enemy could create an opening on the wall that was large enough, the entire force of Poodles, Goats, and Rams could flow through it and make their way to the gate. They would open it for the Boars from the inside.

Some of the Poodles broke down the hill and bounded onto the backs of the Boars and then onto the wall. Unlike the day before when they were only able to get two feet on the wall and then pull themselves up, they landed on the wall with all four paws firmly planted. They were ready to fight or bound into Knight Farm and take evasive action once on the ground.

The first score of Poodles were met by Mastiffs and their necks were perfunctorily snapped.

Howls, yelps, brays, snapping and other sounds of battle filled the air. Each Poodle that made it onto the wall fought toward the middle on either side of the gate. Lord Winston noticed that the Poodles were focusing on the gate while the Goats and Rams leapt up from the far end of the line of Boars.

"Mastiffs to the gate," Lord Winston ordered.

Sir Nelson directed fifty Mastiffs to the gate. As they made their way into a collective group of twenty-five on either side, Poodles poured toward the area surrounding the gate and bounded onto the wall. It appeared to Lord Winston that there would be so many Poodles that the Mastiffs would be overwhelmed. This would mean disaster. The Poodles would hold the wall surrounding the gate as Goats and Rams of the combined forces joined them. Once a large enough force was amassed on the wall, they would drop into Knight Farm and open the gate. Lord Winston began to wonder what it would be like to end his storied career in disgrace.

As this disturbing thought passed through his mind, and Poodles continued to amass on the wall at the gate, he heard a frightening howl, the likes of which he had not heard for years.

Lord Winston followed his instinct and turned his head toward the sound. Standing at the very spot where the Premier had rallied his troops just minutes before, was the largest wolf he had ever seen. It was the first wolf he had seen in nearly a decade. Twenty more wolves stepped behind the large one and they let out a terrifying, synchronized howl.

The pack of wolves loped down the hill in silence. Lord Winston shuddered. They are so different from Dogs, Lord Winston thought. Their silence belied their vicious character. It was clear they were going to attack the Premier's Boars from behind. For the first time, Lord Winston was confused on the battlefield. Why are they attacking a force that is a hundred times their number? More importantly, why are they joining the battle at all?

As he mulled these questions over in his head, he noticed something strange was happening to the line of Snail Farm Boars just in front of the gate. They began kicking their hind legs in a panic, oblivious to the Poodles who were trying to use their backs as spring boards. Within a couple of minutes of the pack of wolves arriving, the Boars in front of the gate broke ranks and sprinted away from the wall. As the Boars vacated the area just in front of the gate, the reason for their panic materialized out from under them. Cats, at least fifty of them, darted away from the retreating Boars and stumbling Poodles. Their fur stood on end.

They did not stay on the ground for long. Before the Poodles could massacre them, they jumped in unison up onto the wall and found shelter under the legs of the Mastiffs. Now they could help fight the Poodles while using the giant Dogs as protection.

*   *   *   *

Cody stood with the Pack and watched from the woods, North of Knight Farm. They were two hundred yards from the fighting and hidden by a grove of apple trees. The Cats' attack on the Boars had gone perfectly. Cody had been skeptical but Percy had assured him that Cat claws raking over the Boars genitals would cause instant panic. As usual, Percy was correct.

Cody watched Percy and the other Cats scale the wall to safety. He turned his attention to One-eye's pack and they were within fifty yards of the panicking Boars. Cody threw his head in the direction of the fighting and sprinted out of the woods, with the fifty members of the Pack behind him, Bart and his family by his side and Dutch and Alexander a few yards behind the Pack.

Once the Goats, Rams and Boars of Snail and Manor Farms spotted them, Cody yelled at the top of his lungs, "Lord Winston, attack." The ferocity of his voice sent the Goats and Rams on the North edge of the Snail Farm and Manor Farm forces into a tizzy. They did not know whether to turn and fight, or run. The Premier was focused on the wolf pack and did not even look in the Pack's direction.

*   *   *   *

Lord Winston turned to see Cody and the Pack before he heard him. When he heard Cody, Lord Winston was no longer at a loss. He knew exactly what to do. He waddled down the steps along the wall and into Knight Farm. He waddled toward King George, Prince James and Sir Andrew. They stood some distance from the gate, watching the Mastiffs and Cats destroy the Poodles stranded on the wall next to the gate. Too few Poodles made it onto the wall before Percy's Cats caused the collapse of the line of Boars, and now the Mastiffs were killing them or forcing them to jump from the wall.

"Your Highness, Sir Andrew, Prince James," Lord Winston said calmly. All three turned toward Lord Winston. "Please send all the Llamas and Rams over the wall and attack. And don't kill any wolves."

They stared at him, confused.

"I will explain later your Highness," Lord Winston said with confidence.

King George did not hesitate. Moments later Llamas and Rams poured over the wall and into the battle. Lord Winston rambled back up the stone stairs to the top of the wall. He watched the battle for a minute and then shouted with glee, "Schnauzers and Mastiffs into the battle."

Lord Winston jumped down into the symphony of broken bones and terrifying Animal cries.

A thousand Schnauzers and nearly a hundred Mastiffs followed right behind him.

One-eye's pack set on the Poodles and Boars with abandon. Cody, Maggie, Dutch, Alexander, the Horses and the Pack, tore into the forces on the North side of the line. They pushed into the middle of the line adding to the confusion. Llamas, Rams, Mastiffs and Schnauzers dropped among the Premier's confused army. Now the soldiers of Snail Farm and Manor Farm trampled each other trying to escape the vicious torrent.

The Premier could not prevent panic as the Knight Farm forces and their allies overwhelmed his troops with a fierce brutality. He watched silently, as if he thought that by concentrating hard enough he could turn the tide of the battle. When he saw ten of his Boars fall to the wolves, without one casualty to the enemy, he made his decision.

"Retreat," he shouted.

In helter-skelter fashion, the armies of Snail Farm and Manor Farm retreated up the hill. Individual Animals would escape from a Mastiff right into the jaws of a wolf, or they would rush from an oncoming Dog from the Pack only to be stomped to death by a Llama.

The Schnauzers and Llamas continued their pursuit of the Premier's army until they had been driven five miles from Knight Farm, and all the stragglers had been killed. They turned and let the rest of the enemy retreat. A thousand Animals from the Premier's armies lost their lives in the name of equality.

One-eye's pack disappeared into the forest just as quickly as they had materialized. The Hawks brought back news that One-eye's pack had stalked the retreating army all the way back to Snail Farm. They killed and ate stragglers causing an uprising that the Premier barely squashed.

The army of Manor Farm retreated back to the Farm in small groups or as individuals. With no leader, there was no one to keep order. They were all equally responsible for their own safety.

CHAPTER FIFTEEN – PEACE AND PARTING

The night of the battle, all the Animals of Knight Farm, and their Animal allies from Manor Farm, ate hardily and retired early to the comfortable beds in the castle and surrounding buildings. The next evening, King George hosted a feast, the largest in hundreds of years, to celebrate the victory. Cody, Percy and Paulie were the guests of honor.

Cody was required to tell the story time and again of how One-eye had approached him, seeking a way to live undisturbed in the East. Nearly every citizen wanted to hear the story directly from Cody.

"All he wanted was to be left alone, regardless of what the wolf pack did to the citizens of Snail Farm," Cody would begin.

"So we simply looked for a way for both of us to benefit from an alliance," Cody would say. And then he ended his story the same way every time, "War makes for strange bedfellows. The only thing we had in common was a hunger for freedom."

As the evening came to an end, King George invited Cody and Maggie to his private chambers to share a quiet bowl of ale with the Queen, Sir Nelson, Lady Eliza and Lord Winston. Sir Andrew and Prince James stayed behind to entertain the other members of the Pack, Dutch, Alexander and the Horses.

King George and Cody stood alone by a fire built to take the chill off the cool summer night. Cody was on his fifth bowl of ale, and had finally allowed his sadness to push away his anger and anxiety. For the first time since Preston had won the election, over six month before, he let his lungs push the oxygen out of his lungs. He now began to philosophize, which Frank had always loved to listen to.

"I feel as if I am living in some sort of fable created by man," Cody said quietly.

"You mean a fairy tale," King George said, thinking that bantering might bring Cody out of his somber mood.

"No, a fable," Cody said with a smile.

"I am not sure I understand the difference," King George said.

"Fables have a moral."

"Oh, I see and a sense of morality I would think," King George offered.

"Yes," Cody said. "Justice is king, not equality."

"Is that meant as an insult my friend?" King George said, with his black eyes sparkling.

"No, in fact it was meant to be the opposite. If you were not just, you would not be allowed to rule." Cody tossed his head in the direction of

Sir Nelson, Lady Eliza and Lord Winston who were thirstily lapping ale from their giant saucers.

"Ah yes," King George said, "I tried to explain this to Carter and Louis just a week ago. They did not understand my meaning."

"No, because they did not understand that equality has shades of grey but justice does not."

The conversation shifted lazily to other topics, and by the end of the evening, King George and Cody were drinking bowls of ale quietly in Frank's honor.

*   *   *   *

Early the next morning, Cody padded slowly up to the top of the hill overlooking Knight Farm. He spent a moment alone at Preston's grave. The sun still hid behind the hill. Cody watched his breath float over the dirt pile covering the body of the leader of Manor Farm. He tried to visualize the future as Frank would have done. Nothing came to him.

But like a flash an understanding of the past hit Cody. He knew Frank had foreseen the future and knew the Dogs must abandon Manor Farm. Cody finally allowed himself to feel the loss of Frank. With the battle won, Cody allowed himself to suffer.

Cody sat alone until the sun pushed over the hill. As the morning passed, the members of the Pack made their way slowly up the hill, alone or in pairs. They greeted each other quietly and spoke infrequently. When Maggie joined her husband, she licked his face and took her place by his side.

The Cats watched the Pack roam among each other in relative silence. The Cats sat on the high rock wall of Knight Farm. At noon, Percy dropped off the wall and zigzagged slowly up the hill. A half an hour later, Dutch, Alexander, Bart and his family, walked through the massive gate of Knight Farm and joined them at the top of the hill.

The Animals of Manor Farm had gathered on the hill, despite no one calling a meeting. None of them knew whether they were heroes or traitors to their fellow citizens. None of them cared. Cody smiled at Bart when he arrived but then turned his attention back to the might of Knight Farm. After a half hour of silence, the most unlikely candidate decided to state the thought that rolled through all of their minds.

"The Pack isn't returning to Manor Farm is it?" Alexander asked in his deep baritone. The Bull nonchalantly swatted at flies with his tail as he posed the question.

Cody slowly shook his head. "No," he said softly. A tear seemed to well in each of his eyes. Alexander stared in fascination. He had never

178

seen a Dog shed a tear. Cody looked eerily like the humans in the paintings that hung from the walls of Knight Farm. But a tear never materialized.

"You have always had incredible insight, Alexander," Cody said. "Just like Frank."

"But things are different now," Bart protested. "There is no doubt you will be elected leader when we return to the Farm."

"Elections are how humans decide on their leaders," Cody said. "It is a popularity contest based on broken promises and ideology that works only in one's mind. We are Dogs. We don't elect our leaders. We just all know who it should be and accept it. If there is ever a dispute as to authority it is resolved quickly. It may be crude, but it is efficient and, more importantly, much more effective than an election."

The Animals were quiet. They were trying to understand the meaning of Cody's decision; not just for the farm but also for them.

"What will you do?" Dutch asked.

"Head West of Manor Farm, to the plains and valleys on the way to the human lands. There are wild goats and sheep and elk and deer for us to hunt. There is plenty of water flowing down from the mountains."

"What about the other citizens of Manor Farm?" Bart asked.

"I am sorry Bart, but I think we were all naïve."

"How so?" Bart asked.

"To think that different Animals could live together as one," Cody said. "We all think differently. One cannot expect another Animal to think the same way as a Dog and visa versa. It is idealistic and, as the Premier and Preston have demonstrated, unsafe for all of us."

"Are you saying all Pigs are wrong in their thinking?" Dutch asked a little defensively.

"No," Cody said with a slight shake of the head.

"What exactly are you saying?" Dutch asked, trying to understand.

"That Animals approach life, the Man-God, war, peace and all other things differently and it is much too difficult to bridge the gap. Dogs have enough trouble relating with other Dogs."

"So you are giving up?" Dutch asked. His voice was now filled with anger and disappointment. "We just fought this war in vain?"

"No," Cody said, "we fought this war for justice, not for any political cause or any particular Farm."

"But you are giving up on Manor Farm," Dutch said.

"No, we are simply choosing to be Dogs."

"But what about the Dogs of Knight Farm and Snail Farm?" Alexander asked. "They all manage to coexist with other Animals."

"True," Cody said. "They live in a defined structure where Dogs govern other Dogs to serve other Animals. My guess is that if such an arrangement is no longer in the best interest of the Dogs, Lord Winston and Sir Nelson would put an end to the way things currently operate at Knight Farm. I hold out little hope for Snail Farm."

Cody said this as if he expected no further argument. He and Maggie stood proudly and nodded at the others to indicate the subject was closed. Cody turned and headed over the hill. His tail, a bristle of fur, was a beacon to the Pack as they followed him west. A sense of adventure filled their hearts as they trotted after him. There would be no more Dogs at Manor Farm.

EPILOGUE

Fifteen years later, a large German Sheppard, white with grey, lay on a bed of grass in the middle of a beautiful valley. Butterflies filled the short, flowering bushes and the grass looked the color of a chameleon hiding in the leaves. The grass was transitioning from green to white as the season pushed through the end of spring. Dragonflies taunted the fish in the nearby water. Twenty pups, from the age of three months to a year, surrounded him. Most of the pups were black with either short hair or the slightly longer hair of a Sheppard. There were also a few Dogs who were smaller than the others, with longer ears and multiple colors.

"What happened to the Cats, Master Cody?" one of the older pups asked.

"Well, for about ten years after the war I'd see Percy now and again. Usually when the Pack wandered close to Manor Farm as we still did back in those days," Cody said. "The Cats had not returned to live at the Farm but instead to the area around it. You know how Cats become attached to places and not other Animals? So it was with Percy and Manor Farm. They lived on the banks of Beaver Creek. Over time, they destroyed Poseidon's pack of rats despite Pete's pledge to let them be. It wasn't in the Cats nature to abide by such a pact."

"You've told us that Knight Farm and Snail Farm still exist," said the same curious pup, "but you have never said what they are like now."

"Knight Farm remains the same under King George's rule, stable and strong," Cody said. "Snail Farm lives behinds its walls, fearful of the wolf pack once led by One-eye and the free Dogs. Now hundreds of wolves roam the Eastern lands as well as packs of Poodles. After the war, the Poodles fled Snail Farm and the rule of the Pigs."

The pups sat silently for a moment, staring with big, dark eyes at Cody.

"Why did Manor Farm fail Master Cody?" a smaller pup asked.

"I think because the Pack was not allowed to do what it did best, and because the other Animals were not allowed to do what they did best. In the end we sacrificed justice for equality. That was our downfall."

Cody nodded, put his head down and fell asleep. This told the pups the lesson was over. The pups bounded into the grass and fell on each other in mock battle.

THE END